A
Colder
Home

Jillian Maria

- 1 -

<u>SLUGLINE</u>

EXT. RURAL ROAD - AFTERNOON

There is a truck crumpled against a tree. Broken glass litters the ground. Smoke pours from the hood. Faint rock music still plays from the radio.

CLOSE-UP ON: A pale hand dangling out the shattered window. Blood drips from its fingertips into the snow.

WE'RE GOING TO die.

The truck drifts across the barely visible road and hits the shoulder with a jolt, wheels grinding as they wage a losing battle against gravel and ice. Noah leans forward, gripping the wheel in both hands.

"Shit," he mutters, more annoyed than alarmed.

I'm alarmed enough for the both of us. I can picture our deaths perfectly, typed out in the same font as the movie scripts I write. Fitting, since it's a script we're currently risking life and limb to film. I should have known this was a terrible idea. I *did* know, but now it's too late.

At the last moment, Noah coaxes the truck back onto the road. The cargo bed wavers, then straightens. "*Whew,*" he breathes. He's relieved.

I'm not. "Noah, maybe we should call this off."

"What?" Noah shoots me a quick glance before returning his gaze to the road. His eyes, the same shade of brown as mine, are wide and incredulous. "We're almost there. Doesn't make sense to turn around now, does it?"

"I guess not, but . . ." But what? Despite my earlier internal hyperbole, I *hadn't* thought this was such a terrible idea at first. When we'd left Ellis this morning, there'd only been light flurries. They barely stung my cheeks as I helped Noah pack the filming equipment into the truck, and the forecast had called for less than an inch. Nothing life-long Michigan residents like us couldn't handle.

Not to say I was thrilled at the idea of filming *The Widow Ghost.* Personally, I would have been content to file it away with all my other half-finished projects. But Noah insisted. It seemed harmless enough to humor him.

It does not seem harmless now.

I look out the window at what little I can see through the thick white fog and streaking snow. It's the kind of storm that happens once in a lifetime. The kind of storm that ends with a death toll read out by a solemn-faced newscaster to all of those lucky enough to be safe in their homes when it hits.

The kind of storm that feels like an omen to those unlucky enough to be caught in it.

I swallow around the panic-shaped lump in my throat. Beneath my black sweater dress and thick tights, my skin is slick with a cold sheen of sweat despite the blizzard raging outside. "I think we should—"

Noah hits a patch of ice. The truck skids.

My hands fly to my face, eyes squeezing shut in reflex against the inevitable end. As the truck begins to spin, I wonder if we'll have separate funerals, or if Aunt Carla and my mom will deign to get it all over with at once. INT. FUNERAL HOME — MORNING. Or maybe mourning. Two caskets sit side-by-side, surrounded by flowers. Inside, my pale hands are laced over the chest of a brightly colored dress I'd never wear in life, and Noah's habitual red zip-up is replaced with a suit.

Actually, I sort of hope that the damage is extensive enough for a closed casket. The practice of leaving them open is ghoulish, and I don't understand how anyone finds comfort in it. I'd only felt vaguely nauseated at my father's wake, staring at him through prayers I didn't hear and condolences I don't remember. I couldn't stop wondering what sort of state he must have been in for the undertaker to put him back together so *wrong*, his waxy face shaped into an uncanny approximation of what he'd looked like in life.

The tires screech. My entire body braces, waiting for the crunch of metal against bark, and . . .

The truck slows to a halt.

My body unfurls in increments: back slowly easing into the seat, breath returning to lungs, legs releasing from their defensive crouch. When I lower my arms from my face, I see Noah in the driver's seat, his hands still white-knuckled against the wheel, his brown hair tousled.

"We're . . . here." When he smiles at me, he at least has the sense to look sheepish. "You okay?"

"Okay? I saw our *funeral*, Noah."

Noah begins to laugh. I laugh too, because it really does sound melodramatic when I say it out loud. Also, the leftover adrenaline from our near brush with death has me fighting off hysterics.

"You would be thinking about death, fucking goth," Noah says, with all due affection. "Come on, help me get the equipment out of the trunk."

He flings open the car door. A chill runs down my spine, one that has nothing to do with the cold wind that rushes into the cabin of the truck. "Are you sure you want to film this?"

Noah pauses, halfway out of his seat. His wide-eyed stare is the same one he used to give me when we were children and I suggested maybe *not* going along with one of his half-baked plans. It's his patented *'you're being crazy, Cleo'* stare. "Are you kidding me? We're already here."

"But the cast isn't," I argue. "And if the storm

keeps on like this . . . obviously, no project is worth risking their lives for. But especially not this one. We're just making this on a whim, Noah. For fun."

Honestly, I hadn't taken Noah that seriously when he first suggested making *The Widow Ghost* a reality. I'm surprised he went through the trouble of finding a filming location for it, and I'm even more surprised that he found a cast and crew willing to work on it. They're all mutual friends of ours, which helps. But I have to imagine that they have better things to do with their time than risk their lives in a freak snowstorm for a dead-end passion project with no pay.

Noah's expression flatlines. As if he might, for once, be taking my words to heart. But the moment I think my cousin has finally found his common sense, it's gone, replaced by a grin. "It'll be fine, Cleosaurus." He punctuates this latest nickname by reaching out and giving my ponytail—this month dyed a pale blue-gray—a familial yank. "You worry too much."

Before I can say anything else, he's up and out of the truck.

I don't know what I was expecting. Noah may be fantastic at directing horror movies, but he'd never survive one. If a masked killer cornered him in a dark cabin, he'd react with that same blasé optimism. *It'll be fine.*

My stomach gives an uneasy lurch. The car may not be in motion anymore, but I still feel like we're sliding across the ice. Like any moment we'll meet our doom, our vision too choked by fog and snow to see it before it's too late.

"Hurry up, Cleopoke!"

I sigh. The wind rips my car door from my hand, and snow immediately swirls into the cab, stinging my cheeks in icy pinpricks. I squint against it as I step out of the truck. My feet slide out from under me the moment they make contact with the icy driveway, and I have to grab onto the door handle to keep myself from christening this endeavor by eating absolute *shit* on the pavement.

Which would be terribly on brand, I suppose. The universe is not shy about humbling me.

"This movie is cursed," I tell Noah as I round the back of the trunk in careful, mincing steps. I have to raise my voice to be heard over the wind.

Noah snorts. "Your face is cursed."

I scowl, even though I'd *meant* the words with the same melodramatic humor as my quip about our funerals. I can recognize, on some level, that I'm jumping to extremes. But I hold that knowledge in the same part of my brain that knows, logically, that there are no monsters hiding beneath my bed at night.

It may be true, but that won't stop me from making sure none of my limbs dangle from beneath the covers after the lights are out.

We're parked at the end of a long driveway. The home where we'll be filming *The Widow Ghost* is, at this point, only a vague dark shape. The snow is too thick to look at it straight on. Closer to us is a sedan, already coated with ice.

"Are the homeowners here?" I ask. I hadn't been aware that we'd be filming for an audience, and the idea makes this whole proposition feel even more horrifying.

Noah shakes his head. He returns his clapboard to the box it fell out of during our expedition across the ice. "No, that's Declan's. He and Rhiannon must have beaten us here."

The last time I saw him, Declan had been driving a passed-down minivan. I suppose it makes sense that he's gotten a new car in his three years since heading off to college, but it still seems a bit strange to me. Stranger still is the second half of Noah's statement. "Rhiannon rode with him?"

Rhiannon is sixteen—two years younger than me—and I'd only met her after Declan graduated. I've never seen them interact, but Noah's worked on films with the both of them. According to him, they're constantly at each other's throats.

When I voice this to him, he scoffs. "What? No, they're good friends, really." He hands off my camcorder, still secure in its case. "Five bucks says they're arguing when we walk in."

"You have a very strange definition of friendship," I tell him. But there's no real disdain in my voice. The camera rests at my hip when I sling the bag over my shoulder, and its familiar weight is a comfort.

Arms laden with boxes, we start our slow trudge up the icy driveway. The closer we get to the house, the more it comes into view, its dark siding stark against the snow. In spite of its rural location, there's something distinctly suburban about the shape of it: two stories with tall windows flanking the door. It's got the sort of liminal familiarity of a place I might have stayed briefly as a child.

There's only one thing I can say about it. "It's creepy." I force a shiver for emphasis. "I'll give you this much, it's perfect for *The Widow Ghost*. Where on earth did you find this place?"

Noah grins. "Craigslist."

"Jesus. We're going to get murdered."

"If I go first, get it on camera."

When he wants to, Noah can be just as morbid as me. I try and fail to fend off a laugh. "Ah, of course. Nothing like that sweet, sweet posthumous publicity."

The chill works its way into my bones, numbing my fingers and the tip of my nose. Despite its unsettling aura, it's actually a relief when we finally get inside and out of the cold.

After the bright white of the snow, the house's interior is impossibly dim. Dark spots dance in front of my eyes, and there's a faint buzz in my ears. I'm almost dizzy as feeling rushes back into my wind-numbed appendages.

While I struggle to orient myself, familiar voices echo.

"You're ridiculous." That's Rhiannon, frustrated.

"I'm just saying!" And that's Declan, amused. They're arguing after all.

I suppose it shouldn't surprise me that they

manage to push each other's buttons. Rhiannon will argue until she's proven her point a thousand times over; Declan will argue just for the thrill of it.

Beside me, Noah snickers and holds out his hand. I slap my palm to his in a pantomime of handing over a five-dollar bill, and he tucks the imaginary cash into his pocket. It's a ritual we've performed hundreds of times since childhood.

"If you're going to kill each other, *please* wait until Cleo gets her camera out," he calls into the kitchen. "We were just talking about how a murder would really spice up the marketing."

By now, my eyes have begun to adjust. We stand in an entryway with surprisingly high ceilings and wainscoting along the walls, wooden floors overlaid with thick rugs. There's a kitchen to our immediate right, and a hallway to our left that seems to lead to a living room. Above us is a second-floor balcony lined by a wooden banister.

I'm struck by how lived-in this place feels. The wood floors are well-maintained, and the air doesn't strike me as stale or underused the way it sometimes does in hotel rooms or rentals. An umbrella hangs on a hook by the door, and the fridge in the kitchen is overflowing with magnets from tourist traps: Mt. Rushmore, Niagara Falls, the Grand Canyon.

It's from this kitchen that Declan steps, heeled boots clicking against the floor. He wears tight dark jeans and a gray off-the-shoulder sweater, silver eyeshadow sparkling against his brown skin. His dark hair is artfully coiffed. He's grown into himself in the years since I last saw him in person. He's always been confident, but there's something new in the way he holds his body. He came out as non-binary recently, and I wonder if *that* has something to do with this change, although his name and pronouns remained the same. Perhaps self-actualization is what lends him this new air of assurance.

He seems impossibly, distantly mature, even though he's only a few years older than me. Frankly, it's a bit intimidating. But then he smiles, and I see my friend. The same senior who, three years ago, took one look at the artsy, angsty, wannabe-goth freshman and decided to take her under his wing.

"Cleo, *darling*," he coos, swanning into the hallway. He speaks in a pseudo-transatlantic accent. I'm fairly certain it's only partially ironic at this point. "It's so wonderful to see you again. Where have you *been*?"

I smile, accepting his hug and the air-kisses he presses to both my cheeks. "Where have *I* been? You're the one who graduated."

Not that it's stopped him from seeing Noah. Or Rhiannon, for that matter. And I suppose I've had opportunities myself. Noah has tried to convince me to play cinematographer on countless projects over the years, dangling the names of friends in front of me like lures. But the timing has never been right. We only tried working together once, when we were fourteen, on a stereotypical slasher film called *Slaughter!* It didn't get far. Frankly, I'm surprised this one hasn't blown up similarly in our faces. Yet.

Again, the image of the storm outside as an omen returns to me. I fight a shiver.

Declan doesn't seem to notice. He slings a companionable arm around my shoulder, giving me a gentle squeeze. "I suppose you *do* have a point. Well, come along then. Rhiannon and I have been using the kitchen as our base of operations."

Base of operations, apparently, is code for *dumping ground*. The kitchen is long and narrow, with pale yellow wallpaper and a wooden door at the far end, and we've taken over nearly every inch of the floor. Boxes overflow with wires and mic packs. Bags are full to bursting with clothing, groceries, and miscellaneous set dressing. There are light bulbs and reflectors, boom mics and other filming apparatus I don't even know the name of.

When I suggested that everyone in the cast and crew bring their own clothing to hang in the closet, hoping to imply that the haunted house had claimed more victims prior to the start of the story, I thought I was being overindulgent. But the boxes strewn across the kitchen are even more so. Why do we need light bulbs and set dressing when the house already comes with all of that? It's overkill for a project like this one.

Noah whistles. "Damn, we've got our work cut out for us if we want to start filming tonight."

He sounds amused but not surprised. Had he known they'd be bringing all of this?

Rhiannon sits at the kitchen table, fussing with a

portable recorder. Faint blue light from the screen shines against her dark-skinned face and yellow hoodie, reflecting in her round glasses and in the metal beads woven into her braids. She glances up when we walk in. "Hey. Do you need help unloading your equipment from the truck?"

She directs her question to me, not Noah, for some reason that I can't parse. "Huh? Uh, no. This is it." Noah and I only have a few boxes between us: prop blood, copies of the script with loose production notes, a surprisingly organized shot list and a schedule in a binder from Noah, along with a few other miscellaneous tools like the clapboard. And, of course, my camera in its rightful place at my hip.

"Hm." Rhiannon cranes her neck to look into the boxes. "Who's bringing the tripod then?"

"Tripod?"

"To stabilize while shooting."

"Oh." I grip the strap of my camera bag in both hands. "I've never used one of those. I guess I just thought I'd hold the camera, like I always do . . ."

Although most of my completed filming experience boils down to candid shots taken at parties or events, or quick vignettes turned in for school assignments. A whole movie? That's far more ambitious. Looking at all of the equipment Rhiannon and Declan bought, I can't help but worry that I'm woefully unprepared to rise to the task.

Noah shrugs. "The camcorder has built-in image stabilization. You've seen Cleo's work in class, right?

You know it'll look great."

The vote of confidence doesn't feel all that comforting: *it'll look great* spoken in the exact same cadence as his earlier *it'll be fine*. I'm not sure if this convinces Rhiannon, but she turns back to her recorder with no further argument.

Declan smiles. "You're still working with that camcorder? Goodness, I haven't seen that since . . . graduation, I suppose." His silver eyeshadow sparkles as he raises his eyebrows. "It's perfect, I'm sure. Analog horror is all the rage these days. The judges will love it."

"Judges?" I laugh a little, thinking this is the set up to one of Declan's jokes.

Beside me, Noah goes uncharacteristically stiff, his normally easy smile becoming noticeably forced. It reminds me of the time Aunt Carla caught us trying to sneak out of Thanksgiving to go see *V/H/S/94*.

"Well, naturally," Declan says. "For—"

"Heeeeeeey," Noah interjects, subtle as a lead balloon. "Cleo, did you see how cool the balcony looks from the first floor? The shadow the banister casts is creepy as hell, you've got to check it out."

His hand clamps around my forearm. Beneath Declan and Rhiannon's bemused gazes, he drags me out of the kitchen.

The hallway is dim. There's an overhead chandelier, but it's off at the moment, which means that the only light comes from the kitchen and what thready gray sunlight manages to get through the storm. It's not enough for the banister to cast *any* shadow, much less one worth remarking on, but Noah makes no attempt to rectify the situation. He just stands there, flickering shadows of snow from the tall windows playing across his sheepish smile.

"Noah," I say.

"Cleo," he responds, mirroring my tone. No nickname, which is a terrible sign.

I fold my arms over my chest. "What did Declan mean about judges?"

Noah's sheepish smile widens. "Surprise? I signed us up for *Horrorfest*."

"You—what?" I must have misheard him. Because it *sounds* like he just admitted to submitting this mediocre mess of a film script to the horror film festival we've been fans of since we were preteens, and that's an utterly ridiculous notion. "You said that this was casual! That we were doing this for fun!"

"I know, I know! But then I checked the submissions page, and what do you know, they were open! And the deadline just happened to line up with the filming schedule . . ."

"Oh my god." I pinch the bridge of my nose. So much of his behavior over the past few weeks—his uncharacteristic determination, his unflappable excitement—is suddenly put into a new, horrific context. "*That's* why you were so dead set on starting today. It was . . . I cannot fucking believe . . ."

There's a long beat of silence as Noah lets me stew in my own frustrated anxiety. But, finally, he breaks it.

"What's the big deal? We'll still be making the movie like we planned. This doesn't change anything."

"It changes plenty! I didn't think anyone was going to see this! If I'd known, I would have . . ."

Well. I would have refused, most likely. *The Widow Ghost* is a simple script. I'd written it as an exercise in playing with my favorite tropes, without giving much thought to plot or substance. As a result, it's painfully derivative and downright clunky in places. I was only willing to go along with this production because Noah pitched it to me as a practice piece.

But anything more than that?

"You should have told me."

Noah sighs, cheeks puffing out in a slow exhale. "I'm sorry, okay? But I knew . . . I *know* you're going to have a great time. Trust me, okay? It's all going to work out."

How can he say that so easily? He has to remember our first attempt at filming, back when we were younger. He watched that production fall to pieces. He got a textbook education about how things aren't always fine, how they don't always work out. So how can he look at me now and be so unflappably optimistic?

I'm not sure. But I also don't know how to argue with him when he's like this. I sigh long-sufferingly instead. "When we get murdered in the creepy Craigslist house, I'm going to use my dying breath to tell you that I told you so."

Noah laughs. He claps me on the back. "Oh, come

on, already. We've got a lot to do if we're going to be ready for filming by the time the actors show up!"

He vanishes back into the kitchen. I make no move to follow him.

It's not the house I'm worried about, of course. Not really. How long will it be, I wonder, before the rest of the cast and crew realize how woefully inadequate I am? How long until they regret getting involved?

Above me, something skitters. Because of course this place would be infested with rats on top of everything else, I swear that I—

But the face that peers over the banister at me is too large to be a rat's. Two eyes, sunken into a pale face, glitter out at me from the shadowy slats of the balcony. Pale hands wrap around the beams, their limbs bent at impossible angles. There's a wet shine in the darkness, one that might come from a string of saliva.

Or teeth.

My heart stutters. I pull in a breath, stumbling back. But before I can even think to exhale that breath in a scream, the figure vanishes. Only darkness remains. Darkness and silence, save for the ever-present howl of the wind outside.

- 2 -

MISE-EN-SCENE

CLOSE-UP ON:

An empty hallway, doused in shadow. A strange figure crouches behind the banister. The light shifts. The figure is gone. But low, foreboding music continues to play over the scene, and the shadows seem darker than ever.

I STARE AT the empty hallway. The figure does not return.

I must admit, there is a distinct possibility I imagined it. It wouldn't be the first time I dreamt up a creature lurking in the shadows, stalking my every step. It's a hazard of the trade, being a horror writer. I don't know if my stories will ever scare others, but I do an excellent job of scaring myself over nothing.

Unless it *isn't* nothing.

I'm agnostic to the existence of ghosts outside of fiction, but if any house could be haunted, this one is a prime candidate. It has the right shape for it, all hidden corners and strange shadows. It's basically begging for some unfortunate specter to stalk its hallways, wailing mournfully in tune with the wind.

"Cleorama! Are you coming, or what?"

"I'm assuming 'or what' is not an option," I shoot back. My voice is, I'm glad to note, relatively steady. And if I'm being honest, the idea of supernatural intervention isn't half as frightening to me as the idea of watching *The Widow Ghost* crash and burn.

Noah appears in the entrance to the kitchen. His silhouette in the low light could almost be dignified, if not for the grubbiness of his zip-up sweater and the untied laces of his shoes. "Well, it's not like there's anywhere else you can go."

He says it like a joke, but I can read between the lines. We're here, and Noah is my ride home. I have no choice but to move forward with this, no matter how much of a waste of time it may be.

I spare the balcony one more glance. Still empty. I almost certainly imagined what I saw, but I still have to hunch my shoulders against the chill that creeps along the back of my neck.

Rhiannon is sorting through mic packs and takes little note of my arrival. Declan, leaning against the counter, seems a bit more interested. "Are you okay, darling? You look pale."

Is he asking because he's concerned, or just because he's hungry for gossip? Knowing Declan, it's probably a mix of both. "I'm fine." I have no intention of explaining the *Horrorfest* situation, or inviting questions as to *why* I find the idea so unappealing. I grope for an alternate excuse. "I thought I saw something on the balcony. It startled me, is all."

Declan's eyebrows raise, brown eyes sparkling more than his dramatic eyeshadow. "Is that so? Could there be an uninvited guest haunting these halls? Perhaps our titular widow ghost is more than mere fiction."

Rhiannon scoffs. "Oh, please."

If anything, her dismissal seems to encourage Declan further. He hoists himself up to sit on the counter, his long legs dangling against the cupboards below. "Oh, *Rhiannon*. Are you really going to dismiss the possibility of paranormal activity so quickly?"

"Obviously. Ghosts aren't real." Rhiannon turns, arms crossed over her chest. "It was probably just a shadow or something. Right, Cleo?"

Even though I'm the one who *started* this conversation, it's still a bit of a shock when she addresses me directly. "Oh. I mean, yeah, maybe?" I'd be willing to let it go there, but Rhiannon's gaze is so disapproving that I feel the need to add, "Probably?"

Declan hums, a disapproval so put-upon that it circles back around into irony. "No vision, either of you. Where's your sense of drama? Just *think* of what a haunted filming location could add to our production."

Noah chuckles, scratching the bridge of his nose. "I'll stick with a living actress for our ghost. Easier to direct."

Sensing that it might be best to move the conversation along before it starts a genuine argument, I ask, "Who did you get to play the ghost, anyway?" There are three roles in *The Widow Ghost*, and I know the other two: Andrea and Zander, old friends of ours. But the owner of the titular role somehow never came up during planning.

Noah grins. "Oh, she was a dancer in the spring musical I directed. You'll love her, trust me." Straightening, he claps his hands together. "Anyway! Let's get started with—"

A muffled clatter cuts him off.

I'm still keyed up enough from what I saw on the balcony that I jump, hands reflexively curling into fists. Noah's the only one close enough to actually notice, but because he's Noah, he immediately draws attention to my overreaction by chuckling. "That came from the basement, I think." He nods toward the door at the far end of the kitchen. "Probably just a draft."

"Or a ghost." Declan wiggles his eyebrows. "Moving from the balcony to the basement is quite a feat, but it's probably easier for those of us who are less . . . corporeal."

Rhiannon sighs, long-suffering. "Are you going to be like this the *whole* time?"

The wind howls, and the entire house groans in response. Declan laughs. It's a really rather convincing Vincent Price impression, so over-dramatic that even Rhiannon cracks a smile.

The wind dies down, but the house doesn't quieten. In fact, the noises from the basement get louder.

Thump. Thump. Thump.

My stomach drops, panic setting in before my conscious mind even registers what I'm hearing. It's the same anticipatory panic that clutched at me when Noah's truck started to fishtail, and a moment later, I realize why.

Those are footsteps.

There's someone—or something—in here with us.

Thump. Thump.

Noah catches on a second too late. "What—"

The door opens.

A woman steps out. Her clothes are splattered in *something*—dried blood?—and the hand not occupied in carrying a large canvas is holding something silver and sharp that glints like a weapon. Her eyes lock on me. For a moment, I consider the irony of a horror writer getting murdered by a knife-wielding killer.

Then the woman shrieks, and she drops her weapon. Which is, I must concede, a very uncharacteristic thing for a knife-wielding killer to do.

"Oh my god," Noah says, his conciliatory tone only further dampening my suspicions. "Michelle? Are you okay?"

The name is unfamiliar to me, but Noah clearly knows her. I have to conclude that she must be the owner of the house. I hadn't seen her car in the driveway, but that doesn't mean much. Maybe she simply doesn't have one, or maybe I'd been too focused on making it through the blizzard to see it.

"Who—wait. Noah, right?" She massages her chest with her newly free hand. The other still clutches the canvas, knuckles white. "You're . . . the one making a movie. You were here last month. Location scouting, you called it." She pushes her auburn hair back from her face, revealing the hints of gray at her temples. "I thought you weren't coming until the eighth?"

Noah laughs. It's his awkward laugh, but hopefully it isn't as noticeable to this woman as it is to me. "Uh, it *is* the eighth." He shakes his head. "I'm sorry I didn't let you know we were here! I just assumed you were out of town."

"Oh." For a moment, Michelle looks dazed, as if she's not quite sure where she is. But then she chuckles. "You must think—You must think I'm crazy. But I completely lost track of time. I meant to leave this morning, but I got . . . caught up."

There's a strange glassiness to her eyes that doesn't go away no matter how much she blinks. Upon closer inspection, the splatters on her clothes are darker than dried blood would be, more black than brown. It could be dirt, but the canvas in her hand makes paint more likely.

"Well, that's okay!" Noah's cheer sounds almost hysteric in the wake of her quiet, quavering voice. "I can introduce you to the crew, anyway. Everyone, this is Michelle Barlow, the house's owner, who is nice enough to let us film while she goes on vacation. Michelle, this is Rhiannon, our sound mixer" — Rhiannon nods, looking almost as uncomfortable with the situation as I feel— "Declan, our costume and set designer" —Declan waves, removing himself from the counter with as much tact as he can manage— "and Cleo, our cinematographer and script writer."

I clear my throat. Something about this woman's bloodshot gaze unnerves me. "Hi."

"It's . . . nice to meet all of you." Michelle smiles. In spite of the gray in her hair, the lines around her eyes and mouth are very fine. "I'm sorry, I'm such a mess, I just wasn't expecting . . . well, it's like I said."

"Oh, hey, don't worry about it. It's fine." Noah nods at the canvas in her hands. "What do you have there?"

"This? Oh, it's, um. It's a painting I was working on." Rather than turn it to face us, Michelle clutches the canvas closer to her chest, hiding what's on the other side even further from view.

Noah doesn't seem to notice her reluctance to share. "Whoa, you paint? That's so cool, can I see?"

In spite of the way she frightened several years of life off of me, I begin to feel a bit sorry for Michelle Barlow. Her face twists, and I can't tell if it's an attempt to fend off laughter or tears. "You—You *can*, of course. But I was actually going to throw this one out, it . . . it wasn't turning out how I wanted, so I . . . well, see for yourself."

Slowly, she turns the canvas around. The painting

has the air of one of those staged family portraits, with three people standing against a dark red background. But only one of them is rendered in any sort of detail: a blonde woman in a white dress. One hand is splayed against her collarbone; the other is curled around her stomach. There are purple bags under her eyes, but there's a sharpness in them. Her lips are pressed into a thin, tight line.

Beside her is a shorter woman, or maybe a young girl. Her blonde hair suggests that she's related to the first woman, but it's impossible to make out any further inherited similarities. Michelle didn't get that far in painting her. Her face is blank and featureless, a blob of pale skin.

The final figure seems taller than the other two, but that's all I can make out. Thick black paint obscures their face and a good portion of their body.

"I got a little frustrated toward the end, there," Michelle says sheepishly.

I surprise myself by speaking. "Once, I got so frustrated with a script that I set all my notes for it on fire, so, uh, don't worry about it."

"Oh, man, your mom was so mad." Noah snickers. "Anyway, Cleo's right. We've probably all got you beat in the drama department."

"Well, most of us," Rhiannon adds.

"Debatable," Declan goads.

The banter does seem to put Michelle a bit more at ease. Her grip on the canvas loosens slightly. "Well. There are more paintings in my studio downstairs, but, um. I'd prefer you didn't go in there. It's . . . It's superstition, I guess, but it's my space, you know? It was originally built as a storm shelter, so sometimes I *had* to let the rest of the house in when it was an emergency, but I really prefer . . ." She trails off, blinking. "I'm sorry. You're not here to listen to me ramble."

"Well, no studio snooping, got it." Noah makes a dramatic cross over his chest. He once made the same gesture when promising to save a slice of Aunt Carla's cake for me. He promptly ate it, but seeing as how he was eight years old at the time, it seems unfair to bring up now as he smiles winningly at Michelle. "Hey, if you were just going to throw that painting out anyway, can we use it?"

Michelle's eyes widen, what little calm she had before vanishing. "What?"

"I'm serious! I know you didn't mean it, but this is kind of great set-dressing for a horror movie."

"It does have a certain air to it," Declan says, looking interested now. "It would look quite striking hanging in the hallway, right below the banister."

"Oh, well . . ." Michelle's eyes dart around the room, as if looking for a savior. But none comes for her any more than one came for me when Noah snagged *The Widow Ghost* out of my pile of incomplete manuscripts and demanded we film it. "I . . . It's fine, sure."

She hands over the painting. Declan takes it, turning it over in his manicured hands. "Fantastic.

Although I must say, that particular hallway doesn't need much help feeling ominous. Tell me, Michelle, does your house have a sordid past of some kind?"

Rhiannon sighs, and Declan's grin grows wider. But Michelle doesn't seem to find any humor in the situation. Her face grows pale, and that glassiness returns to her eyes tenfold.

"Did you see something?" she whispers.

It's as though the temperature in the room plummets, and the mood with it. Declan had obviously been fishing for a lighthearted, campfire-type ghost story. Not the sort of story that would bring the homeowner to near tears.

Noah clears his throat. "Cleo thought she saw something on the balcony," he says. "But it was probably just a shadow."

"A shadow . . . Right. Of course. It's . . . It's a very strange coincidence, that's all." Michelle swipes a hand over her face. It remains dry, but there's a twitchiness to her expression. Her lips twist, but instead of a sob, she barks out a nervous laugh. "Sorry, it's just, well . . . my mother, she hung herself from that balcony."

There's a pregnant, awkward pause, broken only by the shuffle of fabric as Michelle fidgets. Finally, Noah coughs. "Shit, I'm so sorry. Was it . . . recent?"

People always say the strangest things when they find out that someone close to you has died. I've experienced weirder comments since my dad's passing. But I suppose I can't judge Noah. I certainly wasn't rushing to fill the silence with anything better.

"Not recent, no, no," Michelle hurries to clarify. "It was decades ago now. My sister and father had just died in a car crash, and she . . . well, it was a lot for her. My father, he . . ." She trails off, her eyes drifting off toward the basement door. I get the distinct sense that she's trying to pull herself together.

It's uncomfortable, watching this stranger struggle so openly with her emotions. I know that I'd feel mortified in her shoes. I wish that we could give her privacy in this moment, but simply walking out of the room would be rude. The others seem as frozen as I am, most of them avoiding eye contact.

Finally, Michelle breathes in, blinking rapidly. "Anyway! It really isn't . . . I mean, it was so long ago, so it's not . . . I'm keeping you from your movie, aren't I! I should let you get to it, and I should really . . . really get going, huh?"

"Oh, right! Yeah, absolutely!" Noah nods, palpable relief in his tone as he turns to the rest of us. "Let's get going. Declan, let's get this painting hung up. Rhiannon, you can get the lights set up in the living room. Cleo, you grab those clothes and get them hung up in the closet. Alright?"

"Okay." Set dressing is not, strictly speaking, my job, but I'm not about to argue with an opportunity to clear out of the room. I fumble with various duffel bags and totes as the rest of the crew files out.

Michelle hovers. "I need to clean up downstairs," she says. "But then I'll be out of your hair. Is that okay?"

"Of course! Um, take your time." I pause, torn between wanting to flee and feeling obligated to stay. The air in the room feels expectant, somehow. Heavy with words not said. In a movie, this would be the point where the homeowner would give a warning that falls on deaf ears. When Michelle regards me, I'm almost sure that she's going to talk about the shadow I saw on the balcony.

Instead, she smiles. It's so shockingly genuine that I almost forget the awkwardness. "Are you really making a horror movie?" she asks.

"Oh! Yeah. Yeah, we are." If I had a hand free, I'd be fidgeting with something. "It's nothing special though. I mean, the script is not my best. Really, it was nice of you to let us use your house for something as silly as this."

"Well, it was hard to resist. Horror is my favorite genre." Michelle tucks a lock of hair behind her ear. There's a wistful tone to her voice, something sweet and gentle. "I suppose it's a bit morbid, but I've . . . I've just always loved scary stories, ever since I was a little girl. I guess I never grew out of it."

In spite of myself, I smile. I know other female horror fans exist, but I haven't met many of them, and none of them older than me. I wonder what my mom, who frequently derides my interests as "unladylike," would have to say about Michelle.

"Me, too. There's something fun about being scared when you know it's all fake, I think." I could continue along that train of thought for quite a while, but my arms are starting to ache from the combined weight of the bags I'm holding. "Sorry, I really need to get these upstairs. And you need to get going too, right?"

"Right. Of course." Michelle nods. "I'll let you . . . get to it, then."

The conversation feels distinctly unfinished. But I don't stop Michelle as she returns to the basement, shutting the door behind her. I only readjust my grip on my bags and head in the opposite direction, up the stairs to the balcony above the first floor.

And if I *do* happen to glance at the banister as I go, all I see are plain wooden railings. Nothing more.

- 3 -

<u>**CALL TIME**</u>

UPSTAIRS, THERE ARE three bedrooms. Only the largest has a walk-in closet suitable for filming, but I suppose that's all we'll need.

There's no clothing inside, which strikes me as a bit odd. Surely Michelle wouldn't have had to pack all of her clothing for a vacation? This must not be her room, despite being the nicest. Then again, if it used to belong to her parents, I can't blame her for not wanting to sleep here. Just the thought puts a chill down my spine.

In the back corner of the closet is a stack of canvases. None of them are as large as the one Michelle hauled upstairs, but they're the same material. Is this where she stores her extra supplies? Curious, I turn over the top-most one in the stack.

It's not extra supplies at all. It's a finished painting. In it, a woman stares out with bulging eyes and a mouth stretched in a silent, eternal scream. Blood drips down her face in lurid, obscene strokes. It's objectively well-painted, but what really thrills me is that it's familiar: this is a scene from *Carrie*. It isn't a direct recreation of the movie. Carrie's face in this painting is rounder, more plain. But the wide, staring eyes are what made Sissy Spacek's performance memorable, and those are rendered here in full glory.

Carrie was less conventionally attractive in the book, I believe. I remember reading an article once that argued the importance of that part of her character, urging casting directors of a remake to take it into account. Maybe this painting is Michelle's way of bridging that gap.

Flipping through the stack gives my theory more credence. The next paintings depict a scene from *Silence of the Lambs*, then *Frankenstein*, then *The Exorcist*. They all blend classic images from the films with more canon-accurate elements from the source material.

I can't stop smiling. Michelle *said* she was a horror

fan, but I hadn't expected to find such enthralling proof of that fact. It's too bad she's almost certainly gone by now, because I'd love to pick her brain about some of these pieces.

Even if she was still here, I probably wouldn't say anything. I wouldn't want to hold her up.

I pause at the final painting in the stack. It takes me a moment to place: it's *House of Usher*, blending the original short story by Edgar Allen Poe with the Vincent Price movie. Although outside of the character appearances, it doesn't look much like the scene from the movie at all. In the film, Rodrick Price dangles out the window while his revived sister strangles him to death, her hands bloodied from climbing out of her grave. That's not what's happening here. Here, Rodrick opens his arms to Madeline, pulling her closer even as her collapsing, blood-stained body crushes him. Behind them, paintings hang sideways as cracks run through the walls.

Is this how it went in the short story? I only read it once, years ago, but I seem to recall Rodrick near madness in his terror of Madeline. He doesn't look terrified here. Instead, there's a tired desperation in his expression, almost a resignation. Madeline's back is to us, so her face offers no further insight.

The other paintings delighted me: the blood, the body horror, the haunts. But this one is unnerving in a distinctly less fun way. There's a weight to it, from the crushing fall of Madeline's corpse to the way the walls crumble behind her and Rodrick. I almost expect the canvas to be heavier when I lift it to turn it around.

I can't leave these here. They're wonderful, but they'll clutter up the shot. Leaving the bags of clothing to deal with later, I heft the stack of canvases into my arms, careful not to damage them.

When I return to the balcony, Declan and Noah are standing on the first floor, right below Michelle's newly hung painting. As bad as I feel about Michelle's reluctance, I do have to admit that it's going to look fantastic on film. In the darkness, the woman's eyes seem to move, and the unfinished faces of the figures next to her take on strange, inhuman shapes.

Noah looks up at me. "What do you have there?"

"Paintings," I say. "They were being stored in the closet. What should I do with them?"

"Would any of them make good set dressing?"

He *would* ask that, even without Michelle here to give permission. I shake my head, coming up with an excuse on the spot. "These all have IP in them. I wouldn't." I consider showing them off but decide against it. It feels right, somehow, to keep these as a secret between Michelle and me.

Thankfully, Noah doesn't press it. "Go ahead and put them in the basement, then. Not like we're filming any scenes down there, and that's where Michelle's studio is anyway."

It makes enough sense to me. I walk toward the kitchen.

Declan raises his eyebrows. "Do you want one of

us to accompany you, darling? Venturing into a basement by yourself in such a home . . ."

I'm a little surprised by how quick he is to joke about it, considering what we just heard. Then again, Declan's never been the type to take anything seriously for long. I honestly admire how quickly he's able to brush things off.

Noah grins, getting in on the joke. "Hey, yeah, that's not very final girl of you. Sydney Prescott would be ashamed."

The *Scream* reference, more than anything, pulls a smile out of me. It's one of the first horror movies Noah and I watched together, and it's gained a bit of a soft spot in our banter. "I have never claimed to be the Sydney Prescott of this operation," I say. "If anything, I'm the Casey Becker."

Cannon fodder who exists only to die a gory death in the first scene? Far more likely.

"Aw, don't sell yourself short, Cleoface! You're at least Randy Meeks, easy."

I laugh, holding up the paintings in lieu of a proper response. "I'm going to get these downstairs."

Some of my resolve falters when I open up the basement door. The stairs downward are narrow and wooden, a little uneven. A chill wafts up from the stone flooring, bringing with it the smell of must and old cigarettes. Between that and the dimness, it calls to mind one of those ancient, seedy types of bars. For all of my joking, it makes me uneasy.

I glance down. At my feet is a metal tool—what I'd

mistaken for a weapon in Michelle's hand. As I pick it up, I see that it's a spackle, its edge coated in black paint. Holding tangible proof of my tendency to jump at shadows doesn't quite make going into that dark basement a pleasant prospect, but at least it breaks my paralysis. I walk downstairs.

The basement is unfinished, and it is cold. Within seconds, the tip of my nose begins to ache, an involuntary shiver radiating from the base of my neck. Plenty of houses don't heat their basements, but should it be *this* cold? I swear, the chill down here is sharper and more cutting than it is outside among the flurries and ice. It's not quite so cold that I can see my breath, but in all fairness, I can't see much of anything. There is one single high window, coated over with a thick crust of ice. Only a little light breaks through, pale and blue.

A dusty lightbulb hangs from the ceiling, a chain beside it. I pull it, and it flickers to dim life.

What it reveals is fairly average: mostly shelves and old storage, nothing of note. Perhaps the strangest thing is the door on the far wall, one that I can only assume leads to the art studio. "Michelle?" I try. But there's no answer. She must have left when I was upstairs.

I hesitate. Michelle wanted to keep her art studio private, but surely she wouldn't mind me leaving these there? I'll just open up the door and lean them against the wall. I won't even have to look inside.

Only when I try the doorknob, it's locked. I frown.

Were there hard feelings about Noah strong-arming her into letting us hang the painting? It wouldn't surprise me if she didn't trust us not to poke around, after all that. Guilt sours my stomach, even though I'd been determined *not* to snoop.

I lean the paintings up against the wall by the door instead, setting the spackle down as well. As I bend over, I hear a noise from the other side, in the studio. A strange shuffling sound, like something scratching at the wood.

"Hello?" I pause. There's no response. "Michelle?"

Silence reigns. But the hairs on the back of my neck are all on end. I'm struck with an oppressive feeling: not just of being watched, but *monitored*. As though, in spite of all evidence to the contrary, I'm not alone down here. It's like I just got into bed after a horror movie marathon, and now I'm left alone to imagine terrors lurking in the dark.

Shivering, I hurry back upstairs.

The next few hours are such a whirlwind of preparation, there's no time to dwell on that feeling. Lightbulbs are swapped for ones that look better on camera, stingers are placed strategically, and boom mics are tested in every room we plan to film in. The set is already mostly dressed as is, but Declan's brought a few key pieces: a strange antique bust for the living room, a creepy doll for one of the beds. Plus there are plot relevant props to place, like the scrapbook Andrea's character finds in the final scene. Seeing that come to life, when before it only existed as words on a page, is surreal.

This is far more work than we ever did while filming *Slaughter!* It's overwhelming, and it's strange to see how expertly Noah takes charge, ticking off items on a checklist in his binder with remarkable professionalism. I know he's had plenty of experience since our ill-fated venture four years ago. But I'm just not used to seeing this level of organization from him. He certainly doesn't approach schoolwork with this kind of determination. Aunt Carla probably wouldn't recognize him either.

We've done just about everything but dress the kitchen when there's a knock at the front door. Noah, deep in conversation with Rhiannon, glances up. "Probably Zander and Andrea. Andrea said she'd bring dinner. Cleo, can you get it?"

"Sure." Setting down my camera, plugged in and charging, I move to the hallway.

It's freezing when I open the door. I wince as Andrea and Zander hurry in, Andrea balancing pizza boxes in one hand. She hoots. "Holy wah! That wind is a nightmare."

I peer over her shoulder. The sun has fallen, but I don't need it to see that the snow is still falling fast and hard. "The storm hasn't gotten any better, then?"

"What do you think, eh?" Andrea's always had a bit of an accent, having grown up in the upper peninsula before moving to Ellis, but two years at Michigan Tech have thickened it. "I thought we were goners. Didn't you, babe?"

"We had some close calls," Zander agrees quietly.

On the surface, the two couldn't be more different: Zander with his pale cheeks reddened by the cold, his wide blue eyes and his windswept blonde curls; Andrea with her clear olive skin, her narrow features and her sleek black bob. Zander's dressed in preppy pastels with a thick scarf around his neck, while Andrea wears a snow-caked brown bomber jacket and steel-toed boots. But years of dating have left their mark: they move in tandem with ease, Zander catching the pizza as Andrea sheds her coat.

"Well, I'm glad you guys made it," Noah says, appearing in the kitchen entryway. "I'm saying that because of the pizza, by the way."

"Fuck you and the horse you rode in on," Andrea says, no real venom in her words.

Zander smiles at me sweetly as he lines up her boots alongside his by the door. "It's good to see you again, Cleo."

"You, too." I smile back, but there's no real warmth in it. I'm thinking of the snow outside, the storm. *We had some close calls.* Andrea and Zander made it here safe, but we're still waiting on a final actress.

Is that how this production is going to end, then? Not with my own death in a car wreck, but someone else's? It makes a horrid kind of sense. After all, that's what happened during *Slaughter!*, when . . .

I don't want to think about it. But I can't think about anything else.

I barely manage to pick at my slice of pizza, too nervous to enjoy it. Eventually, I can't sit still anymore, so I examine the remaining bags on the counter. They're full of food to use as set dressing.

It's a good thing we have it, because the pantry is empty. I'm a little surprised to see just how bare it is. It makes sense that Michelle would clear out her fridge before she leaves for vacation, but why would she get rid of shelf-stable items?

Declan shrugs when I bring it up. "Perhaps she's frugal," he suggests. "Open up some of those boxes, would you, darling? Make it look more lived in."

I obey. It's a poor distraction as time ticks by and no actress appears. I wonder how it's going to happen. Will the hours go by with no word, or will the police come by to deliver the bad news? CLOSE-UP ON: red and blue lights spilling across the snow.

Finally, when Noah heads out into the hallway, I follow him.

"Hey," I say. "Has the ghost actress texted you or anything?"

Noah frowns, stopping in his tracks. "I guess she did a while ago. But she's probably running late, it's fine."

I stare at him, wondering how he can be so monumentally dense. "Noah, the roads are terrible."

Noah's gaze skates over me, toward the window. "Zander and Andrea made it fine."

"Andrea said they almost went off the road. *We* almost went off the road."

"And we all made it fine!"

"What if *she* didn't?"

Noah shakes his head. "She would have let me know if she got in an accident."

"Not if . . ." I swallow. I feel like I should be on the other end of the camera for this conversation. Filming it at a distance, not having to be the one to say it. "Not if she can't."

"Oh, relax already." Noah leans against the wall next to me, nudging my shoulder with his. "First you're jumping at ghosts, now this? Save the blood and guts for your scripts, Cleodrama."

But he's worried. Too late, he's worried. I can see it beginning to bloom behind his eyes, like a slow-seeping poison.

"We should have cancelled," I whisper.

"Cleo—"

"I warned you, in the truck. I *said*."

Noah's expression pinches. Finally ready to take me seriously, for once. Only then light floods the dim hallway. Headlights. They shine in through the tall windows by the door like a beacon, or a searchlight.

Noah's expression relaxes, nascent fear melting into exasperated relief. "See? What did I tell you? You worry too much." He boops me on the nose before heading to the living room.

I stare at the windows as the headlights fill them, then cut out. Even with my fears proven false once again, I can't shake off the persistent anxiety. Not the way I could back in the truck, or the hallway, or the basement. It lingers on the back of my neck like a cold, clenching hand.

I head back into the kitchen. Declan is putting away pizza boxes as Zander and Andrea finish changing into their costumes. Rhiannon fusses with their lav mics, threading cords beneath Zander's university hoodie and Andrea's pale sweater. "Is there anything else I can do?" I ask.

"Could you give the fridge the same treatment you gave the pantry?" Declan asks. "I already filled it, but make it look less staged."

"Sure." I take the fridge door from him, letting banter wash over me as I examine its contents.

I open the milk and pour some of it down the drain, then open a box of butter sticks. I keep my back to the kitchen as the door opens, and Noah hollers a greeting to our final arrival. I glance over my shoulder as she steps into view.

My heart seizes in my chest.

The girl standing at the entrance of the kitchen is my age, wearing a soft pink scarf tucked into a light gray jacket. Her honey-blonde curls look perfect in spite of their windswept appearance, and the cold has only done her pale skin favors, adding a rosy flush to her cheeks and full lips. Her green eyes are bright and curious as she takes us all in.

Declan whistles. "Well, well! Miss Isobel Vernier, as I live and breathe. How have you been, darling?"

Isobel beams, a bright smile that scrambles my brain like a bad signal. "Oh my god, hi! It's been *way* too long." She swans into the room on lithe dancer's legs, hugging Declan like they're old friends. Which they probably are—he and Noah have worked on enough of the same stage shows. Isn't that where Noah met her?

Noah, who never told me the name of the actress who would be playing our titular ghost.

Noah, who is now looking at me with the *smuggest* fucking grin.

I've been doing my best to dismiss my fears of any paranormal entities so far. But if this house isn't already haunted, it's about to be, because I'm going to kill him.

Isobel, mercifully unaware of this silent exchange, continues to chatter brightly with Declan. "I'm so sorry I'm late, the roads were a total nightmare! But oh, here, I got your text so I brought this." She holds up a large tote bag. "It's, like, a bunch of clothes, you said you wanted them for set dressing or something?"

Sensing the opportunity for escape, I get to my feet. "I can take your clothes off!" All heads turn to me, and I can *feel* the heat rushing to my face, body reacting to the embarrassment before my brain has the chance to catch up. Jesus. This is why I'm better behind the camera, where it's expected I'll keep my mouth shut. "I mean, I can take your clothes. Can take the clothes off your hands, it's—um, Declan probably wants to get started on makeup, so I can handle these." I'm rambling. I'm prattling on like an idiot, in fact, and I haven't even introduced myself. "I'm, um, Cleo, by the way. I wrote the script and I'll be behind the camera, so . . ." So her job will be to ignore me. Probably for the best. "So I can handle set dressing."

Isobel smiles. Small and polite and for my benefit, which makes me want to die a little. "Oh, sure. Cleo. Didn't we have, like, Algebra together freshman year?" Lamely, I nod. I'm a little awestruck that she remembered me at all. "Right, totally! Good to see you again. Here." She hands over the bag and gives me a wink. "This isn't how pretty girls *usually* ask to get into my pants, but, like, I'll take it?"

"I. Right. Thank you." My brain, helpfully, refuses to process that. I'm viewing this whole scene as if through the lens of my camera, objective and clinical. AERIAL SHOT ON: a perfectly normal and platonic clothing hand-off. "I'm just going to take this, then."

I clutch the bag and flee.

I make it about halfway up the stairs before I have to pause to catch my breath. I'm used to making bad first impressions, but even for me, this was a colossal failure. I'm seriously considering going outside and burying myself under a snow drift when Noah walks out of the kitchen, grinning.

"Nice."

"You!" I hiss. "You did this on purpose."

Noah laughs, which does absolutely nothing to quell my fury. "Okay, look, I didn't tell you because I thought it would be funny, but I didn't think you'd react like that! I thought that crush was freshman year stuff!"

"It was! It is! I haven't even thought about Isobel in years!" Which is both true and a lie. We haven't had any classes together since freshman year, and nothing came of the hours I spent staring at the back of her head in Algebra, captivated by her bright smile and cheerful confidence but unable to work up the nerve to talk to her. I've seen her in passing since—in the halls, and once when I went to see a show that Noah directed. But we never talked.

Still. Isobel is the first girl I ever had a conscious crush on: the one that made me realize I was bisexual. That's not the sort of thing that stops meaning something. Even if those feelings faded before I did anything with them, they're still important to me. They're part of what makes me who I am today.

I can tell none of this to Noah. Instead I say, loftily, "You're too heterosexual for me to explain this."

Noah snorts, leaning a shoulder against the wall. "I didn't *just* do this to fuck with you. She's actually talented, and the best person for the job. Don't you trust me?"

"About as far as I can throw you," I grumble, leaning against the banister. Above us, the half-finished painting looms, eerie in the low light. "If it weren't for the storm, I'd consider stealing your keys and making a run for it."

Noah rolls his eyes, poking me in the cheek. He pulls away when I move to bite his finger, unfazed and amused. "Oh, quit being so fucking dramatic. Do your thing behind the camera, and Isobel will do her thing in front of it. It'll be great."

Sighing in defeat, I hold up the bag of clothes. "I'm going to put these upstairs."

Noah goes back into the kitchen, and I walk up the stairs. Just before I reach the top, I hear the bright peal of Isobel's laughter.

I can only hope she's not laughing at me.

$$- \mathbf{4} -$$

<u>**DUTCH ANGLE**</u>

```
INT. CLOSET - EVENING

A girl steps inside with a bag of clothes.
She hangs them up with no fanfare. Everyone
watching is utterly convinced of her absolute
normality. There is nothing to suggest that
she is, in actuality, panicking.

The fact that she is in a closet, of all
places, has no thematic relevance whatsoever.
```

I SORT THE new clothes into the existing ones, and while doing so, I try to make peace with the current state of affairs.

So. Isobel Vernier is our ghost. I'm going to have to talk with her. I'm going to have to *work* with her. What if she thinks the script is terrible, and that I'm a horrible writer? What if she's going to look down her nose at me for being interested in such morbid, creepy things in the first place?

I take a deep breath, trying to stop my pessimistic

thought spiral in its tracks. She wouldn't have agreed to do this if she didn't like horror at all. She might not be a huge fan—Rhiannon isn't, I know, and I don't think Zander or Andrea have any strong feelings about the genre—but she wouldn't be here if she absolutely hated it.

And, okay. Maybe she was my first crush on a girl, a crush so big and useless that I couldn't even bring myself to do more than stare at her from the back of the classroom. But that was years ago. I'm older, more mature. This is fine.

I breathe, acclimating myself to the inevitable reality: I'm going to make this movie, with these people. There's no getting out of it.

A hanger clatters to the floor. I jump. *Right.* I'm going to be making this movie, with these people, in a house that seems more haunted by the moment. Maybe ghosts should frighten me more than spending time with an old crush, but honestly, the situation is so ghoulish that I start to laugh instead.

I lean against the door as I get myself under control. The fit of laughter calmed me somewhat. I suppose that, since I'm here, I might as well make an effort to make the best movie I can. I don't have a chance of impressing someone like Isobel, I'm sure, but if I focus all of my energy on it, perhaps I can at least manage to not *completely* embarrass myself.

It's just a few weeks of filming. I can handle this.

Taking one last fortifying breath, I make my way back downstairs, following voices into the kitchen. I walk in at the exact moment Isobel unbuttons her jeans and pushes them down.

I *cannot* handle this.

"Hello, Cleo!" Andrea, her finished makeup lighter than what she usually wears, turns to face me. "You came back just in time to take Isobel's clothes off, eh?"

The comment sets off a round of good-natured laughter. I will the floor to swallow me whole, but naturally, the world is not so kind.

"I think she's doing a fine job of that on her own," I manage. "Uh. Not that I'm looking, or anything."

Isobel giggles. "I mean, I can't blame you. This ass doesn't quit." She wiggles her hips with typical theatre kid bravado.

"Um." I say, eloquently.

"Aw, don't feel bad, Cleo," Zander says kindly. The worn university sweater looks odd on him, considering his usual preppy wardrobe. "We knew what you meant."

Noah snickers, and I shoot him a glare.

He sobers, but it has little to do with my expression. He claps his hands together once. "Okay! Status report. How close are we to getting started?"

"Once Isobel's costume is on, I just have her makeup left," Declan says.

"And her lav mic is all I have left to set up," Rhiannon adds.

Noah looks at me expectantly, and I startle. "Oh! Um, my camera should be finished charging. I'll be ready once I grab it?"

The others are so organized, my answer feels weak in response. But Noah doesn't call me out on it. He just smiles sunnily, excitement radiating off of him in waves. "Awesome! Let's finish up so we can get rolling."

I scurry to the living room and grab my camcorder off the charging cord. It takes much less time than either Declan or Rhiannon's jobs, and I'm antsy when I return to the kitchen. I don't just want to stand around and wait for them. They already must think I'm an amateur; there's no need for them to think I'm completely useless.

I check the fridge. I'd abandoned the job of setting it up when Isobel arrived, but it looks fine enough to me, if a bit less disturbed than the pantry.

A box on the bottom shelf catches my eye. It's a twelve pack of beer, which I'm a little surprised to see. I mean, Declan turned twenty-one a few weeks ago, so it's not like he bought it illegally. But alcohol is expensive. Why waste the money on something like that? I hope no one plans on drinking it. No one else is old enough, and besides, I doubt anyone is going to do their best work while buzzed.

I open the box and pour one of the cans down the sink. Amber liquid cascades out and down the drain. There's something hypnotic in the way it swirls, in the scent of alcohol hitting stainless steel.

For a second, I'm transported back into a memory overlaid in film grain. EXTREME CLOSE-UP ON:

Another kitchen sink, another brand of beer. A little girl standing on a chair, pouring cans down the drain while her father isn't looking. He'll yell at her for it later, but she's just a kid, and she doesn't know any better.

"Cleo! Earth to Cleopatra!"

I blink, shaking my head. "Sorry. Zoned out."

Noah grins at me. "Getting another script idea? Attack of the killer beer cans?"

I laugh. I start to stuff the can deep in the trash before realizing that I don't actually *have* to hide it. "No new scripts. Just thinking about *The Widow Ghost*."

"Nice." Noah flips open his binder and checks the call sheet. "We're starting with the scene where Halley and Patrick are exploring the house for the first time. Originally I wanted to film the shot where they walked in here, too, but how about we save that for after the storm calms down? No need to make you guys walk out in that, plus the wind'll probably mess with the audio anyway."

So he *can* acknowledge the storm. I don't have time to dwell on that bitter thought as the others file out. I wipe my sweaty palms on my dress, pulse hammering in my throat. We're actually doing this, aren't we?

"Is your full name really Cleopatra?"

I turn. Isobel looks up at me, her dramatically made-up face covered by a black veil.

Maybe that distance makes it a little easier to form actual sentences. "Uh, no. That's just Noah being dumb." I clear my throat. "My full name is

Clementine, but everyone calls me Cleo." Everyone alive, anyway. I manage not to add *that* little overshare by some minor miracle.

"Clementine," Isobel lilts. "That's a pretty name."

This girl might be trying to murder me. "Thanks! Isobel is a pretty name, too, I think. Very, um, sophisticated. It suits you." I need to stop talking. And, thankfully, I have an excuse to. I scoop up my camera, holding it to my chest. "We should probably get started! Like Noah said."

Isobel hums and drifts past me, her gauzy black skirts swirling around her legs like a storm cloud. Perhaps by the end of this venture, I'll manage to have something resembling a normal conversation with her.

Noah sets to work getting the actors in place. We all stand silently as Rhiannon records room tone, and Declan makes some last-minute touch-ups on Zander's makeup. I check the viewfinder of my camera, adjusting the ISO settings until I get the lighting the way I want it. I'm a bit surprised to see that the battery is only at 73%. Had it come unplugged at some point while it was charging?

"Cleo! You good to go?"

"Huh? Oh, yeah." I put worries about the camera battery out of my mind. I should still have plenty of life left for tonight's shoot.

"Awesome! Places, everyone."

Rhiannon fusses with the portable recorder while Declan obligingly holds the boom mic out of frame. Zander and Andrea stand at the doorway as if they've just entered the home, and Isobel tucks herself into the corner, head tilted at the exact right angle to conceal her expression. She takes a breath, then becomes still—so still that she almost blends in with the scenery. There's something graceful, artful in the way she holds herself. I know at once that Noah told the truth: she *is* the best person for the job.

I stare at the viewfinder, canting the camera just slightly to the left. Hitchcock used this technique, called a Dutch Angle, in many of his movies. I don't pretend to be anywhere near his prestige, but I hope that the odd shot will telegraph at least *some* unease to the viewer.

Noah holds up the clapboard in front of the lens. "Scene two, take one. Action!" He slams the top down.

"Hello?" Zander—only he's Patrick now, Patrick in the lens of the camera—cups his hands around his mouth. "That's weird. Where did that woman go?"

"I'm not sure," Andrea—now Halley—looks around. "She was definitely waving us in, but . . . I don't see anyone here now."

Her eyes skate over Isobel, not seeing her. The camera hardly sees her, either: just the hem of her dress in the very corner of the shot. I hold on that angle as Halley and Patrick pass, staying there just for a beat longer than necessary. And then, right as Isobel begins to move, I pull the focus away, following Halley and Patrick instead. I may want a proper cut there, and make a mental note to try that with my next take.

"Well, let's try to find a phone, anyway," Patrick

suggests.

"I'm not sure how I feel about just barging into someone's home," Halley says.

"She invited us in. Besides, we need help. The car's not working."

"I know you're right. I just don't like it."

I step away, pulling the camera back. Halley and Patrick walk into the kitchen.

"Something about this place makes me uneasy," Halley murmurs.

I wrinkle my nose. What was I thinking? Andrea's a fantastic actor, but even she can't deliver *that* anvil believably.

"Cut!" Noah calls. "That was great. Let's run it again."

"Could I try and film it from the second floor?" I ask. "I want to play with perspective a little." Maybe with creative enough camera work, the viewer will be less put out by how amateur the script is.

Isobel makes a quiet noise from beneath her veil. "Totally cool," she coos. She's almost certainly just being kind, but the praise does still make my heart flutter embarrassingly.

"I don't see why not," Noah says. "Let's run it again."

So we do. I shoot the entire scene from above, crouching down and aiming the lens between the wooden slats of the banister. It's a bit disorienting, staring down at the tops of Halley and Patrick's heads like this. For the third take, I shoot it above the banister instead, as if someone is standing at the top of the stairs and watching them.

We do a few more takes from the first floor. I start to get into it a little, nerves replaced by the pure enjoyment of making something. But even in the flow of things, Isobel impresses me. She hovers on the very edge of the frame, as if she knows naturally where the shot ends. She's a little more visible in the overhead takes, but still just as graceful, flitting about the shadows with a dancer's ease.

Michelle's painting stands sentinel over the scene. It lends an unsettling air to the whole production that's almost enough to make up for the weakness of my script. I still think it was rude of Noah to use it, but I can't help but be glad that it's there.

"I think we've got it in here," Noah says. "Let's move into the kitchen. Cleorama, how're things?"

"Good." I check the camera's battery life. 45%. I frown. "The camera's battery is going faster than I'd like."

Rhiannon glances at the screen. "Maybe it's time for a new camera," she says. "That one's getting old."

I grip the camcorder a little tighter. She has a point. It was already an older model when I got it for my fourteenth birthday, and that was four years ago. But it's been with me through a lot. Sure, I haven't tried to actually film a movie since *Slaughter!*, but it's been my constant companion at parties and on vacations, capturing little vignettes whenever the mood strikes.

It's not that I'm sentimental. It's just that I'm not ready to get rid of it while it still works.

Besides, cameras are expensive, and it's not like I can expect Mom to get me a new one whenever the next holiday rolls around. The fact that she agreed to let me have one for my birthday that year, knowing the kinds of movies I'd want to make with it, is nothing short of a miracle.

I don't know how to say any of this to Rhiannon, so I swallow down my response as we move to the kitchen.

It's brighter in here, harder for Isobel to hide. She stands back in the hallway instead, staring in from the darkness. With her black veil covering her face, it's suitably unnerving.

Noah holds up the clapboard. "Scene three, take one. Action!"

Halley and Patrick enter the kitchen. "There's no phone anywhere," Patrick complains. "What are we supposed to *do*?"

"It's strange," Halley says. Her gaze is distant as she examines the bare kitchen table. "This place . . . it *looks* like someone lives here, but it doesn't *feel* like someone lives here. Do you know what I mean?"

Patrick glances to her. "I do. And that woman who invited us in . . . Do you think she was even there?"

"I'm not sure." Halley looks at him. "I'm scared, Patrick."

Patrick's gaze softens. I know it's not a look that Zander has to fake. He goes to Halley, pulling her in by the waist. "Do you want to leave?" His fingertips caress her face, a casual intimacy.

She leans into the touch. "And go where? The car's not working. And there's nothing else around for God knows how long." She takes a steadying breath. "Let's just stay long enough for your phone to charge."

"Good idea." Patrick presses his lips to hers.

"Cut," Noah says after a moment.

Andrea pulls Zander in closer, kissing him harder than Halley would dare. The way that Zander melts against her isn't particularly Patrick-like, either.

"Cut!" Noah says, laughing. "Hey, quit making out! We've got a movie to make!"

"It's not that I have a problem with heterosexuals," Declan says, voice dripping with irony. "I only wish they'd quit shoving it in my face, you know?"

I cover my mouth to smother my laughter. More laughter drifts from the hallway, and I'm surprised to see that it comes from Isobel: her shoulders trembling beneath the heavy black velvet of her dress, her smile a sharp, wet shine beneath her dark veil. She's got a nice laugh, open and unpretentious. Does it mean something, that she's laughing at a gay joke? The embers of my lingering crush do *not* need that fuel.

Andrea shoots Declan the bird as she pulls away from a red-faced, giggling Zander. "Kiss my happy pansexual ass," she says with no real rancor. Declan snorts and blows her a kiss.

"Okay, okay, let's rein it in," Noah says. "Ready for another take?"

Zander offers Andra a hand, leading her back into the hallway. As Declan resets the scene, I ready my camera, peering through the viewfinder. Noah holds up the clapboard.

"Scene three, take two," he says, "Action!"

We go through the scene again. I try a few different angles, trying to make it more visually interesting. Still, this is one of the weaker scenes in the script. I kept it in as a placeholder: knowing that I needed Halley and Patrick to decide to stay the night in the house, but being unable to come up with a decent reason why.

Zander and Andrea do some heavy lifting, bringing their natural chemistry to the roles. But the writing still feels hollow, and I wish I'd had time to come up with something better. I can't imagine audiences on the edges of their seats during this scene, eager to see what happens next. It's just boring.

I step around the kitchen table, catching the edge of the outside hallway in the shot. At least that isn't boring. Isobel, hovering in her spectral black dress, is a marvel. Her eyes glitter hard and ominous from beneath her back veil, her shrouded expression one of dark intensity.

Just before I pull the camera away, a second pair of eyes peer out over her shoulder.

Isobel's performance is still impressive, but it pales in comparison to those eyes. Because there's nothing alive in that flat, shining gaze. They're the dead eyes of roadkill, but they aren't senseless. They see. They *understand.*

They're staring at *me*.

And then they vanish—along with everything else.

My stomach lurches, but it isn't the world that's vanished. Just my view from the camcorder screen. "Fuck."

"Uh, cut?" Noah laughs, the sound a little nervous. "What's going on, Cleolinda?"

I look up, half expecting to see that specter still looming over Isobel's shoulder. But she's alone in the hallway.

"Um . . ." I look down at my camera. The viewfinder is still dark. "My camera died." What else can I say? Whatever I saw—or thought I saw—is gone now. It only left behind the goosebumps on my arms and the hairs sticking up on the back of my neck, and those aren't worthy of comment.

"Oh, shit," Noah says. He peers at the viewfinder himself, as if expecting it to turn back on. "That was fast."

"Yeah. We can wait for it to recharge, but . . ."

But that will add time, and it's already late. And if the camera *keeps* having issues, it will add even more delays. Delays that our catastrophically tight filming schedule won't allow.

None of this would be a problem if we were filming this as a passion project, the way it was supposed to be in the first place.

"Okay, okay," Noah says in the tone of someone watching his *Horrorfest* ambitions go up in smoke. "We'll call it for tonight, then head out early tomorrow morning to buy a new battery for the camcorder, and try to make up shooting . . ."

"Tomorrow's Sunday," Rhiannon says. "The electronics store in Ellis is closed on Sundays. I don't know what's around here, but . . ."

"I don't think anything's going to be open tomorrow," Andrea says. She's squinting at her phone. "Looks like they're setting a snow emergency for Cheboygan County. That storm's something else, eh?"

Outside the tall windows by the door, the blizzard rages. It makes me wonder how any of us will even get back to Ellis in one piece. Our luck has to run out eventually, doesn't it? A death would be a fitting end to this production. The only end, really. I've felt the weight of it all day, haven't I?

Deep down, I knew we were doomed from the start.

Noah frowns. He's staring out the window, snowflakes flickering in the wet shine of his eyes. For a moment, I think he might finally understand what a terrible idea this has always been.

But then, he lights up.

"I've got it!" He slams his fist into his palm. "Let's just stay here!"

I frown at him. "What?"

"I mean, for a few days at least. We've got food. We've got clothes. And if we're on set all day, we'll be able to get ahead of schedule even if your camera does keep acting up! We should still get a new battery when we can, but there's no point in going out in all that snow."

He adds this casually, as though he hadn't brushed off my concerns while we were actively in danger of dying. Then again, that was when the storm was a hindrance to filming *The Widow Ghost*. Now, it's an excuse to keep at it for longer.

I just don't understand. Why does this movie mean so much to him?

Isobel shrugs. "I'm fine with it? I wasn't, like, super looking forward to driving home in all that anyway." She jerks a hand toward the frost-coated window.

The others make noises of assent. I should be happy. It's not as if I *want* to risk life and limb in Noah's truck tonight. But still. I can't help thinking about the shadow I saw on the balcony. The eyes staring out at me from the viewfinder. That awful feeling in the basement.

I don't want to sleep here. Even if every single one of those incidents *were* just passing flights of fancy, a product of my horror writer's brain on overdrive. I don't want to be here at all.

But I am here. And one look out the window at the storm tells me that staying in this house, no matter how unnerving, is the lesser of two evils.

I force myself to breathe in. "Fine," I say. "Let's stay."

- 5 -

<u>CINEMA VERITE</u>

PATRICK
Aw, babe, don't worry. Everything will
look better after a good night's sleep.

(Excerpt from THE WIDOW GHOST, written by Cleo Moss.)

A QUICK CALL to Michelle is all it takes to seal our fate. Noah gives us the rest of the night off, assuring us that we'll be able to make up filming and then some with the new schedule.

The house has three bedrooms. Two of them have a single full bed, and the third has two twin beds. "That's enough to sleep six," Noah says. "But there's seven of us . . ."

"I can take the couch," Rhiannon offers. "Would rather have a room to myself, anyway."

"Cool, that's one problem solved." Noah claps his hands together. He's smiling, still pleased and giddy with the idea of staying the night. "Now we've just got to divide up the bedrooms . . ."

"Zander and I can share one," Andrea suggests. "That's pretty much a given, eh?"

"Yeah, okay, you two can take the bigger bedroom," Noah says. "As for the rest of us . . ." His smile morphs into a truly shit-eating grin. I find that I don't care for it at all. "Declan, how about you and I take one bedroom, and Isobel and Cleo can take the other? Split it between girls and, uh . . ." He falters, visibly remembering Declan's recent coming-out at the last possible moment. "Not-girls?"

"Ooh, nice save," Declan says, half-sarcastic and audibly amused. "I'm fine with that."

"Great!" Noah flashes a thumbs up. "You and I should probably take the room with the twin beds. I kick. As long as you ladies don't mind sharing a bed?" He turns to me, radiating smugness.

Somewhere in my next script, a messy-haired brunet is going to meet a gruesome, bloody end.

"That works for me," Isobel chirps. She's removed her veil, and she looks unfairly beautiful in her dramatic make-up. This unfairness is only compounded when she turns to me and *winks*. "As long as you're not going to be, like, weird about sharing a bed with a lesbian? Not that you seem like the type, but you know!"

That's. Well. That is information about Isobel that I have, now. "You're . . . I mean, you . . ." Isobel squints at me, and I realize that I probably *am* coming across a little homophobic. "No, it's not like that! I'm not like that. I mean, I *am* like that! Like you. Not exactly like you. I'm bisexual. Not that it matters, because obviously we're just sharing a bed, we're not . . . It's fine!"

And I thought the time I tried to come out to my mom had been a disaster.

"Sounds like we're all set, then!" Noah is positively gleeful. I've given him enough comedy material to last him months. "Good night." He drags a bemused Declan away.

This leaves Isobel and me alone in the hallway. Before the silence can get too painfully awkward, she smiles a bright actress's smile. "Do you care if I take the bathroom first? I, like, *really* want to wash this makeup off."

"Oh! Yeah, no problem."

"Thanks! You're the best." She blows me a kiss and swans off.

I am not going to read into it. Declan calls everyone *darling*; that doesn't mean he's flirting. Theatre nerds are just like that. And it's not like I've made a stellar impression so far. There's no reason to believe that a blown kiss was anything more than cheerful reflex.

The bedroom at the end of the hall is too ubiquitous to be anything but a guest room. The comforter is a plain pale blue, with a matching rug on the floor and a single chair in the corner. The only art on the wall is a simple landscape, a meadow with a tiny waterfall. I recognize Michelle's talent in the strokes, but it certainly doesn't have the personality of her horror series. Even the unfinished painting in the hallway shows more passion.

I plug in my camera, breathing a sigh of relief when it seems to hold a charge. Maybe there was something wrong with the outlet I used downstairs? The issue doesn't have to be with the battery. Although that would be my luck.

Once I'm assured that the camcorder at least somewhat works, I sit at the foot of the bed. The mattress dips under my weight as I settle, soft but firm. It's comfortable. More comfortable than braving the storm. At least, that's what I try to tell myself.

Sighing, I pull out my phone and dial my mother.

She answers before the first ring ends. "Cleo? Are you alright?"

I wince, both at the worry in her voice and the quickness of her response. I expected her to be in bed, not waiting for my call. "I'm fine," I tell her. "I'm sorry. I should have called you earlier."

"It's so *late*." The disapproval in her voice cuts as cold as the frosted-over windowpane. She doesn't acknowledge my apology. "When are you coming home?"

I breathe out as surreptitiously as I can, not wanting Mom to pick up on my anxiety. "We're, um, not." I hurry on before she can draw any conclusions. "I mean, the blizzard is really bad up here. None of us feel comfortable driving home in it, so we just decided to stay here. You don't have to worry, we're filming in a really nice house. We've got food and clothes and everything like that."

Silence on the other end of the line. I resist the urge to fill it, fidgeting with the black hem of my dress. Finally, my mother sighs. "So you're staying at a stranger's house?"

"Noah called her," I say. "She doesn't mind."

"Are you sure that's safe, Cleo?"

I open my mouth. Then I close it. I try not to think of glimpses of eyes or snatches of shadow. If I'm honest, I feel anything but safe in this place. But then I look out the window. Snow buffets the glass, the wind howling a forlorn tune. I shiver in spite of the radiator. "It's safer than going out there, I think."

Mom sighs again. "I guess I am glad you're not driving in that," she admits. "Just be careful. Keep me posted." Her tone turns into a prickly, care-worn frustration. "I don't know *why* you let Noah talk you into this. You'd be better off focusing on something less . . . morbid."

I scrunch up my face. "I hardly think my preferences in genre caused a *blizzard*, Mom."

"That's not what I meant and you know it," she says, although I'm utterly unable to see what else she *could* have meant. "I'm just saying. I don't understand it."

I breathe out carefully. She's just worried. It doesn't make her disdain sting any less, but it's not worth a fight. "I know, Mom," I say. "Look, I'll be careful, I promise. I love you."

Mom sighs again, but she doesn't push it. "I love you, too."

I hang up. In the quiet, the howling wind sounds almost like a voice.

Are you sure that's safe?

I'm not, of course. Even if I'm being dramatic and the house *isn't* haunted, there could be a thousand things wrong with it. Faulty wiring. A broken fire detector. Hell, with the roads this bad, even a slip down the stairs could prove fatal. It's not as though anyone could come to our aid in this weather.

Are you sure that's safe?

Are you sure that's safe?

"Cleo?"

I startle. Isobel stands in the doorway, towel-drying her damp curls. She wears a simple white t-shirt and leggings, and her face looks clean and fresh, not plagued by the same acne that's haunted me since I was fifteen. She probably eats a lot less grease than I do. She probably has a skincare routine.

"Are you, like, okay?" Isobel asks.

"Yeah, I'm fine!" I jump to my feet. "Sorry, I'm just going to, uh . . . yeah." I toss my phone. It bounces against the mattress before landing on the floor. I briefly consider the merits of picking it up before deciding that, actually, the floor is where I wanted it all along. "Be right back!"

A shower does little to rinse away my embarrassment. After I'm done and changed, I grip the edges of the bathroom sink, staring at myself in the mirror. It's not a pretty picture: acne clusters scrubbed red, dark circles under my eyes. The collar of my old Joy Division t-shirt has gone ragged from one too many washes, and my pale blue-gray hair is stringy and over-processed. Compared to Isobel, I look like something the cat dragged in.

Behind me in the reflection, something flickers. I whirl. Nothing there but the shower curtain. For a moment, I'd sworn that it twitched, but that's ridiculous. I'm alone. I'd know if someone occupied the shower. I was just *in* it.

And, still, my traitor mind conjures up the perfect horror movie picture: a masked killer, gripping the shower curtain in one hand and a knife in the other. CLOSE-UP ON: the blade glinting in the light.

The curtain twitches again. I bite back a scream.

I cannot keep doing this. I storm to the shower curtain, full of the kind of bravado possessed only by the truly exhausted. I tear open the curtain to reveal *nothing*, no killer, no knife, just slightly damp shower walls and a dripping faucet.

"Get it together, Cleo," I mutter. If I'm going to be sharing a bed with Isobel, I'm going to have to put these creeps out of mind. The last thing I want to do is look more ridiculous in front of her than I already do.

There's a knock at the door. Noah's voice drifts from the other side. "Quit mooning over yourself, Cleosaurus, I have to take a piss."

I sigh. No use putting off the inevitable forever, I suppose. I open the door.

Noah groans in relief. "Oh, thank fuck. I was about to go all Jack Nicholson on your ass." He contorts his face into a terrible grin. "*Heeeere's Johnny!*"

This reference to *The Shining* isn't half as charming as his *Scream* joke earlier. "Ugh. That's a little on the nose, isn't it?" I gesture out the tall windows flanking the front door. Snow collects wet and thick against the bottom, eerily reminiscent of the Overlook Hotel.

Noah laughs. "Oh, man, you used to *hate* that movie. Is getting snowed in like this your nightmare scenario, or what?"

"Every day with you is a nightmare scenario," I deadpan. "And, for the record, there is no 'used to.' I *still* hate *The Shining*."

"Aw, but the elevator scene is such a classic!" Noah makes a dramatic 'whoosh' noise, miming blood pouring from an elevator. "You've got to admit that there are some fantastic shots."

He has a point, but I refuse to budge too much. "I can admit that without liking it."

Noah makes a dismissive gesture, but he disappears into the bathroom without further argument. I return to the bedroom.

Isobel sits in bed, her face illuminated by the blue light of her phone. She glances up when I come in, smiling. "Hey! What movie were you guys talking about out there?" She blinks, then giggles. "I wasn't, like, eavesdropping or anything. Noah's just kinda loud."

That manages to make me laugh. "Fair." I sit on

the other side of the bed, half expecting her to flee. When she doesn't, I pull myself in. It's warm beneath the blankets from her body heat, a fact that I feel extremely normal about. "We were talking about *The Shining*. The movie by Stanley Kubrick? It's based on a book by Stephen King, but honestly, they're like two completely different things. King even said . . ." I'm getting off-topic. Always a danger, when talking about horror films. "It's a long story. But anyway, that's what we were talking about."

Isobel makes a quiet, thoughtful noise. "I think I've heard of that one. Is that the one with the kid riding the tricycle through the hallways?" I nod. "Yeah, okay! I should probably watch more horror movies sometime. It's not a genre I know super well, but it's not like I'm not interested or anything. Ooh, maybe you can give me recommendations! Although it sounds like *The Shining* wouldn't be one of them."

"Uh, I don't know, I wouldn't *not* recommend it?" I scratch the back of my neck. "It's not a bad movie, I don't think. I just don't like it."

Isobel cocks her head to the side. "Why not?" Her green eyes are wide and curious, focused on me like she actually cares about my answer.

I chew the inside of my cheek. "Well, as far as adaptations go, it took a lot of liberties with the source material. I'm a writer as much as I am a cinematographer, so that always rubbed me the wrong way. Also, the actors in that film weren't treated very well. It's said that Kubrick intentionally frightened

Duvall—the lead actress—to get a more 'authentic performance.' But that always felt like a weak justification for cruelty to me. If you hire an actress, shouldn't you trust her to do a good job?"

I'm talking entirely too fast. And I know I'm taking on a *tone*—what Mom calls my "lecturing voice." She hates it, says it makes me sound condescending. But Isobel doesn't seem to mind. She only laughs, soft in the low light. "Well. Good to know you're not going to try to, like, murder me in the name of method acting?"

Isobel Vernier just made a joke at me. A *morbid* joke. I'm grinning before I can help myself. "I mean, you're doing a great job just on your own. I don't need to force it." Isobel visibly preens under the praise in a way that manages to come across as endearing instead of conceited. "Anyway, sorry for getting on my soap box there."

"It's okay. I like your soap box." Isobel settles in, laying on her stomach and folding her arms beneath her chin. She looks up at me from this angle in a way that sets my heart skipping. "So, if you're not a fan of *The Shining*, what horror movie is your favorite?"

"Oh, uh . . ." I pause, thinking. I don't want to recommend anything too weird to her—if she's not familiar with the genre, I don't want to send her running right off. "I mean, it's hard to pick, because there are so many different kinds. *Scream* and *Friday the 13th* are classics if you want a good slasher, *Poltergeist* and *The Ring* for haunting, *Psycho* and *Get Out* are great psychological horrors. *The Exorcist* and *Rosemary's Baby* are solid religious horrors, or there's *The Thing* and *Alien* if you want science fiction? If you want something a little more recent I'd probably suggest *The VVitch* or *Midsommar*; *The Uninvited* is a little older but I think it still holds up . . . *Insidious, Lake Mungo,* and, oh, obviously, *The Blair Witch Project* is a found footage that's . . ." I trail off, face heating up as I realize how *long* I've been talking. "I'm sorry, I'm rambling."

Isobel giggles, but it isn't a mocking laugh. "No, no, don't apologize. I'm living for it, I love the passion." She tilts her head to the side. "But, like, I wanted to know what *your* favorite movie is."

"Oh." The tips of my ears burn. I hope that the dim lighting is enough to conceal my blush. "I mean, it's hard to pick just one. But if I had to, maybe *Oculus*? There's some really gorgeous camera work in that one, and it's got a dual timeline that I think is well done and disorienting in a genuinely creepy way, and . . ." I breathe, pulling myself back from the brink of another ramble. "Anyway, I just like it."

"That sounds cool. I'll have to check it out." She sounds like she actually means it, like she's not just saying it to placate me.

I sink a little deeper beneath the blankets, lowering myself closer in inches. "What's *your* favorite movie?" I ask.

Isobel makes a face. "I mean, you're totally right, it is hard to pick just one!" She wrinkles her nose. "If I'm being honest, it's probably, like, *The Wizard of Oz*? I've loved it since I was a kid, and I put it on whenever

I need a pick-me-up. Maybe a little less edgy than what you like, though."

I smile. "I mean, *The Wizard of Oz* is a classic. I'm not going to judge you for that."

Isobel looks up at me, her gaze teasing. "You're not going to go all 'not like other girls' on me?"

I snort. "Hardly. I enjoy horror movies, but it's not like I have a superiority complex about it." I sink a little more. My head is almost level with Isobel's now, and I lower my voice as if I'm sharing a secret. "I may have, on occasion, even teared up when Toto gets stolen by Miss Gulch."

Isobel buries a squeal in her pillow. "Oh, my god, right? I used to get so upset by that as a kid!" She peers out, smiling. "Anyway, I guess my favorite genre is probably movie musicals and, like, romances and stuff, but I do like some thrillers and horror movies! I really liked *Black Swan*."

"*Black Swan* . . . that's the one where the ballerina goes crazy under the pressure of her role, right?" Isobel nods. I press my head against my pillow, facing her. "I'm surprised you like that one. Does it hit close to home at all?"

"Well, yeah. But that's why I liked it so much!" Isobel giggles. "I mean, *besides* the sapphic sex scene. Representation is important."

A laugh comes out of me that more resembles the startled bray of a hyena. I should probably just roll out of bed right now. Maybe I could hide under it, or maybe I could keep rolling until I reach the front door.

Burying myself in a snowbank feels like the appropriate reaction to this.

Undeterred, Isobel continues. "But, like, yeah, ballet is hard, you know? And that kind of perfectionism can totally eat you alive from the inside-out. So the movie got super uncomfortable to watch in places, but it was a *good* uncomfortable, you know? I think it's important for art to be like that."

"Like what?"

"Honest," Isobel says. There's an intensity to her voice, a sincerity that radiates from her skin like light. "Like, if you're gonna portray something serious like that, it should be unflinching, right? I always try to bring that to my roles. Like, I want to make people feel something. I want to make them think." She looks at me. "Don't you feel the same way about writing?"

"Oh." The question surprises me. "I . . . uh, yeah. I guess I do."

I say so, but in truth, I've never really thought about it that way. I just can't imagine disagreeing with Isobel, when she says it like that.

"That's what good art does," Isobel says. There's a real passion in her voice. "It's honest even when it's hard, or scary. When I think of the art that's stuck with me, that's the thing I think about the most." She giggles. "Now I'm on *my* soap box."

"I don't mind." I smile a little, echoing her words from earlier. "I like your soap box."

"Thanks." She yawns, her teeth glinting in the low light. "I guess it's time for me to call it a night. Do you mind?"

"Oh! No, of course not." I settle in, tucking myself fully beneath the blankets. "Goodnight, Isobel."

"Goodnight, Cleo."

– 6 –

<u>CONTRAZOOM</u>

```
INT. BEDROOM - NIGHT

Shadows creep across the wall, marking the
passage of time in ominous drips. Sometimes,
those shadows almost look like long, reaching
hands.
```

I CAN'T SLEEP.

I'm in an unfamiliar bed, in a stranger's home, with only the vaguest assurance that I'm allowed to be here. Isobel breathes deep and even beside me, and my hyper-awareness of her body heat is just one more thing competing for my attention. It's a perfect storm for insomnia.

I'm no stranger to sleepless nights. Mom says it's all the scary movies I watch. To be fair, she isn't exactly wrong in her assessment: fear keeps me up more nights than not. And this house—with its sordid history and dark shadows—gives my brain plenty of ammunition.

I roll over, trying and failing to find a comfortable position. It's silly, but on nights like these, I sometimes like to entertain the idea that one day someone will tell me that a movie of mine made them lose sleep. Any horror writer knows that's the ultimate compliment.

I can't imagine it tonight, however. It's hard to think that I'll ever make a movie that frightening, especially while working on *The Widow Ghost.*

The plot is so simple. Halley and Patrick are on a road trip when their car breaks down. They're beckoned inside by a woman in black, but when they arrive, they find the woman has vanished, although her specter lingers in the shadows. Compelled by forces they don't understand, Halley and Patrick stay in the home. Patrick starts behaving strangely, then vanishes. While searching for him, Halley finds a scrapbook with photos of all the house's victims. The woman in black, seen clearly for the first time, appears out of the shadows and wraps her hand around Halley's mouth. The final shot of the movie is of the scrapbook falling to the ground, still open on the last page: a photo of Halley and Patrick staring dead-eyed at the camera. Blood splatters across the paper, and the camera cuts to black.

I can see it all in my head. Wide shots and close-ups and all sorts of odd angles, keeping the scares in the periphery until the last possible moment. It *looks* like a good film, when I imagine it. But it's missing something. I can't imagine *The Widow Ghost* making anyone feel the way *Black Swan* made Isobel feel. The way *Oculus* made me feel. The way so many other horror movies have made other people feel.

It's not good enough. Not honest enough?

Isobel believes that trait to be the hallmark of a good movie. I'm inclined to agree with her, especially as I imagine all the ways *The Widow Ghost* comes up short. There's nothing honest about it. It's a hundred different horror tropes, all of them done better by other writers.

None of this would even bother me if Noah hadn't made the ridiculous decision to sign it up for *Horrorfest*. I wouldn't be picking at every single one of its flaws like a vulture over roadkill.

I roll again, facing the wall. The snowflakes cast flickering, ghostly shadows as they batter the window. It's like living in a television filled with static.

I burrow deeper under the blankets. Beside me, Isobel stirs. Am I bothering her with all of my tossing and turning? I can't seem to keep still, any more than I can lull my brain into quiet. Even when I make a sincere effort, my legs twitch with pent-up energy.

If I keep up like this, I'll wake her for sure. Carefully, I slip out from beneath the blankets. I step out into the hallway and cross over to the bathroom. At least there, I can move around without bothering anyone.

The bathroom lights are disorienting after so long in the dark. I blink against the brightness, but even after my eyes physically adjust, my vision retains an oddly fuzzy quality. The strange, lightheaded sensation is a familiar companion on sleepless nights. I peer into the mirror, and the pallid face that stares back at me looks more like a recording than a reflection. It doesn't look like a stranger, but my weary brain doesn't quite register it as *me*.

How would I go about capturing this feeling on film? Would a lens filter be enough to communicate the strange, disconnected sensation of staying awake past the threshold of physical exhaustion? Perhaps it would require something more creative: a distortion of frame rates, odd cuts and near-imperceptible inconsistencies. Maybe something as subtle as shooting on a wide-angle lens.

Kubrick did that in *The Shining*, didn't he? I don't like the movie, but I still picked up that particular piece of horror movie trivia from somewhere. Dad, maybe? I hear it in his voice, a low baritone rumbling over the movie's ominous title music.

That's right. The only time I watched *The Shining*, I watched it with him.

I'm never sure what I'm supposed to feel in moments like these. Horror movies were so important to both of us. Watching them was one of the few things we could actually do together. Shouldn't a memory like that stir up *something* now that he's gone?

Sometimes, I worry that I got over his death too quickly. I cried the first night, when I came home to police cars crowding my driveway. But that was all. During his funeral, I felt more like an actor playing at grief than an actual mourner. Even now, sleep-deprived and raw, his memory doesn't inspire tears. Just a dull discomfort that almost feels like dread.

The wind howls, and the house lets out a long, forlorn creak. As the gust dies down, it lets out a shorter one, the kind of noise that any house would make as it settles back into its foundations. No cause for alarm.

Until it makes the same noise again.

And again.

And again.

Creaaaaaaaak. Creak.

I shiver. *The Widow Ghost* will never frighten anyone, I'm sure, but Michelle's story has burrowed under my skin. Now there's a story that's honest. Honest in the sense that it's true, of course, but honest in a different kind of way, too. It was hard to listen to. It was *real*.

Creaaaaaaaak. Creak.

My brain—my treacherous, ridiculous, horror-writer's brain—has no problem imagining what waits for me on the other side of the door. INT. HALLWAY — NIGHT. The specter of a long-dead corpse hangs from the memory of its noose. The rope creaks as it sways, carried by inertia and the small drafts of wind that creep through the gaps in the window.

Creaaaaaaaak. Stringy hair dangling, only half-obscuring a bloated face.

Creak. Pale toes hanging limp above the wooden floor.

Creaaaaaaak. A chest gone still and breathless.

Creak. Fingertips ragged and bloodstained from a final, desperate struggle against rough rope.

CLOSE-UP ON: Those fingertips, twitching. Because in a house like this, on a night like tonight, who could expect such a soul to stay still and dead?

Fear wells up in the back of my throat, aching and tasting of copper. It doesn't matter that the ghost only exists in my imagination. I know I'm being ridiculous. But logic has little to do with horror, as I've lived my life steeped in it long enough to know.

So what do you intend to do, Clementine? The voice that floats up from the pit of my brain is hectoring, tetchy with exhaustion. *What is your grandiose plan? Are you going to sleep on the bathroom floor, hiding from your own imagination?*

Of course not. It wouldn't be comfortable, and besides, someone would probably find me in the morning. I don't want to have to explain to any of the others that I spooked myself out of going to bed.

The over-bright bathroom is at once a sanctuary and a prison. I can't stay here. I know that. But the idea of leaving, of turning off the lights and stepping into the disorienting dark hallway, fills me with irrational, stomach-swooping dread. It's as if I'm caught between fight or flight with no way to enact either.

I force myself to move, despite my stiff limbs and panic-slicked throat. In the back of my mind, the last bastion of rationality babbles on, assuring me there's nothing to be afraid of. But that rationality is not in charge of my movements. Instead of opening the door, I press my ear against it, palms flat against the wood.

There's nothing. No creaking, no whispers, no ghostly wailing into the night. Only the wind and the same dull thrum I'd hear with my ear pressed against any surface: a quiet noise indistinguishable from the sound of my own blood pumping.

Because there's nothing there.

Because I'm being ridiculous.

This should be the moment where the fear breaks. This happens all the time, and if I let it stop me in my tracks indefinitely, I'd never leave the house. I should be able to fling open this door as easily as I'd flung open the shower curtain. As easily as I'd walked into the basement.

I almost do it. Really, I do. But then, I hear it: a quiet scrabbling, scratching sound on the other side of the door. It's distant, and it's muffled. But it's there.

It could be the house. It *could* be. Mice in the walls, a tree branch against a window, the radiator rattling. There are a thousand simple, harmless, mundane explanations. But my mind isn't interested in the mundane. It is all too happy to once again conjure up the image of the woman on her noose. Only now she isn't lifelessly dangling, oh no. She's trying to climb up here. And that noise, it's her fingernails against the banister, right before the wood meets the carpet.

Another creak. The house settling, or the balcony protesting against the force of her clutching hands? Is that soft *shirring* sound a curtain rustling in the breeze, or her clothing slipping between the railings? Is that groan the foundation settling, or the creaking of bones that should be resting beneath the earth?

And there—*there*. The unmistakable *thud* of a body hitting the carpet.

I hold my breath. There's no convincing myself that this isn't real. That I made it up out of whole cloth, sleep deprivation mistaking the thrum of my own pulse for something sinister. Not with what comes next.

Thump. Thump.

That *sound*. Any horror addict knows it. It's practically a cliche: "things that go bump in the night." It's the sound of an intruder. The sound of a child with a nightmare that will go uncomforted. The sound of someone coming to tell you bad news too urgent to wait until daylight. It's the sound I heard in the smallest hours of the morning when Dad would rummage around in the kitchen, sneaking trips to the liquor cabinet when Mom wasn't awake to scold him.

Thump.

The sound of something that should not be.

Thump. Thump.

Footsteps, while everyone is asleep.

Thump. Thump. Thump.

Footsteps, coming closer.

CLOSE ON: Stumbling, clumsy feet across the carpet. Barefoot, probably. I can't imagine that Michelle's mother put on shoes to hang herself.

Thump. Thump.

Thump.

She's right outside the door.

What would the heroine of a horror movie do in this moment? It's hard to imagine a proper final girl being in this position. These sorts of scares—long and drawn out and full of tension—can only be paid off by her far more expendable kin. There's only one way this scene ends, and I'm not on the right end of the camera to survive it.

It might be better, kinder even, to get it over with.

I open the door.

The hallway is empty.

I stare into the darkness for one second, then two, then three. Any moment, I'm sure, the ghost will appear. It will be a jump scare worthy of even the most stoic audience members. But the hallway remains still and silent. And the longer I stand, the longer reason has to reassert itself.

No ghost is going to get me. There's nothing there.

I let out a shaky sound that could only charitably be called a laugh. "You're being ridiculous, Cleo." Even at a whisper, my voice is louder than the footsteps I heard. Or thought I heard. Already, the fear—the *hysteria*—that gripped me in the bathroom is fading, leaving behind only a quiet sort of embarrassment that borders on amusement.

Thank God Noah isn't awake to see this. I'd never live it down.

To prove to myself how ridiculous I really am, I step to the banister. Nothing there, of course. No rotting corpse-ghost hanging at my feet. No hands clinging to the railings. No fingernails scrabbling against the wood. Only the portrait on the wall, keeping watch over the shadow-choked hallway below.

I lean against the railing, staring out across the gap. The storm seems to be abating some. Snow still falls, but it's no longer a blur of white streaks carried on the wind. Instead, fat, thick flakes float past the tall windows on either side of the door. Ice accumulates on the bottom of the glass, mist creeping up like a final breath.

It's hard to make out much else. I can't see our cars, but considering how long it's been snowing, I can only imagine that they're buried by now. Digging them out will be an exercise in frustration.

The realization settles over me like a lead weight. Even once the storm lets up, we're not going anywhere soon. The roads won't be clear right away. And with the inconvenience of having to dig out our cars, how easy will it be for Noah to convince the rest of the cast to stay for the duration of the shoot?

It's bad enough to imagine one or two nights in this place. But weeks?

I groan, rubbing my eyes. I'm too tired to come up with a solution for this. I should go back to bed. See if exhaustion can beat out paranoia long enough to catch at least a few hours of sleep before the night is over. I step away from the banister, glancing once more down to the first floor in a reflex as thoughtless as breathing, and—

Someone's there.

I freeze. The figure standing downstairs is a woman—too pale to be Rhiannon, too slight to be Andrea, too tall to be Isobel. I can grasp those surface-level details, can tell that she isn't someone I know, but trying to actually perceive her is like trying to hold water as it slips through my fingers. She has all the substance of the afterimage that comes from staring into a light for too long.

She is there. But she is also not there.

And she is looking at me.

This is the moment where a final girl would run. The ghostly threat would give chase, and the final girl would have limited options. Her best bet would be to run back to the bedroom, shut the door, and wake her love interest for the final showdown. Yes, I can see it now. CLOSE ON: Fingertips, poking along the bottom of the closed door.

Would those fingertips be ragged and bloody? Like they dug their way up from a frozen grave, or like they clawed at a noose in a reflex of survival?

I'm not sure, because I don't run. And the ghost doesn't give chase. She stares with her indistinct not-face for a few more seconds. Her arms move, but not in a way that any arms *should* move. They *twitch*, is the best way to describe it, a single shuddery lurch upward that ends as soon as it begins. She makes a noise, I think. A noise that sounds like a breath, so quiet that it's almost swallowed by the wind.

And then, she vanishes.

I take one step backward. Another. SLAM CUT TO: Our unfortunate character colliding with the ghost that's suddenly teleported behind her. Only when I whirl around, there's no ghost, no scare chord. Only the wall with its faintly peeling wallpaper.

"I didn't see that," I whisper. It sounds good, so I say it again. "I didn't *see* that."

I'm tired.

I'm in an unfamiliar place.

I have an overactive imagination, and it's an imagination that's already predisposed to scaring the absolute living fuck out of me.

All this is true. And none of it changes the fact that I saw a ghost.

I creep back into the bedroom, slipping under the blankets. Beside me, Isobel breathes deep and even, unaware of the anxiety that thrums beneath my skin.

For a moment, I have a selfish, childish desire to wake her. But it's not as if there's anything she can do about my current predicament. At best, she'll call me crazy and go back to sleep. At worst, she'll try to see for herself, and who knows what would happen to her? I can't risk it. I can't wake her.

All I can do is wait for morning.

– 7 –

<u>SHALLOW FOCUS</u>

(Excerpt from THE WIDOW GHOST, written by Cleo Moss.)

T HE NIGHT TAKES an eternity to end.

I trace the unfamiliar shapes of the bedroom with my eyes, on alert for any deviations in the silhouettes of the furniture. My body jerks back into wakefulness the second I manage more than the lightest of dozes, imagining the specter of a ghostly face hovering inches from my nose. Not even Isobel, her body warm beside mine, can distract me from my fear.

The sky lightens from black to gray in stop-motion increments. It's around 6 a.m. when I finally give up on sleeping for good. I peel myself out of bed, stiff and heavy. Isobel slumbers on, unburdened by my restlessness.

No ghosts greet me on the stairs, and no specters linger in the hallway. But I'm not alone. I'm surprised to find Noah in the kitchen, bent over his binder. A cup of coffee steams to his left, and he's got a highlighter clamped between his teeth.

He spits it out when he sees me. "Good morning, Cleeping Beauty!" He blows a raspberry before I can respond. "Yeah, I know. Not my best." He takes an enthusiastic swig of his coffee. "How'd you sleep?"

His energy makes it obvious that the two of us had very different nights. I give a noncommittal grunt as I cross to the coffeepot. In a rare show of mercy from the universe, it's still full. "What are you doing up?" I've never known Noah to be an early riser.

"I'm reviewing the shot list," he says. "Figuring out what to prioritize with the new schedule. We'll probably have to work around your camera's battery issues for another day, though. Snow emergency is still on, and it looks like the storm's not letting up until tonight."

I glance at the window. The snow has slowed more since I last checked, but it's still coming down at a respectable clip. I don't think the plows or the salt trucks are going to be able to get to us anytime soon.

We're trapped here. In spite of the mug clutched between my hands, I shiver.

"We'll be able to make up any lost time easy, though," Noah continues. "And it's not like we have to leave for good once the storm ends. It's lucky Michelle's out of town and doesn't mind us sleeping here. I can't believe how perfect this place ended up being, seriously."

I tap my fingertips along the edges of my mug. "It's creepy."

"I know," Noah says, grinning. "Isn't it great?"

"I mean . . ." What *do* I mean? The coffee isn't touching my exhaustion, leaving my thoughts uncoordinated and sluggish. My head and mouth both feel dull, as though shot through with some kind of numbing agent. "Are you really okay with sleeping here?"

Noah raises an eyebrow at me. "We don't really have a choice, Cleossandra." He gestures at the window. Thick snowflakes gather along the bottom of the pane. The ones not stuck fast to the glass tremble with each gust of the wind, catching the early morning light at blinding angles.

"I know, I know. The storm. But . . ." But Noah isn't suggesting just waiting out the storm. This is exactly what I was afraid of last night, and now, the prospect of spending weeks on edge like this is unbearable. "I don't think we should stay here longer than we have to. It feels wrong."

"Wrong?" Noah's frowning now. "Michelle gave us permission."

"I'm not worried about Michelle. I mean, I am, but it's . . ." I pull in a frustrated breath. None of my words are coming out right. "Noah, someone *died* here."

Noah lets out a small, unbelieving sound that stops just short of a laugh. "Oh, come on."

"I'm serious, Noah. Last night, I—"

"I know what's going on." Noah looks at me over the rim of his coffee cup, so smug and indulgent that I have to resist the urge to hurl mine at his head. "You're getting in your own head about the movie again, aren't you? Seriously, it's going to be great! Admit it, you had fun filming all those different shots yesterday."

"That's—That's not what's going on here." How can he be so dense? I know I'm not at my best level of communication right now, but it's like he's purposefully ignoring what I'm trying to say. "This isn't about the movie, I'm trying to tell you—"

Declan appears in the kitchen entrance, sleep shirt slipping off of one lithe shoulder. "Good morning, darlings," he says around a yawn.

"Morning, Declan." Noah brightens, his attention shifting as though I hadn't spoken at all.

"I saw a ghost last night," I say.

Declan stops in his tracks. Noah looks at me with abject disbelief, his voice aghast. "What?"

"I . . ." I rub my face. I hadn't meant to come out and *say* it like that, but frustration and exhaustion got the better of me. "I couldn't sleep. So I walked out into the hallway and I saw it. There." I point vaguely over Declan's shoulder. "It stood in the hallway for a moment, and then it disappeared."

I'm not doing the experience justice. Trying to describe what I saw is like trying to write one of my scripts: like I'm shoving my hands into soil, digging blindly through the muck for the right words. Only the right words don't come. Instead of horror, Noah just reacts with mild confusion. And Declan looks actively thrilled by the news.

"Oh, this is *fantastic*." He rubs his hands together, brown eyes sparkling with mischief. "Wait until Rhiannon finds out."

"Easy, now." Noah laughs. It's not at all his usual laugh, more akin to how he sounded when talking with Michelle. "We've got a job to do here. Besides, Cleo was probably just dreaming. Isn't that right?"

"I . . ." What can I say? Am I convinced that I *wasn't* dreaming? It had been rather surreal. There are details that aren't clear even when I search for them. Was the specter's hair blonde or silver? Had it been standing at the foot of the stairs, or framed by one of the tall windows by the door?

My memory of the encounter is dreamlike. And, yet . . .

"I don't think it was a dream."

Noah makes a tiny, unconvinced noise. "Maybe you were awake. But that doesn't mean anything. Remember when we watched *Child's Play* during that camping trip? You woke me up at 2 a.m., convinced that Chucky was trying to climb into your sleeping bag."

I scowl. "That's different. We were *nine*."

"Still." Noah spreads his hands out. "You gotta admit that you jump at shadows, Cleophobia. Am I wrong?"

He's not. And he isn't even telling me anything that I didn't think during that moment in the hallway. It's possible that what I saw last night was in my imagination. But it's also possible that it wasn't. And either way, I don't want to stay in this house any longer than strictly necessary. I just wish Noah would accept that, and not try to convince me that this is all based on filming jitters.

It all comes back to that. To *The Widow Ghost*, a movie that isn't even important. Even though Noah, for some reason, seems to believe it is.

"You aren't listening to me," I try. Ironically, it sounds like something Halley would say.

"You're fine." He stands, gathering his binder up in his arms. "Look, let's forget about all this ghost stuff, and focus on making a kickass movie. I promise, you'll have so much fun, you'll forget all about it by the time tonight rolls around." And with a single boop to my nose, he strides from the room.

Declan clears his throat delicately. "Darling, I mean this with all affection, but the fact that you didn't sleep *shows*."

I groan. "I'm aware." Great. I'm exhausted, terrified, and more than a little annoyed by how easily Noah brushed me off. Now I get to add embarrassment into the mix. I probably look as though I got hit by a train. What will Isobel think?

It's a ridiculous thought. I have it anyway.

Declan *tsks.* "Well, we can't have that. Come along, then."

He drags me into the downstairs bathroom, where he's stashed his kit for safekeeping. Without a word, he takes out a pale foundation and gestures for me to sit on the closed toilet. I do so, and he sets to fixing my face with a careful, practiced hand.

"Thanks," I say quietly.

"Well, I can't have you looking so tragic in present company," he says. "Truly, I'm surprised that it was fear that kept you up, and not more amorous endeavors. Isobel tends to go for the artsy girls."

"I—wait, really? I mean, never mind. It doesn't matter." The last thing I need to do right now is overthink every interaction Isobel and I have had thus far.

Naturally, overthinking is exactly what I do. She *did* seem interested in my artistic opinions. Was that her way of flirting? Suddenly, I'm worried I didn't answer correctly. That I gave responses that were too simplistic, not intelligent enough. Maybe I talked too much about myself without asking her enough questions in return. She'd want them returned, wouldn't she?

"Could you postpone your bisexual crisis long enough for me to get this eyeliner on you?"

I splutter. "I'm not—I don't—"

"Cleo. Darling." Declan taps my nose with the handle of his makeup brush. "I was there when you were a freshman, remember? You doodled 'Cleo Vernier' in your notebooks when you thought no one was looking."

I'd forgotten about that. Maybe it would have been better if I had died from a ghost-related mishap last night. It would be preferable to the mortifying ordeal of having to confront *that* particular memory. "Oh, fuck."

"I mean, that's certainly one option," Declan says, apparently unfamiliar with the concept of mercy. "Maybe offer to take her out to dinner first, though."

I choke on air, so violent that Declan actually has to pause what he's doing to my face. "That's not going to happen," I say once my voice returns. "I mean . . ."

I trail off, unsure what to say. Isobel and I had a conversation last night. But that's all it was. She didn't escalate things or give any sort of indication that she wanted me to do so. Maybe she was flirting at the beginning. But I must have failed in some way, turned her off without even meaning to.

Come up short, like I always do.

It's a dramatically self-loathing thought, even for me. Probably the sleep-deprivation talking. But that doesn't mean there isn't a kernel of truth in it.

"Isobel may be into artsy girls. But she's not into *me*." I jab a finger into Declan's chest. "And so help me, if you try to play matchmaker, I'll—"

"Now, now!" Declan holds up his hands, laughing. "Darling, you know me better than that! I won't get involved. I'll simply be watching from the sidelines, enjoying the drama that unfolds." He shakes his head. "Really, it's a delightful thing to observe. Light and dark . . . artist and muse . . . how terribly romantic. I can practically hear the wedding bells. Or the wedding *night*—"

"Stop talking," I say. My face is so warm, I'm afraid that the newly applied foundation might melt right off of it. "*Stop* talking."

Declan lets out a dramatic, long-suffering sigh. But he must take some pity on me, because he drops the subject as he tilts my face up to the light, one finger curled under my chin. "Fine. If you don't want to talk about your burgeoning romance, we can revisit your paranormal experience. Did you *really* see a ghost last night?"

I eye him. "Why? So you have more ammunition when you bicker with Rhiannon?"

"It's not bickering, darling! It's a spirited debate. Pun very much intended." I chuckle despite myself, and Declan's teasing grin softens around the edges. "Anyway, I am genuinely interested. Humor me?"

Come to think of it, I do remember Declan having a passing interest in the paranormal. I just hadn't realized that it was sincere. It can be difficult to tell what's sincere with Declan, sometimes. I remember admiring that about him, when we were younger. I liked how mysterious he was, had wanted some of that unflappable affect for myself.

If only I had the nerve for it.

"I don't know *what* I saw," I admit. "It happened

so fast, and . . . Noah is right, I was really tired. I guess I could have imagined it." Downplaying it feels natural, like the right thing to do. Even though a knot of fear remains lodged between my ribs, aching. "Do *you* think it could be a ghost?"

"It's a definite possibility." Declan gestures for me to close my eyes, and I obey. "The house certainly has the history for it. Like something out of one of your scripts, don't you think?"

"That's true, I guess." It feels strange to talk about so candidly. In movies, the ghosts are usually people who have been dead for hundreds of years. Not ones who died in living memory, with daughters left alive to grieve.

Why should it feel so different? I'm not sure. I only know that it does.

"What do you think about it?" I ask as Declan finishes my eyeshadow and I'm allowed to see once again. "If the house is haunted, I mean. Isn't that scary?"

"Not particularly." Declan turns my face this way and that, putting on the finishing touches. "Ghosts in fiction are often dangerous, because they function as a useful metaphor for the things humans *actually* fear—mortality, death, etc. In real life, they're far more benign."

"Oh." It's a surprising answer, robbed of Declan's usual irony. "You sound like you've thought a lot about this."

Declan shrugs. "What can I say? I've found myself

particularly fixated on the topic lately. It's fascinating, really. The history alone provides some positively wonderful reading material. I've spent more than one night with my nose in some book or another on the subject."

"Huh. That does sound interesting." Back when he was in high school, Declan was never much of a reader. It's a strange reminder of the fact that we haven't seen each other in years. I've gotten updates through social media, of course, but there's bound to be parts of him I don't know.

I wonder if Noah knew about this. He's kept up with the others better than I have, working on movies with them. Maybe that's why he reacted the way he did when I told Declan about the ghost in the first place.

"At any rate, I don't find ghosts frightening," Declan says. "I find them fascinating. What would convince a soul to linger on past its time? What is that existence like? The possibilities are endless. And there's no evidence in real life to suggest ghosts are dangerous, so what is there to fear?"

He has a point. When I saw the ghost, she didn't do anything particularly threatening. Does that mean I don't have to be afraid, even if she is real? "That's probably a good way to look at it," I admit. "It might help me sleep at night, if we're really stuck here."

"At least for the foreseeable future, that seems to be the case." Declan hands over a tube of black lipstick. "Here, you can keep this. You're lucky I couldn't decide between this and red for Isobel, or you might have to forgo your signature look."

"Thanks," I say, half-sarcastic. But I can't help but turn genuine once I look at myself in the mirror. "Seriously, thank you."

Declan's managed to make me look presentable. There's still exhaustion glazing my eyes, but he's covered my dark circles and evened out my skin tone, making me look far less haggard.

"Happy to help, darling." He steps behind me. "You may be the one behind the camera, but that's no excuse to not look your best!"

He nudges my shoulder. It reminds me of simpler times, jokes traded over lunch. Sometimes, I feel as distant as a ghost, left behind while my friends move on. But in moments like this, I'm able to believe that's not true. Somehow, it makes the whole situation with the haunting less frightening, too.

"Let's go," I say. "I should check on my camera."

- 8 -

<u>MIRROR SHOT</u>

CLOSE-UP ON:

The television. In the gray glass, we see movement. The GHOST descends on PATRICK. But the reflection is too warped. We can't quite make out what she's doing to him.

He cries out. But his cry is cut short.

(Excerpt from THE WIDOW GHOST, written by Cleo Moss.)

THE CAMERA'S BATTERY works.

It's a small mercy, because problems plague every other aspect of the morning. First, we try to shoot a scene in the closet, but the ceiling is too low to keep the boom mic out of the shot. Noah knocks over and shatters one of the prop sculptures that Declan brought when we film in the living room. Zander nearly falls down the stairs during a hallway scene, and while he's fine, it's a sobering reminder of how bad things could be if a real injury were to happen. Outside the window, the sky is still choked in gray clouds and thick snowflakes.

By the time late morning rolls around, we're all on edge. At least, I am. Exhaustion makes it difficult to face even small problems with any amount of grace.

"Okay," Noah says. He rubs the bridge of his nose, eyes scanning over his binder. "One more scene, and then we'll cut for lunch. Next up on the list is Patrick's death, so let's head to the living room."

My stomach drops. "Can we do another scene?" I ask. "I don't think I'm ready for that one yet."

Of all the shots in *The Widow Ghost*, Patrick's death is going to be the toughest to pull off. I want it filmed in the reflection of the television screen, leaving it somewhat ambiguous as to what exactly happens to him once the ghost grabs him from behind.

Mirror shots are, in the best of circumstances, difficult. It takes time to find an angle where the camera doesn't show but the action is still visible. Even at my best, it would be a nerve-wracking proposition. And now, running on no sleep and lingering anxiety, I am about as far from at my best as I can be.

"What? You'll be fine." Noah waves a hand. "Besides, the lighting in the living room is perfect for a shot like that right now."

I fight back a stab of irritation, knowing that I'm being mostly unfair. It's not Noah's fault that I'm operating at a deficit, even if it *is* his fault that I'm here in the first place. I breathe out and force my voice to come out even. "Fine. But don't say I didn't warn you."

Noah takes this in as much stride as he does my other warnings. Which is to say, he ignores me entirely and hustles us all into the living room.

During the silence while Rhiannon records room tone, I examine the television. The model is big and bulky, from the nineties at the latest. Its curved screen is sure to pose a unique set of challenges while filming. I know without testing it that its glass surface feels fuzzy when it's on, like you're pressing your fingertips against a layer of dust even when it's clean. My grandma used to have a television like this one. Dad always used to complain about how the picture was never clear enough.

"Cleorama? You ready?"

Noah's voice pulls me out of my thoughts. I bite back a groan. "Let's give it a shot," I say dubiously.

I'm right to be dubious. Figuring out the shot is, as expected, an absolute clusterfuck. Zander, Isobel and I spend what feels like an eternity shuffling in different positions, trying to find an angle that works for the scene. I can feel the judgement radiating off of the cast and crew, and as the minutes tick by, it gets harder to convince myself that it's all in my head.

A better filmmaker would probably have a more sophisticated technique for this. But my editing skills are minimal, and I didn't bring anything to make the process easier. The others *have* to wish that they weren't dealing with such an amateur right now.

Finally, I sigh. "I think this is as good as we're going to get." In the viewfinder, Zander is more or less how I imagined, but Isobel is invisible as she hovers behind him. Hopefully she'll appear when she steps up to overpower Zander, but with today's track record, I doubt things will go that smoothly. "Let's try it, I guess."

"Is now a bad time to ask for a bathroom break?" Zander says in his sweet, quiet voice. It's enough to get the rest of the room laughing, which is probably his aim. He has a way of doing that, of noticing when the tension is getting too thick and easing it in a way that comes across as natural.

I'm wound a little too tight for it to help me, but I smile for his efforts anyway.

"Alright, alright, quiet on set," Noah says good-naturedly. He holds the clapboard in front of my camera. "Scene eleven, take one. Action!"

In the viewfinder, Patrick jerks suddenly, crying out. But Isobel doesn't materialize. Her black costume keeps her from showing up on the screen.

"Cut." I pinch the bridge of my nose. "This isn't working. I can't see Isobel at all."

"Okay, no problem," Noah says. He sounds so calm it almost makes me more frustrated. "Declan, could you adjust that reflector there, see if we can get more light on Isobel?"

Declan makes an affirmative noise, and a moment later, the lighting shifts. Isobel's black-cloaked figure becomes more apparent.

"Let's try again," Noah says. "Scene eleven, take two. Action!"

This one is better, at least in the sense that it's technically visible. But instead of coming across as haunting like I imagined it, the scene just seems sort of silly. "This isn't right at all," I say, playing back the footage for Noah.

He nods, his expression thoughtful but far from defeated. "Yeah, I see what you mean. I think it's the way Isobel is grabbing him." He jogs back to the actors. "Hey, Isobel! Instead of grabbing his shoulder, try wrapping your arms around him from behind."

"Like this?"

"No, no, *really* get into it, like . . ."

I stare at the camcorder. Noah's direction to the cast fades away to a hum of white noise in the background. In my viewfinder, the gray surface of the television warps and wavers, as though reflecting far more than Zander and Isobel's blurry figures. I strain my eyes.

There's something there.

"Cleopoke? Can we try again?"

I startle. The television screen is normal, both in real life and in my camcorder. Last night, this probably would have been enough to send me into another spiral of fear and anxiety. But the fear doesn't come. Maybe it's the daylight, maybe it's the people, or maybe it's just that I'm too exhausted to be scared, but all I'm *really* feeling is a desire to get this over with.

"Ready," I say.

"Scene eleven, take three. Action!"

Take three becomes take four, and take four becomes take five. By the time we reach take ten, I'm thoroughly convinced that I won't be able to translate the shot in my head to real life. In some takes, the movement is too vague; in others, it's too defined, robbing it of any ambiguous horror. Noah suggests that maybe it's Patrick's scream that's the problem, and Zander replaces it with a truly harrowing gurgle. It helps, but it's still not right.

"Scene eleven, take eleven. Action!"

The ghost descends on Patrick, black fabric swallowing him in slices as she wraps her arms around him. His body twitches.

"Cut!" Noah calls. "Cleoberg, how are we looking?"

"I don't *know*," I groan. "It's just . . ."

It's just that there's something *missing*, here. Something that no amount of fussing with the composition or settings will fix. I can't make this work, no matter how hard I try.

My eyes sting with frustration. Part of me just wants to snap and demand to call this whole thing off. But it would be unfair to take out my exhaustion-fueled crabbiness on everyone else. "It's just not working," I finally say. "You guys are perfect, I'm the one who can't get this stupid shot right. I'm sorry."

"Hey, no apologizing! You're totally fine." Isobel's valley-girl accent sounds a bit off, coming from beneath her ominous veil. "I think you're doing great!"

"We all know how these things can be," Zander assures me. "Don't worry about it."

Their kindness makes me feel worse, not better. They're trusting me with so much. Their images, their reputations. And in this moment, I don't feel worthy of any of it.

A quick glance at my camera makes matters worse. "My battery is starting to go again." My voice wavers against my will, and I hiss out a breath. "Fuck." I'm being over-the-top. I *need* to dial it down, but I can't seem to help it.

"It's about time to break for lunch anyway," Noah's voice is indulgent, like he's talking to a tantruming child. "Let's take a breather and regroup after food."

The others head into the kitchen. I linger in the living room, muttering an excuse about needing to charge my camera. The truth is, I feel too raw right now to be around them. The exhaustion is part of it, but only a small part. There's no way I can sit around a table with the others without bringing down the mood.

Instead, I sit on the floor of the living room, my camera plugged into a nearby outlet. The carpet beneath me is worn, the baseboards coated in a layer of dust. Out the living room's only window, I can just barely make out the shape of a tree, weighted down in heavy ice. It sways with the force of the howling wind.

Last night, that howl had sounded so ominous.

Now it almost feels mocking. As though it wants to remind me that there's no escape from this doomed excuse of a production.

The problem goes far beyond this single shot. Even if I do manage to get it right, or find a suitable alternative, what comes next? I've never actually finished a movie before. I've never tried editing the things I shoot for fun, and my school assignments only ever required minimal effort.

The idea of pouring over all of these takes, polishing them and trying to shove them into a coherent narrative feels terribly overwhelming. And worse, it feels pointless. Why bother wasting all of that effort on a script that isn't even particularly *good*?

I lean against the wall, reviewing footage of the mirror shot. On some level, I recognize that I'm wallowing, and I'll probably just end up making myself feel worse. But I keep looking anyway. Forcing myself to face the reality that Noah seems so ready to ignore.

All of the mishaps, the near misses, even Zander's almost injury, they all point to one thing: this movie is doomed. It has been, right from the start. No wonder I find it so hard to work on.

It's odd, because making *Slaughter!* never felt like this. Oh, looking back on it, I can see that the script had flaws, and the shots I'd managed to get were far from perfect. But they hadn't felt that way at the time. I can't compare that single night of filming to anything else. It sounds dramatic to say, but at the time it really felt like I was experiencing the first day of the rest of my life.

I'd *enjoyed* making that movie.

I suppose I was younger, and more naive. Unable to see the problems for what they were. Probably, the movie would have fizzled out and failed, even if it hadn't been for . . .

The mirror shot footage is still rolling. I'd stopped paying attention to it, but as Noah's clapboard drops, something brings me back. It's the take after I saw something in the glass. It hadn't worked at the time, but now that I'm playing it back, I'm having a hard time figuring out what went wrong with it. The lighting is right. I can *see* Zander and Isobel's shapes in the television's surface.

This shot should have worked.

But there's still something wrong with it.

I rewind and play back, giving the shot my full attention this time. Zander and Isobel grapple with just the right amount of clarity. It's exactly the shot I had in my head. Only there's one thing I didn't account for. A third figure, standing in front of the actors, translucent but impossible to ignore.

I pause the footage. The figure, its features indistinct except for its eyes, glares right into the camera.

Right at me.

It could be a trick of the light, I suppose. But after everything I've seen in this house, that thought doesn't hold much weight. It should scare me. But, somehow, it doesn't.

I rewind the footage again, letting it play. How could I have missed this in the moment? Even indistinct, the raw emotion in the figure's eyes is impossible to ignore. What I've been playing at, this figure does for real. This is the sort of shot that could get someone to feel something. This is honesty.

It's everything I've been trying to do, distilled into a single look.

And I have it on camera.

"Hey." Andrea appears, Zander at her side. "You coming, or what?"

"We brought you food, in case you wanted to stay here instead," Zander says. He is, in fact, holding a plate with a sandwich on it.

"Oh. Thanks." My stomach gurgles, reminding me that I'm running on a single cup of coffee. I take the plate, balancing my camcorder on my lap. "I was just reviewing footage."

Well, what I'd really been doing was moping. But that feels distant now, unimportant.

Andrea leans against the wall, tilting her head. Black hair shadows her face, but there's a kindness in her stance. I have no doubt that she was the one who suggested bringing me food. She's always been like that, a maternal streak perfectly married with her proactive nature. "Find anything usable?"

I look down. On the camcorder screen, the ghostly figure stares, captured in a moment of pure, unfiltered menace. Only that menace no longer feels directed at me. Not when it's in service to reaching an audience.

"Yeah," I say quietly. "I think I have."

113

– 9 –

<u>**APERTURE**</u>

<pre>
                    PATRICK
              (slow, trance-like)
        It's too late already, isn't it?

HALLEY stays sleeping beside him. She doesn't
hear. But something seems to be listening,
all the same. The GHOST hovers in this shot,
just out of focus in the background.

                    PATRICK
               (still in a daze)
        I knew it. I was never going to be able
        to call for help. Help never comes.
</pre>

(Excerpt from THE WIDOW GHOST, written by Cleo Moss.)

NOAH HOLDS THE clapboard up to the camera. "Scene six, take one."

We're back to filming, in the main bedroom this time. Noah accepted it at face value when I told him that one of the mirror shots we filmed earlier worked. I kept any mention of ghosts to myself.

Noah was so quick to dismiss me this morning, and I don't want to argue the point with him.

Everything is in place for the next scene. Patrick's jacket sits sprawled at the foot of the bed, leaving Zander in just jeans and a t-shirt. Andrea stands outside in the hallway with a fluffy white towel wrapped around her body. She wears a strapless top and biker shorts beneath it, since we won't actually be showing anything scandalous on camera.

Isobel is tucked behind the wardrobe, her lithe form melting into the shadows. Even with the camera trained on her, I can barely make out her shape in the darkness.

"Action!" Noah calls, and he drops the clapboard.

In the viewfinder, Patrick stares out the window. His expression is strange: not quite confused, but distant somehow.

On cue from Noah, Halley speaks from the doorway, off-screen. "Baby? What are you looking at?"

"Does the sky seem . . . too light to you?" Patrick asks. "It's still nighttime, isn't it?"

It's barely past 1 p.m. at the moment. The idea is to film the scene again at night, then cut between the two in the final edit. Although I worry that the overcast sky will rob the scene of most of its sting. The daylight is muted, not nearly as jarring as I'd like.

"It *is* night," Halley says, walking into frame. "I don't know what you're talking about."

I try to imagine the scene abruptly cutting to night

as Halley appears. The idea seemed unsettling when I wrote it, but now I'm not so sure. What if the audience just thinks it's a continuity error? Everything about the filming looks so amateurish, after all.

Everything except, maybe, the apparition caught accidentally in the mirror shot.

Patrick turns from the window, smiling as he focuses on Halley for the first time. "Never mind. How was your shower?"

"Fine. Hot water works great." Halley shakes her head. "It doesn't make sense. Full kitchen, working electricity, running water . . . a closet full of strangers' clothes. But I'd *swear* that nobody's lived here in years. It's weird. Don't you think it's weird?"

"Weird . . ." Patrick's gaze drifts off for a moment. Drifts in the direction of the wardrobe where the ghost in black hides. I don't let the camera reach her, but I let it get close. In the viewfinder, Isobel's shadow spreads across the carpet like an infection. She sways gracefully. The hem of her skirt flits into frame, then away.

It's almost like we're dancing: her in her dress, me with my camcorder. I lead, always keeping a careful distance from actually capturing her. And she matches me step for step, nearly playful in the way she evades me.

"Patrick?" Halley calls, and I pull the camera back to her.

Patrick blinks, roused. "Sorry. What were you saying? I got a bit distracted by the view." He smiles.

The gaze that trails down Halley's body is too warm to be properly lecherous.

Halley makes a noise that isn't quite a laugh. "How's the bed?"

"Fine," Patrick says. He hasn't checked it.

"Are you sure? I don't want bed bugs."

"Hm. You've got a point, Hals." Patrick puts on an expression of mock-thought. "I think this is going to require an inspection. A very thorough inspection."

This time Halley does laugh, shoving Patrick back on the bed. He goes willingly enough, pulling his shirt over his head. I move the camera just before Halley's towel can drop low enough to show Andrea's bra. I pan slowly across the room as Halley and Patrick giggle, landing on the wardrobe. The shot lingers for a beat longer than it should as Isobel drifts out from behind it.

In the final edit, I'll cut right before she's visible. For now, though, I see all of her in the viewfinder: her veiled face uptilted, her spine arched, her limbs moving with a dreamy, distant grace. She doesn't walk so much as she glides, her whole countenance giving the illusion that she's floating above the ground beneath her skirts.

"Cut!" Noah shouts. Isobel drops her stance, rolling her shoulders, shifting her legs. No longer a ghost, but a girl. She glances at the camera—at *me*—and winks, lifting up her veil to do so.

I make a noise that I sincerely hope Rhiannon's audio equipment doesn't pick up and look away.

"That was great, you guys," Noah says. "Let's reset and give it another go."

Zander's hand has found an easy place on Andrea's hip. He gives it a squeeze as she slides off of his lap; she pauses to press a brief kiss to his temple. It's a far more chaste display than last night in the kitchen. Maybe because the scene itself is so intimate. I'd considered leaving it out—I didn't want it to be gratuitous—but at the time of writing, it felt important. A moment of connection to give the story's later events more weight.

"Scene six, take two," Noah says when everyone is back in place. "Action!"

They run the scene again. Zander and Andrea bring their easy chemistry to the characters, but I can't help but feel like the script, once again, works against them. Art is supposed to be honest, after all, and I can't honestly say I have much experience with this kind of intimacy.

It's not like I haven't come close. There was Adrian, who drove me to a secluded spot well-known for illicit adolescent rendezvous after a date. A year later there was Madison, my first girlfriend, and a night where we sat side-by-side under the same blanket in her basement, bathed in the light of a movie neither of us had been watching. In a script like the ones I write, either would have the perfect opportunity to escalate. But in real life, there's no script. No lines to read, no stage directions to follow. And scripts never mention the *nerves*.

With Madison, I feigned utter fascination with the movie I can no longer remember. With Adrian, I spewed out a panic-fueled info dump on urban legends of hook-handed murderers. No such danger had materialized out of the trees, but I *did* effectively kill the mood.

Still, watching Halley and Patrick flirt in front of the camera, I can't help but wonder what it would be like. To reach out and touch someone, instinctively, without fear. To let myself be touched in return.

"Cut!" Noah calls. "How are we feeling? Good for one more take?"

"Yeah," Andrea says. "But can we take five first? I need to go to the little actress's room."

Noah snorts. "Sure, okay. Everyone take five."

Most of the cast and crew end up taking advantage of the break. Rhiannon and Zander head downstairs for water refills. Isobel follows them and vanishes down the hallway. Declan heads into the bedroom he shared with Noah, and after a few moments, I can hear him holding a one-sided conversation in Spanish.

Only Noah remains in the bedroom, pouring over his binder with the end of a highlighter clamped between his teeth. It's strange seeing him so focused.

I don't have much to do. The camcorder battery holds steady for now. So I walk into the hallway for air, leaning against the banister. It's strange, to think of the horror that engulfed me barely twelve hours prior. That horror isn't gone, exactly, but it has lost its edge. Dulled by exhaustion, maybe. Or something less definable.

Outside, the storm, too, continues to calm. The sun is doing its best to break through the oppressive gray, even if it doesn't quite manage it. By tomorrow, I imagine it will have better luck.

Still, the snow falls, slow and hypnotic. As I watch it swirl, the sounds of conversation around me turn muffled and vague. My vision warps, as if caught by the same wide-angle lens that Kubrick was so fond of using in *The Shining*. There's an odd, fleshy click in my ears whenever I blink.

"Hello? Earth to Cleozoo!"

Noah waves a hand in front of my face, and I startle. I didn't hear him leaving the bedroom, much less approaching me.

"Sorry." I rub my eyes, shaking the grogginess from my head. "I was falling asleep on my feet."

Noah scoffs. "We're only on day two of filming! You're not allowed to be this exhausted yet, we've still got weeks left."

I grimace. "Maybe if I can get a proper night's sleep, it won't be a problem." I glance at the window again. "Do we have to keep staying overnight here? It feels . . ." I stop myself before I make the mistake of mentioning hauntings again. "Uncomfortable."

Noah shrugs. "I mean, it's convenient. But, hey, once the snow emergency lifts, we can take it to the cast with a vote. How's that sound?"

I can't argue with that. "Alright."

"That's the spirit." Noah nudges my shoulder.

"Now, come on. We're back at it."

Indeed, the rest of the cast and crew made it back to the bedroom while I was in my exhausted fugue state. I hope no one else tried to get my attention while my mind was a thousand miles away. Sheepishly, I pick up my camera, and Noah positions the clapboard in my view.

"Scene six, take three," he says. "Action!"

The clapboard drops. Patrick stands in the viewfinder, the shadow of the ghost in black clinging to the corner of the frame. I can't help but be impressed all over again with Isobel's performance. There's something genuinely unsettling in the way she's holding herself this take, her proportions strange and her movements unnatural. A chill runs down my spine.

"Baby?" Halley calls from off-camera. "What are you looking at?"

I'm supposed to cut the camera to Halley now, but instead, I let it drift toward Isobel. Such a fantastic performance deserves to be immortalized. And, besides, letting the camera focus on her in this moment serves as a visual answer to Halley's question.

"Does the sky seem too light to you?" Patrick asks, and I pull focus back to him.

The rest of the scene plays out. Patrick and Halley talk past each other at first, then come together in a moment of pure, gentle intimacy. Only when the scene ends, Isobel goes off-script. Instead of drifting out from her place behind the wardrobe, she stays tucked in the darkness, lurking, waiting. She does something with her veil, because all at once there's an eye glittering out from the darkness, glaring at the camera with such sharp intensity that I barely hold back a gasp.

It's more effective than any jump scare. My heart rate spikes, and it's only thanks to years of practice that the camcorder doesn't drop right from my grasp. Isobel admitted to me last night that she hasn't watched a lot of horror. Where on earth did she learn *that* trick?

"Cut!" Noah says.

I lower the camera, looking into the darkness. Isobel's veil has shifted, covering her face again. "Wow, Isobel," I offer. "I mean, just . . . wow. That was . . ."

"Sorry, what?"

I turn. Isobel stands in the doorway of the bedroom, her black veil pulled back from her face. She smiles, sheepish.

"I didn't realize we'd gotten back to filming," she explains. "I didn't want to, like, interrupt the take or anything. So I figured one without me lurking would be okay . . .? Like, totally sorry if I messed it up, it's just that these skirts are kind of a lot to move around in, and . . . yeah."

My stomach drops. Isobel wasn't behind the wardrobe? Even after everything I've seen in this house, the realization chills me. It's one thing to catch a glimpse of a strange shadow while I'm alone. But the figure behind the wardrobe had seemed so real. I hadn't even questioned it.

Apparently, neither did the others. ". . . Okay, what the fuck," Andrea says. "Isobel was definitely behind that wardrobe. We all saw it, eh?"

"Must have been a trick of the light," Rhiannon says.

Most of her attention is focused on her portable recorder, so she doesn't see the rather dangerous grin that spreads across Declan's face at this pronouncement. "A trick of the light," Declan says. "That's a skeptic's answer, darling."

Rhiannon scoffs. "Please. Let's *not* get started on the ghost conversation again."

"Again?" Zander asks.

"Oh, right, you weren't here for *that* particular reveal." Declan spreads his fingers out, wiggling them in a mockery of fright. "It turns out, this house has quite the sordid history. Isn't that right, Rhiannon?"

The question is pointed, but Rhiannon doesn't rise to the bait. "That doesn't prove anything."

"Nothing back there now," Andrea says. She's peering behind the wardrobe wearing only her strapless bra and shorts, towel left forgotten on the floor. "But what do you mean? We talking crazed serial killer? House built on an ancient—"

"Nothing quite that gruesome," Declan interrupts, "but tragic nonetheless. Apparently, the house's former owner hung herself on that . . . very . . . banister." He points out the door at the hallway beyond.

Shuddering, Isobel steps inside the bedroom, as if to put distance between herself and the scene of the alleged death. "That's so sad," she says. "How did you find that out?"

"Her daughter told us," Declan says. "She seemed rather . . . out-of-sorts. Nervous, even. And Cleo saw something strange just last night, didn't you, Cleo?"

I startle. At some point during the conversation, I raised my camcorder and started watching it through the viewfinder: clinically, at a distance. It's shocking to be addressed now, a stark reminder that I'm more than just an impartial observer in this scene.

Slowly, I lower the camera to look Declan in the eye. "I don't know what I saw."

Rhiannon rolls her eyes. "You didn't see anything, because ghosts aren't *real*."

"And what about Michelle's behavior?" Declan challenges.

"Do you think she was just . . . grieving?" Zander offers, still sitting on the bed.

For a moment, Declan doesn't know how to respond. Neither do I. Michelle lost a mother, and I've lost a father, so I'm in a perfect position to understand her. In theory. But if I'm being honest, my grief never looked like *that*. I don't jump at even the vaguest mention of him. I don't go out of my way to tell people what happened, as if the truth of his death is burning a hole in the pit of my stomach. When someone *does* bring it up, I mostly just feel uncomfortable. Like if I don't react the way they expect me to, that there must be something wrong with me.

Michelle didn't look grieving. She looked *scared*.

Noah clears his throat. "Well, Isobel is here now," he says, "so let's get one more take with her and then move onto—"

"You want me to go *back* there?" Isobel eyes the wardrobe. "I mean . . . yeah, okay. Totally." She takes a deep breath and squares her shoulders, hands curling briefly into fists. "I've got this."

She sounds less than confident in this assessment. I chime in. "I don't think we really *need* another take. I got all of the ghost footage I needed from the first two, the last one was really just extra coverage." There's no need to force Isobel to do something she's uncomfortable with, after all. Besides, everyone seems a little nervous to be in the room right now.

Honestly, I'm nervous, too. This all felt less real when I was the only one seeing it. Easier to brush off? That's not quite right, but I don't know how to describe it. All that I know is that the others' nerves are rubbing off on me, bringing me closer to the paralytic fear that clutched me last night.

Noah looks at me. For a moment, he seems genuinely frustrated. But then his expression smooths out so quickly, I wonder if I imagined it. "If you say so," he says. "It's probably better to keep things moving anyway. Come on, let's film the scene where Halley goes looking for Patrick in the guest room next."

The group hurries from the bedroom with the

same air that they might run from a cheap scare at a fake haunted house. I linger, although I'm not sure why. Despite what I told Isobel, I'm struck by the distinct sense that I'm not done here. I just don't know why.

My thoughts are too slow, too sluggish to make sense of. It's far too early for it, but part of me wishes we could just call off filming for the rest of the day. Even if it means putting us further behind schedule and making us spend another night in this house. I feel as though I could actually sleep now, if only I was given the opportunity.

I'm exhausted.

I blink. At some point, I managed to drift over to the wardrobe. Its shadow is imposing, a gaping maw along the back wall. I'm still frightened by what I saw here—by what we all saw here. And yet, I don't flee. That dichotomy has always been a part of my nature, I suppose. I am easily frightened, and yet, I seek out things that will frighten me. Usually, that tendency is restrained to my choice in fiction.

But is this really so different?

In the moment, it feels no different at all. Especially when I raise my camcorder, peering at the world through the viewfinder. Like this, I find, it's easy to see everything happening here as a story. Like just one more scene in service to *The Widow Ghost*. Or, maybe, something even better.

Something more honest.

I hit record and let the camera peer behind the

wardrobe.

There's nothing there.

Slowly, I back away. My mind is foggy, strange. I'm relieved, yes, but also strangely cheated. The same feeling as when a movie fakes me out on a jump scare. It's an odd sensation to experience in real life.

Because this *is* real life. Why had I felt differently?

"Cleo!" A voice calls from downstairs. I shake my head, clutching the camcorder close to my chest.

"Coming!"

– 10 –

ROOM TONE

```
EXT. HALLWAY - AFTERNOON

It's silent. Only it isn't, is it? What's
going on?
```

WE CONTINUE FILMING. Noah makes a surprisingly strong effort at keeping us on task, but it's a losing battle. The morning's tension is back with a vengeance, and this time, the rest of the cast seems less willing to shrug it off. All the lighthearted banter between takes is gone. Rhiannon is positively snappish, and Isobel keeps glancing over her shoulder every time she has to tuck herself into some dark corner.

In short, the fun has gone out of it. As the sun sets and day gives way to night, even Noah seems over it all.

"Okay," he says, rubbing his temples absently. "Let's do the scene where Halley and Patrick argue

128

next, and then we'll break for dinner. Andrea and Zander, you guys head upstairs and start walking down when I call action. Rhiannon, are you ready to record room tone?"

"Yes," Rhiannon says. Her voice is curt.

"Okay, great. Quiet on set."

Usually, it takes Rhiannon less than a minute to capture the ambient noise necessary for later editing. This time is different. Thirty seconds tick by, then a minute, then two. The silence morphs from routine to awkward to uncomfortable, worried glances exchanged amid silent fidgeting and confused shrugs. Still, no one breaks the silence.

I grip the camcorder. My chest is tight with fear, although I'm not quite sure what it is I'm afraid of. I just know that something is wrong here.

Finally, Rhiannon snaps. "I know what you're doing. Would you *stop*?"

She glares at Declan. He throws up his hands, looking just as confused as I feel. "What did I do?"

"You're messing with the room tone somehow," Rhiannon hisses.

"Whoa, whoa." Noah inserts himself between the two crew members as though he actually expects them to come to blows. "Let's take it easy here. What's going on?"

Scowling, Rhiannon plays back the recording.

The room tone should be almost silent. But it isn't. Beneath the hum of the radiator and the slight buzz of the chandelier lights, there's a whisper. It's too quiet to make out any words, but the sound of it is unmistakable. It's a voice.

"Holy wah," Andrea mutters. "That'll put a chill down your spine, eh?"

She's right. All the hair on the back of my neck stands on end, my heart racing as if preparing to flee. There's something horrific about that voice. Its steady drone is chilling, unnatural. The kind of voice that should instinctively repel someone, with the same uncanniness found in some computer-generated faces.

And yet, there's a part of me that wants to listen closer. To try and pick out words from that haunting, near insectile drawl.

Rhiannon cuts the audio, her movements near violent. "It's obviously Declan."

"What?" Declan's smiling, but it's an incredulous smile. Like he can't believe what he's hearing. "Rhiannon, darling, how on earth would I have—"

"Don't 'darling' me," Rhiannon retorts. "I don't know how you're doing it, okay, but you're the one fixated on ghosts. This is just . . . *unprofessional*."

Her anger is more frightening than the audio. This is starting to take on a similar cadence to the fights my parents used to get into, especially when Dad was drunk.

Declan raises his hands, palms out. "I'm not doing anything. Honestly, is the idea of something supernatural going on so difficult to believe that you'll believe that I'm *sabotaging* us over it?" He actually sounds offended by this, although it's difficult to tell how genuine it is.

"No one's sabotaging anything," Noah says. "Look, let's just focus on filming the scene, we can get room tone later."

But Declan isn't finished. "No, no. We're going to settle this. Rhiannon, I have a proposition for you."

Rhiannon raises an eyebrow. "What?"

"You're so certain ghosts are fake. So why don't we put that belief to the test?" He turns to the rest of the group with both hands spread, as if stood under a spotlight. "Let's conduct a seance."

Isobel utters a small laugh. "A *what*?"

"It's quite simple, really. We commune with the spirits, ask questions, see if we get answers." He shoots a sidelong glance at Rhiannon. "And when we do, you can stop interrupting our shoot with *baseless* accusations."

Rhiannon grumbles something unintelligible under her breath. But incredibly, some of the taut anger seeps out of her body language. Her voice, when she raises it, is more cautious than caustic. "And when nothing happens, will you stop messing around?"

"You won't hear a single ghost-related peep out of me." Declan mimes zipping his lips shut.

Slowly, Rhiannon begins to smile. Her frustration is outdone, it appears, by the opportunity to prove Declan definitively wrong. "Sure. You're on."

"Excellent." Declan laces his hands beneath his chin. "What about the rest of you? We ought to have a consensus for such things."

"Why not?" Andrea's grinning now. "Sounds kinda fun, eh?"

"I'm in, too," Zander says.

"Is it, like, safe?" Isobel asks.

"Of course, darling," Declan assures her. "I've done my research on the subject. I'll ward against any unwelcome guests." Rhiannon snorts at this, which he elects to ignore.

"Okay. Might as well go for it, then." Isobel begins to smile. "Filming a ghost movie in a haunted house . . . it might make a good story one day, right?"

"That's the spirit," Declan says. Then, off of Rhiannon's glare, "If you're waiting for an apology, darling, you're not going to get one. I *never* apologize for puns."

"Look, I hate to be the bad guy here," Noah interrupts. "But we *do* have a film to make, remember? We're already on a pretty tight schedule . . ."

"What, we didn't make any of that up today?" Andrea asks. "Cleo's camera barely malfunctioned . . ."

I hold the camcorder to my chest. It's ridiculous to feel defensive, because Andrea's pointing out an objectively good thing. Only Noah's looking at me like I've done something wrong. Or maybe like he expects something more from me. I haven't the faintest idea what that could be, so I stay silent.

"I'd been wanting to get more ahead, but . . ." Noah sighs. "I *guess* we can take a break after dinner for this. Just so that we can put all of this ghost stuff to bed." He looks at me then. "Cleo, what do you think?"

I open my mouth. Close it. Think of the figure in the hallway, the shadow behind the wardrobe. The barely-there glimpses on my camera that are better than anything I've managed to capture on purpose. What *would* happen, if we called them to us? It's a frightening thought, but it's one that I can't turn away from.

"I think we should try it," I say. "It might make good behind-the-scenes footage, if nothing else." I hold up the camcorder. Maybe, if I appeal to Noah's sense of filmmaking, it will improve his mood about the whole thing.

I'm not sure if it works, but he *does* acquiesce. "Let's do it after dinner, then. But for now, let's focus on the movie. Now, Rhiannon, if you wanted to try the room tone again, I bet . . ."

Having a plan in place removes much of the tension that's been building since we shot the bedroom scene. The banter between Declan and Rhiannon becomes genuinely friendly again, and we're able to get through the scene without incident.

Noah seems cheerier by the time we finish. When we do finally break for dinner, he grabs me by the shoulder. "Do you think you can grab some B-roll while the others are cooking? Get ahead of it, so we don't fall *too* far behind schedule over all this."

"Uh, yeah, sure." Honestly, I'm not sure why he's stuck on this. Surely, we can't be veering that far off course. Part of me wants to ask if he's okay, but knowing Noah, he'd deflect with a joke. Emotional vulnerability rarely plays a part in our conversations. "No problem."

He claps me on the shoulder before heading into the kitchen. I grab my camera and survey the hallway, weighing my options.

"Do you need me in any of this?"

I glance over my shoulder. Andrea and Zander are heading upstairs to change, but Isobel is still in her costume, black veil covering her face.

I consider it for a moment. I don't want to hold her up, but on the other hand, I do want the ghost in black lingering in as many shots as possible. "If you don't mind?" I say. "I'll just need you for a wide take, I think, I'll be focusing on close-ups after that."

Isobel brightens. "I totally don't mind! It's been super fun dancing around the camera like this."

I smile as I adjust the ISO settings. "Where'd you learn to do that, anyway?"

"Dancing? I started when I was, like, super young actually. Ballet's real competitive, you know?"

"No, I mean . . ." I gesture with my free hand, sketching out a crude imitation of her graceful routine. "You always seem to know right where to be. I haven't really had to tell you."

"You have been telling me, though! Well, kind of." Isobel doesn't shrug so much as bob her head. Her honey blonde hair flashes for a moment before vanishing behind her veil. "I just watch your face. You get all focused when you're working, so it's like, when

I hit the edge of the frame, you notice. And I, like, *notice* when you notice. So, yeah."

"Oh." I'm not sure what to make of this revelation. When I film, it's my job to watch other people. I'm not used to people watching me. Never mind watching me that closely. With her face hidden beneath that veil, I hadn't even guessed that she was paying me so much attention. "That's, uh, cool. I just thought you were a natural."

Isobel laughs. "I mean, I am also ridiculously talented, don't get me wrong."

"No arguments there," I admit. Isobel perks up visibly, and I bite back the urge to laugh. It would probably come out embarrassingly shrill. "I think I'm ready. Could you maybe head up the stairs?"

I'm not used to being the one giving directions, but Noah isn't here to do it. No one is here, actually. Isobel and I are alone in the hallway.

Isobel doesn't seem particularly bothered by it. With a nod, she darts up the stairs, holding her skirts as she goes. After a moment of consideration, she tucks herself into a shadowed corner, shifting her weight into that ghostly stance.

Noah not being here means I don't have a clapboard, but it isn't as though there's audio to sync. I clear my throat, mostly for Isobel's benefit. "Um, action," I call.

She stays still for a moment. It gives me time to fix the dark hallway in the viewfinder, panning slow across the shadowed doorways and stairs. It's much closer to the shots I take for fun on my own time, or the work I do for class. It's soothing, in a way. I don't have to worry about where this fits into the overall narrative yet, so I can just focus on making it look beautiful.

Isobel begins to drift. Now that she's pointed it out, I'm aware of how my eyes dart to the edge of the viewfinder. The moment it happens, she pauses, orienting herself along the edge of the frame. It really is like a dance between the two of us, in spite of my stillness. Nerves prickle along the back of my neck at the intimacy of it. But the camera between us offers safety, a certain amount of distance. I don't flee.

I observe, and I let myself be observed.

After a minute of this, I clear my throat. "Cut." I lower the camera. "That was great, thanks. I'm set with the wide shot, so you can get out of costume if you want."

Isobel flashes a smile and a thumbs up before vanishing into our room. Although it's a bit strange and more than a little embarrassing to think of it as "our room." I do my best to push the notion away, along with whatever other tangled emotions it might elicit. Emotions are complicated. Close-ups are easy.

More than easy, they're fun. I've always had a soft spot for shots like this: strange, contextless bites that seem to tell an entire story in just a few moments. I take my time, trying out different angles and settings to find the most interesting way to frame the banister, the overhead light, the doorknob.

I spend a little extra attention on Michelle's painting. I still feel a bit guilty about using it, but it really is fantastic. Doused in shadow, the figures depicted take on an eerie sort of life. The blurry, unfinished surface of the girl's face seems to shift. I can almost picture eyes peering out from the mass of black paint obscuring the man's. And the eyes of the blonde woman seem to follow the camera with a sharp, unnerving focus.

I'm standing halfway up the stairs, capturing it from that angle, when I hear the bedroom door open and Isobel's soft footsteps approach. I expect her to walk right past me into the kitchen, but instead, she pauses. "Want some company?" she asks.

I look up. She's washed her face and pulled her loose curls into a messy bun. Jeans and a slouchy white t-shirt under a long pink cardigan replace the black dress and veil. Her green eyes, no longer ringed by Declan's dramatic make-up, are warm and curious.

I laugh nervously. "I don't think I'll be that interesting to watch."

"I don't mind. I think it's, like, cool to watch artists work." She scrunches up her nose. "Unless this is one of those things where you gotta work alone? Because I totally respect that, don't want to get in the way of your process or whatever."

"Oh! Uh, no, I don't mind." I scratch the side of my neck. "Go ahead."

Isobel smiles. It's a sweet, uncomplicated smile. "Awesome! Cool." She sits down right there on the stairs, propping up her chin in her hands.

I turn back to the viewfinder, but I can feel her curious gaze on me, watching as I fuss with the settings. I try not to think back to Declan's comment on Isobel's taste in women and fail miserably. Is she showing interest, or *showing interest*? Either way, I can't imagine it will last. The process of getting these shots must look terribly dull from the outside.

It would be far more interesting to talk about her. I decide to try. "Can I ask you a question?"

"Sure! Shoot."

I can't help but smile at her enthusiasm. "You say you started dancing when you were very young. What made you decide to go into it? Was it your parents' idea at first, or . . .?"

"Oh, no, it wasn't like that at all. Like, my parents were always super into the arts, but I don't think they ever expected I'd go into them." The stairs creak beneath her weight as she shifts. "My mom's a lawyer, and my dad's a surgeon. I think they both figured I'd end up doing something like that. But they took me to see *The Nutcracker* when I was a kid, and, like, that was it. I just *knew* I wanted to be up on that stage one day. I started begging for lessons that night." There's a smile in her voice. "I think they thought I'd forget or get bored with it, but, like, I was *determined*. I pestered them nonstop for months. Eventually, they gave in."

The mental image of a tiny Isobel digging her heels in is an endearing one. "Why did they take so long? Do they think dance isn't practical or something?"

That's what Mom always says about filmmaking. I never talk about doing it as a career, but that doesn't stop her from commenting on it whenever I bring my camera along to a family party.

Isobel hums. "No, I don't think that's it. Mostly, I think they were worried about some of the more toxic parts of ballet culture. You know, all the *Black Swan* stuff. Which is, like, fair, I've seen a *lot* of that. But they've been good about helping me keep perspective and not get too, you know, wrapped up in that part of it. I like to think I've got a pretty healthy outlook, all things considered."

She says this with no small amount of pride. "How?" I ask.

Isobel huffs. A small smile plays at the corner of her mouth. "Girl, you're getting me, like, dangerously close to soapbox territory again."

"Maybe that was my plan all along," I retort.

"And *now* you're getting dangerously close to flirting."

Warmth swamps my cheeks. "What? I wasn't—I mean, I didn't—"

Isobel laughs. In the low light of the hallway, it peals like a bell. "Oh my god, you're so cute. Who knew the spooky goth who writes horror movies would be so easy to fluster?"

"Who knew the valley girl ballerina could be such a *sadist?*"

Before I can regret my instinctive energy match, Isobel giggles, leaning back on her elbows. "Aw, fine,

I'll play nice." She stretches out her lithe legs in front of her, one heel bouncing idly against the step. "To answer your question, though, it's sorta complicated. People get real elitist and, like, snobby about things. A lot of instructors can be really harsh, and there's a big problem with body image and stuff." Her lips press together. It's not quite a smile, but it's the shape of one. "It's not quite as dramatic as *Black Swan,* but mental health problems are still super common."

"Huh. That sounds intense." I fidget with the settings on my camera, dousing the hallway below us in darkness. "If you started young, there's no way you had any idea about all that. Do you ever regret it?"

"Not even a little bit." Isobel smiles. "I love dancing. I can't imagine not being a dancer. And, like, I'm pretty careful about my own mental health and making sure I don't fall into patterns like that. It's really important to me. It's like . . . I want to be the living proof that you can have a career in ballet without destroying yourself to do it, you know?"

Outside, the wind howls, and the lights in the hallway flicker for a moment. On one hand, I'm worried the power will go out. On the other, I'm sort of thrilled to have gotten that on camera. I'm not sure where, but that shot is going to have to go in the movie somewhere.

For once, the prospect of editing seems almost exciting.

Adjusting the settings to the now dimmer lighting, I focus my attention back to Isobel. "You plan to do ballet professionally, then?"

"Oh, totally," Isobel replies. "I've already applied to most of the top colleges for ballet, I'm just, like, waiting to hear back from them. Julliard is my first pick, but, like, I've got backup options if that falls through."

She sounds so matter-of-fact about it. And not at all stressed. How does she manage it? I haven't even begun looking into colleges yet, even though I know I should. "Doesn't it scare you?" I ask.

"Which part?"

It's a fair question. "I don't know. All of it." I wrinkle my nose. "What if you don't get in? What if you *do* get in? What if you put in all that effort, all that time and money, and then you end up not getting a job? What if it all comes out to nothing?"

Isobel is standing now. She leans easily against the wall, head cocked to the side. "You're, like, kind of a pessimist, huh?"

I flush, in shame more than embarrassment. "Shit, I'm sorry. I didn't mean to, um, bring you down like that." I know I have a tendency to do that. I jump to the worst possible conclusion and run with it. Usually, I only say it out loud when I can turn it into a joke or keep it from bringing down the mood. But Isobel had been so open, so vulnerable. I forgot myself.

But Isobel only laughs. "Oh, Cleo. There's nothing anyone could say to bring *me* down." When she smiles, it's kind. "Besides, it's not like you're saying anything I haven't thought before."

"Oh. Really?" It just seems so hard to believe that someone so confident could ever doubt herself.

"I mean, yeah, of course. There's always the chance that I could fail. It would be silly to pretend otherwise." Isobel cups her elbows in her hands, wistful. "But still. Dancing is everything to me. There's, like, no universe where I don't at least *try*. I'd rather hope and fail than give up before I've even begun, you know?"

I don't think the question is rhetorical. But, in truth, I find myself stunned into silence. I'm used to Noah's brand of optimism: the flippant utterance of *it'll be fine* while doom lurks on the horizon, not just potential but probable. But this is something different. This is looking doom in the eye and walking forward anyway, come what may.

"That's . . ." I swallow. "That's pretty incredible, Isobel. You're really brave. And, uh, I think you're great." I fumble for the right words, wanting to encourage without dismissing the weight of what she said. "I mean, no matter what happens. I think if anyone has a shot at it, it's probably you. You're really talented."

Isobel beams.

Declan sticks his head around the corner of the kitchen entryway. "Dinner's ready." He raises an eyebrow, gaze darting between the two of us alone in the hallway. "Goodness, am I interrupting something?"

Isobel giggles. "Oh, please. You're too much." She

nudges his shoulder playfully with hers as she walks by. In the kitchen entrance, she pauses to glance up at me. "Cleo, are you coming?"

"Yeah." I swallow, my mouth suddenly dry. "Just let me go, um, plug in my camera and I'll be right in."

Isobel shoots me a thumbs up, followed by a wink. She disappears into the kitchen.

Declan stares at me, smirking. I give him a pointed look, as if I can remind him of his promise this morning by gaze alone. He *said* he wouldn't try to meddle between the two of us. He better stick to it.

From the way he laughs as he follows Isobel into the kitchen, I have my doubts.

- 11 -

<u>CHIAROSCURO</u>

TALK SHOW HOST
And now, here to promote her latest film,
it's Cleo Moss!

"SO, WHAT *WERE* you two doing all alone out there?"

Declan shoots an infuriatingly smug smile across the kitchen table. If Isobel wasn't sitting next to me, I'd be glaring at him. So much for watching from the sidelines, evidently. "Isobel was talking about her dance career," I say pointedly. "She's applied to Julliard."

On my other side, Noah groans. "Ugh, don't talk about *colleges*."

His mouth is full of boxed mac and cheese. I grimace, shoving a hand under his chin. "Don't talk with your mouth full, you cretin." Naturally, I immediately follow up this command with a question. "You haven't sent out your college applications yet,

144

then?"

Noah rolls his eyes, swallowing dramatically before speaking. "No, I have. I'm just not sure where to go. Like, do I try for film school right away, or do I try to knock out some gen eds at a community college first?"

"Oh. That's surprisingly responsible of you." I have about five seconds to be impressed by Noah's newfound maturity before he sticks out his tongue at me. It's coated in a thick layer of powdered cheese sauce.

"I've already got a list of colleges I want to apply to," Rhiannon says, nudging her glasses up her nose. "Michigan Tech is my first choice."

Andrea perks up. "Really? Why haven't you come and visited yet, eh? Me and Zander can show you around!"

"She's only sixteen," Zander reminds her. "She's got time."

"Have you declared a major yet, Andrea?" Declan asks. "I seem to recall that you were on the fence . . ."

Andrea's face scrunches up. "Oh yeah, *that* whole disaster. I started out with Mechanical Engineering, eh? That's what Dad does, figured it wouldn't be so bad. But holy wah, I was more miserable than a fly in a glue trap. Dad and I fought about it some, but I ended up much happier when I backed out." She shrugs. "I'm a communications major for now. Figure it'll help me learn marketing skills, if I do try to make a go of this acting thing. And it'll be transferrable if not."

Andrea's story surprises me. She's always seemed so in control of herself. Like she knows exactly who she is and who she wants to be. I can't believe she's talking about her future so uncertainly—and that she's so unbothered by it. If I were in her position, I doubt I'd be half as casual.

"I'm still undeclared," Zander offers quietly. "I was looking into our Theater and Entertainment Technology program, though. I like acting, but behind the scenes work is fun, too. I'd be happy doing that."

"That sounds super cool," Isobel says. Her voice is warm and sincere.

"You're graduating next year, aren't you?" Andrea asks Declan.

"If all goes well," he says. "Honestly, I wish I would have just gone to cosmetology school and been done with it. It would probably serve me better when I do try to break into the industry. But I suppose some of the connections I've made will serve my future career, so it isn't all bad."

"U of M's film program did look good when I came to visit you," Noah says. "If I don't decide to go to community college, that's my first pick."

Noah went out and scouted universities? That's even more surprising than Andrea's story. Aunt Carla is always complaining that he doesn't take school seriously enough. But then again, I suppose my own mother has a laundry list of grievances. Maybe Aunt Carla's nagging is borne from the same instinct that has Mom snarking whenever I bring the camcorder anywhere.

"What about you, Cleo?"

"What?"

The question comes from Isobel. She's looking at me, green eyes curious. "I, like, barfed my future plans all over you, but I realize I never asked you what you were going to do. Totally rude of me."

"Oh, it's fine! My plans aren't that interesting. I'll, um, probably start with community college, sort of figure things out from there."

It's a lackluster answer, especially in comparison to the others. When did I manage to get so behind? It's not as if I hadn't been planning on looking at colleges. Every month, every *week*, I tell myself that I'm going to start. But, somehow, the starting never actually happens. And now, I get the distinct sense that I'm too late.

The others don't seem to see it that way. Andrea even nods approvingly. "Better to take your time than to waste it doing something you don't want to do—trust me."

"In the meantime, you're getting good experience here." Noah nudges me with his shoulder. "Aren't you glad you let me talk you into this?"

I resist the urge to glare at him. Am I *glad* that he lied to me, roped me into doing this, and trapped me in a creepy house in the middle of a blizzard? Of course not. Any experience we're getting is mitigated by the fact that we're doing it for a movie that's still, bar a few key moments, pretty mediocre.

I'd only bring down the mood if I said that out loud, though. Instead, I deadpan, "Of course. There's nothing I love more than being trapped in close quarters with *you*."

Noah snorts. "Aw, you love me."

"It could be a fun story to tell, once your career takes off," Isobel giggles. "Just think about it! Getting snowed in while filming your debut. It's the sort of trivia thing interviewers love, right?"

I can't help but laugh. "You think people are going to interview me about my movies one day?"

Isobel looks wide-eyed at me. "Why not?"

"Well, I mean . . ." I shift awkwardly, caught beneath her gaze. "I don't really think I'd ever get that popular. My movies are just, um, okay, I guess."

Really, I think 'okay' is a charitable description, but Isobel is staring at me like I just insulted her personally. "Whoa, hey, none of that! You're super talented, don't put yourself down."

My face burns. "You're just saying that."

"I am not!" Isobel's voice is shrill. "And even if I am, what I think doesn't actually matter. Like, you've gotta be your own best cheerleader, or what even is the point? I don't like it when my friends put themselves down like that."

"I—oh." I'm not sure what flusters me more— Isobel's insistent complimenting, or the fact that somehow in my blundering, I've managed to get into her good graces enough for her to call me her friend. "I guess?"

"Good girl. Dream big." Isobel pokes my cheek before turning back to her dinner.

Well. *That's* something that just happened. I try to give Isobel's words some thought, mostly so that I don't think too hard about her fingertip on my skin. I have to admit, there's something sort of fun about it. Imagining a future version of myself, glamorous and mysterious, sitting across from a late night talk show host.

Declan threads his hands beneath his chin, smirking. I worry that he's going to say something ridiculous about Isobel and me. But, thankfully, he's got antagonizing someone else on his mind. "The seance would also make a fantastic story."

Rhiannon rolls her eyes. "I cannot wait to prove you wrong."

"Ooooh, strong words!" Declan claps his hands together once, brisk. "Let's put them to the test, then, shall we? Move along, move along."

He wrangles the group into the hallway. Outside, the snow has slowed considerably. Every once in a while, a gust of wind ferries a flurry of flakes past the glass, but once it dies down, the night is stiller than it's been since we've got here.

"Let's do it here," Declan says. "Virginia hung herself from the banister, after all."

Rhiannon gives him a look. "When did you learn her name?"

"I do my research, darling. All obituaries are online these days, and we already knew her last name.

I discovered Virginia Barlow. Survived by her daughter, Michelle, and predeceased by her husband, Gerald, and her daughter, Laura. If Michelle is to be believed, they both died in the same car crash."

I glance up at the banister. Its slatted shadows fall over the hallway, stretching like reaching arms. I shiver. I still feel strange, talking about the death—*Virginia's* death—so casually. I can't stop thinking about Michelle when we do it. The waver in her voice. How pale she grew.

She's not here now, though. So what objection could I raise? I don't even *want* to raise an objection, not really. I voted in favor of this seance. Didn't I?

"Alright, gather around." Declan glances at me. "Cleo, darling, are you going to be part of this experiment, or would you prefer to get video evidence?"

"Oh! I'll film." I'd much rather be behind the camera than in the center of the action. I scurry to the living room, where I left my camcorder charging during dinner.

When I come back, the rest of the group—sans Rhiannon, standing stubborn in the kitchen entrance—sits in a circle around a single tapered candle. I recognize it from the set dressing Declan brought. He kneels in the shadow of the banister, pinching a matchstick between his well-manicured fingers.

"Just in time! How do we look, darling?"

I peer at the scene through the viewfinder, fussing

with the ISO settings briefly before glancing back up. "Ready."

Declan strikes the match. In the viewfinder, the flame grows too bright, briefly throwing off the focus. I adjust just in time for Declan to touch the tip of the match to the candle before shaking it out.

"We are here today to call upon the spirit of Virginia Barlow," Declan says. His voice is grave, but there's cheer sparkling in his brown eyes. "Virginia, if you're here, we'd like for you to make your presence known."

The wind lets out a particularly forlorn howl, and the foundations of the house groan. But not even *I* can twist that into the wail of a lingering spirit. No apparition appears on camera. No ghostly evidence makes itself known. In the viewfinder, my friends just look like a bunch of kids taking advantage of someone else's sad story.

"Join hands," Declan says, sotto voce. Andrea flashes Zander a wink before obeying, and he chuckles. Isobel seems game enough to go along, but the mood is altogether less somber than it should be. I pull the focus back, trying to make the group seem small in comparison to the house. I can create the right mood on my camera, if not in real life.

"Virginia Barlow," Declan calls out. His voice is firm, but a bit too melodramatic—I suppose there's a reason he works behind the camera, and not in front of it. "We just want to know if you're with us. Please, if you're able to, let us know you're here. Could you make the candle flame flicker, perhaps?"

There's a pregnant, hopeful pause. To Declan's credit, the candlelight does flutter quite impressively, but it's been doing that since he lit it.

"Blowing on it isn't helping your case," Rhiannon quips.

"You sound *remarkably* like my ex-boyfriend," replies Declan, not missing a beat.

Andrea snorts. Soon everyone is laughing, what little solemnity remained rapidly dissolving. Noah shakes his head. "Hey, let's call it," he says. "This was a fun idea, but nothing's happening. How about we get ahead on some of the night shots, instead?"

For once, I almost agree with him. I'd wanted to do this as much as anyone, but I can't really remember why. Those moments where I thought I saw something—behind the wardrobe, in the hallway— have the fuzzy quality of a dream. Had it all been coincidence and imagination? And even if it wasn't, what are we hoping to achieve here?

Before I can voice these doubts, Declan speaks. "Oh, let's go for a little longer. These things take time, after all! Perhaps Mrs. Barlow is feeling a little shy."

"Or something's holding her up," Andrea offers. "Traffic in the afterlife, eh?"

"Maybe if we all take this seriously," Declan says loftily, as if he hadn't been the one to crack a joke in the first place. "Let's give it an honest effort. No interruptions. No one can accuse me of not trying."

"Alright, alright." Around the candle, the group

joins hands again. Andrea schools her face into a mockery of seriousness. Declan rolls his eyes at the gesture but doesn't scold her on it. Instead, he raises his voice with slightly more gravitas than before.

"Virginia Barlow," he tries again. "We call upon your spirit. Please, make yourself known."

I'm not sure when the change happens. If it creeps in while Declan is speaking, or if it hits all at once at the end. But as he finishes talking, I realize that the hallway is freezing. Much colder than when we started, and the shadows look darker, too.

At first, I think I'm imagining it. Have I wandered too close to the windows? Maybe that's where the chill comes from. Only when I peer into the viewfinder, the others are affected, too. Zander and Andrea huddle closer, instinctively seeking warmth. Isobel's shoulders tremble. When Declan speaks, a plume of silver mist spills from his lips.

"Virginia." There's a note of uncertainty to his voice now. "Virginia, are you there?"

Outside, the wind howls. Only it doesn't sound like it's coming from outside. And it doesn't very much sound like the wind, either.

It sounds like a woman's voice. A wail.

"Holy wah," Andra mutters. Her dark eyes sparkle in the candlelight. "Zander, do you hear that?"

I hear it. I do.

"Virginia Barlow," Declan says, raising his voice. "If that's you, if you're trying to communicate with us, we're listening! Please, speak to us."

The sound—wind, wail, *whatever*—grows louder. Louder still. I swear that if I strain into the darkness, I might almost be able to make out a word. It almost sounds like it's saying—

Crash!

A discordant sound from upstairs overpowers any ghostly cry. My camcorder shuts off abruptly, viewfinder cutting to black. At the same time, the lights flicker out. Even the candle flame is snuffed in the chaos. Everything is darkness.

Someone curses; someone else screams.

And then, there's a glow: Rhiannon, holding her phone's flashlight in one hand. It illuminates her face in dramatic streaks, harsh in the wake of the candle's gentle flame. "The power just went out," she says. "The storm. It's a coincidence."

A moment later, the lights flicker back on. The radiator clunks and groans. Noah breathes out a sigh of relief. "Thank God," he says. "Being stuck without heat would suck."

"That *sound*, though." Andrea's already up, bouncing on the balls of her feet. "That crash wasn't a ghost, eh?"

She doesn't wait for an answer. She just rushes up the stairs to investigate. Zander stands, anxiously watching as she crosses the balcony. "Babe, be careful . . ."

Andrea ignores him. "I think it came from over here." She disappears into Isobel's and my room, and her voice floats hollowly down to us. "It sounded like . . . oh, shit. Come look at this."

There's an awkward pause before the others obey. I bring up the rear, still clutching my camcorder to my chest.

When something really bad happens, people don't react how you'd expect. They don't yell, and they don't get hysterical. Instead, their voices take on an almost flat affect, as though they've forgotten how to modulate their tone. That's how Mom's voice sounded, that night when I returned home from filming to find police cruisers crowded in our driveway. *"Your father went for a drive while you were out,"* she'd said in that strange voice, emotionless and horrifically emotional at the same time.

Andrea says *oh, shit, come look at this* in the same cadence. A chill creeps up my spine as I follow the others into the bedroom.

Everyone crowds around the window. Peering over their shoulders, I can see the part of the first story's roof that isn't covered by the second-floor balcony. A tree has fallen on top of it. The impact knocked its spindly branches bare, and loose chunks of bark litter the scene of the crime. If the tree had been even a foot taller, it would have hit the second story, too. Maybe even shattered this very window.

"Oh, fuck," Declan says succinctly.

"Is the roof alright?" Isobel asks, peering over his shoulder. The strands of hair not captured by her bun flutter as she leans closer to the glass. It's only then that I realize how badly the wind is still blowing. It howls like a haunted thing, screaming through the cracks of the house.

And it still sounds like a voice.

"I think it's fine." Noah angles his head, inspecting the scene. "I don't see any damage?"

"Any damage *yet*," Rhiannon corrects. "What happens if the roof collapses? That's the living room. I *sleep* there."

"We probably shouldn't stay here," Zander murmurs. "I mean, that looks dangerous . . ."

"We shouldn't go anywhere tonight," Noah says. "I mean, listen to that wind! The storm's slowing down, but it hasn't stopped. Last I checked, they weren't going to lift the snow emergency until tomorrow morning."

"We'll leave in the morning, then," Andrea suggests. "You call Michelle, see if she can send someone out to fix it, and then we'll get back to filming when that's handled. Probably won't get all of it done before winter break is over, but we can film the rest over weekends, eh?"

It's a practical suggestion. But Noah only frowns. "But if we do that, we won't finish in time for *Horrorfest*."

Is he genuinely still stuck on that? The film festival has never seemed less important. And neither has *The Widow Ghost*. How can he still be thinking of that, after everything?

The others think it, too. I can see it in Isobel's pale face, the way that Declan's eyes keep darting to the balcony, as if expecting to see a shadow hanging from the banister.

Something has shifted. The tree is part of it, but not all. It's the same dread I've felt since the drive over here, dialed up to eleven. The sense that something terrible is coming, and there's nothing we can do to stop it. Only now, everyone else can feel it, too.

I hold my camera tightly. Even dead, its weight is comforting.

Noah reads the room. He must, but he doesn't give in. "Listen," he says. "We can't do anything tonight, right? Let's get through the night and check out the damage in the morning. We can decide what to do then."

There's nothing anyone can say to argue with that.

- 12 -

<u>DIEGESIS</u>

```
CLOSE-UP ON:

A set of car keys. They sit on the very edge
of the kitchen table, an unassuming sprawl.
```

EVEN NOAH KNOWS better than to suggest filming after that. Everyone gets ready for bed. Isobel claims the shower first. I sit in our bedroom, swiping between different social media apps without absorbing any of them. Nerves jangle at the base of my spine, compounded by every noise that issues from the other rooms.

I can't stand sitting still. I throw my phone down and pace out into the hallway. The others are similarly restless. Rhiannon talks on the phone in the living room; in the main bedroom, Zander and Andrea hold a muffled conversation. Declan stands downstairs, moving the candle from the seance in odd patterns. Smoke trails from the wick.

I walk down to him, wrapping my arms around

myself. I'm wearing the same t-shirt I slept in last night, and it's colder than my sweater. "What are you doing?"

"Cleansing the space," he says. "Standard practice after a seance, you understand."

I watch the smoke as it drifts into the air, dissolving into nothing. "Do you think we caused the tree to fall on the house?"

Declan laughs. It's loud and sharp and nothing like his usual laugh. "Of course not. It was just unfortunate timing. A shame, too, because I really thought we were going to get something on camera. If only we'd been recording audio, too."

"If only," I echo. There's a strange hollowness in my chest. It's wrong to wish that something more dramatic had happened during the seance, considering how scared everyone already is. And, yet, part of me wishes for exactly that. I don't know what to do with that feeling. I keep walking.

I find Noah in the kitchen, pouring over his binder. He looks oddly haggard in the fluorescent light.

"Are you trying to figure out a new filming schedule?" I ask.

Noah snorts. "We won't need a new filming schedule," he says. "Give everyone the night to calm down, and they'll see there's nothing to worry about. That silly seance got everyone worked up, that's all."

"And the tree," I add.

Noah shakes his head. "No, people are just spooked. But nothing really happened. I mean, the tree thing sucks, but it's not like it did any actual damage. It's fine. Everything's fine."

I bite at my cuticle. I don't want to hold the others hostage here. They should be allowed to leave. But the strangest thing is: I don't think I want to join them. And not because of the movie, which was never really any good. This feels so much bigger than that.

"I have an idea," I say.

Noah looks at me. I try not to wilt under that gaze.

"This house is haunted," I continue. "You can't tell me I'm being ridiculous anymore, not after the seance. Maybe we didn't see a ghost, but something is clearly wrong. Everyone feels it, and I think you do, too."

"You want to give up because of ghosts?" Noah asks.

"Not give up!" This seems to surprise Noah. I hurry on, like I can convince him if I just speak fast enough. "We'll still film. But we'll focus on the ghosts instead. That way, the others can go home if they want."

Noah stays silent for a long moment. "We can't submit a bunch of ghost footage to *Horrorfest*," he says slowly. "You can't be serious."

"I am," I say. "It's not a movie in a traditional sense, so maybe *Horrorfest* won't take it, but somewhere might. And even putting publication aside, I think this is a great opportunity to—"

"No, no, no. We're not having this conversation." Noah slams his binder shut. "You always do this,

Cleo.”

I stare. “What are you talking about?”

“I’m talking about all the times you’ve said no to filming your scripts. Or filming *any* scripts. How many times have you *said* you wanted to film a movie, only to bail out at the last minute?”

I can’t believe what I’m hearing. “Noah, surely you’re not talking about *Slaughter!*” I keep my voice even, measured. “If you’re implying that I quit that on a whim, or that I didn’t have a damn good reason—”

“What? No, fuck, that’s not what I mean.” Noah groans, passing a hand over his face. His skin stretches in a garish mask. “*Slaughter!* was different, obviously. I’m talking about after that. You haven’t even *tried* making a movie since then. You drag that camera everywhere, you’re so *good* with it, but you never use it for anything, and . . . goddamn it, Cleo, I’m no good at this emotional shit, but it sucks to see you like that, okay? I wanted to make this movie because I *care* about you, asshole.”

A chill blooms in my stomach. It feels so much like fear that for a moment I struggle to identify it for what it really is.

It’s anger.

“I don’t recall asking you to come to my rescue, Noah.” My voice trembles. “You’re acting like I’ve been wasting away, locking myself in some mourning-induced stasis . . .”

“Aren’t you?” Noah challenges.

“I’m not,” I say. And then, off his disbelieving look:

"I'm *not*! I've just been busy, Noah. Busy with school, and . . . and . . ."

"Sure," Noah snipes. "Justify it how you want. But I know what I see. Your dad wouldn't want you to give up making movies, Cleo. He loved them. Remember how proud he was of *Slaughter!*'s script?"

"He . . ." This is ridiculous. "It's not like that."

I can't believe we're having this conversation. I knew Noah was attached to *The Widow Ghost*, but I suppose I thought part of him recognized what a doomed endeavor it was from the start. Only now he's acting like this is all so much *more* than what it is, and I don't know what I said to set him off like this. How did we get here?

The wind howls, but it doesn't answer my question.

"Look," Noah presses on. "I know you miss him, I—"

"Noah, stop. I don't . . ." I pause. What am I even supposed to say? That I *don't* miss him? That's obviously a lie. He was my dad; of course I miss him. I just don't miss him the way Noah seems to think I do. The way other people seem to think I should. Even talking about him, now, like this, it doesn't ache the way loss seems to for other people. Thinking about his bright eyes scanning over *Slaughter!*'s script doesn't bring tears to my own.

My primary emotion at the moment is not grief. It's confusion. Confusion, and discomfort at how *earnest* Noah is being suddenly. It's not like him. I don't know what to do with it.

"*The Widow Ghost* is a good movie," Noah tries again, "and he wouldn't want you to—"

"*The Widow Ghost* is mediocre at best and you know it," I argue. "I think it would be far more interesting to pursue—"

"More footage that you'll never use for anything?" Noah shoots back. "You can spin it however you want, Cleo, but you can't fool me. You're just using the ghosts as an excuse to bail, and I don't want to stick around to watch it. If you tell the others to leave, I'll follow them right out the door." He shoulders past me, his voice taking on a mocking edge. "I'll be right back."

His parting quip hangs in the air as he flings open the basement door and storms down the stairs. It's another *Scream* reference. The sort of joke we make at each other all the time. Only his frustration robs the comment of any humor.

I stay standing in the kitchen, stunned. What has gotten into him? This isn't the Noah I know. His erratic behavior almost reminds me, uncomfortably, of how Dad would act when he was drunk. The most random things would set him off, and he'd burst into these strange, rambling arguments that didn't make any sense. Noah didn't seem drunk. His words were sharp, his eyes focused, with no tell-tale sway or bracing against furniture to give him away. But I'm so disturbed by his sudden change that I make a detour to the fridge anyway, checking the twelve pack on the bottom shelf.

The only can missing is the one I poured down the drain.

Well, whatever's gotten into Noah, I don't intend to stick around and subject myself to it any further. Better to leave him alone until he calms down and tires himself out. I go upstairs and get ready for sleep.

Isobel is already in bed when I arrive. The overhead light is still on. When I step on a floorboard that creaks, she startles. "Oh! Geez, I didn't hear you come in."

"Sorry." I hover by the door. "Can I turn off the light?"

"Oh. Well, uh . . ." She giggles at an odd pitch. "I guess I'm a little freaked out by the seance, is all."

I lean against the wall, considering this. "Sure, that makes sense."

Isobel tugs the blanket up to her chin. "I know I'm being, like, totally ridiculous. We can't exactly sleep with the lights on in here."

I smile, hoping it comes across kind instead of mocking. "That would be a bit difficult, I suppose. Hang on, let me see what I can do."

I return to the hallway. The overhead chandelier would be much too bright for sleep, but there are other options. I turn on the bathroom light and crack the door open, so its light spills into the hallway. When I return to the bedroom and turn off its light, the faint glow provides us with some relief. "How's that?" I ask.

"Better, thank you." Isobel giggles as I slide into

bed beside her. "Promise you won't make fun of me for being a wimp?"

"I would be quite the hypocrite if I did." I gesture out into the lit hallway. "How do you think I learned solutions like that? Also, full disclosure: I got maybe an hour of sleep last night because this house freaked me out so much. If you're a wimp, I'm a true, proper chickenshit coward."

Isobel breathes out a laugh. In the dim light, I can't read her expression, but there's warmth in her voice. "I'm sorry. You could have woken me up. I would have held your hand."

My breath catches. Isobel has this habit of tossing out comments like that casually, with just enough of a tease to give her plausible deniability. It never fails to throw me for a loop, no matter my best efforts.

I lay on my side, tracing the edge of her face with my eyes. Trying to catch the minute changes in her silhouette that might offer me insight into how she's feeling. "Do you want to leave?" I ask. "Tomorrow, I mean."

Isobel hums softly. "I don't know. The movie has been super fun, honestly!"

"Really?" It's hard to believe, in our present circumstances. "I hardly wanted to film this in the first place. Noah just has a weird fixation with it because of how our last movie together ended."

"You guys tried to make a movie before?"

Why did I even mention that? For a moment, I forgot Isobel hadn't been there. That she doesn't know. "Yeah, um. We tried making a movie together our freshman year. Declan was involved, so were Andrea and Zander. We didn't know Rhiannon yet, but, um, yeah."

I'm rambling, but it isn't enough to deter Isobel. "What happened?" she asks.

I breathe out. I don't want to be like Michelle about this. I don't *feel* like Michelle. Really, I just feel awkward. It sounds so dramatic when I say it out loud.

"During the first night of filming, my dad died in a car accident. It derailed things. Obviously."

Isobel gasps. "Oh my god, Cleo, I'm so sorry!"

I fight back a wince. "It's fine! I mean, it was a long time ago, I'm okay." I sigh. "But that's what Noah's being weird about. I haven't done a movie since, and he's convinced it's because I was traumatized or something. That isn't what happened, but he's still . . . I don't know." I sigh, rolling onto my back. "I just don't get why he cares so much about this movie in particular. He's worked on plenty of other sets, and he'll work on plenty more."

Isobel is quiet for a moment. "You and Noah are cousins, right?"

"That's right," I say, a bit confused by the direction this conversation has taken.

"So your dad was his uncle. Were they, like, close?"

The question brings me up short. Was Noah close with my dad? "Dad was a big horror movie fan," I say slowly. "We'd all talk about that. And Noah always loved Dad's film recommendations. But . . ." I pause, groping for the right words. On paper, they should have been close. But Dad was never an easy person to get close *to*. There were moments, but they were fleeting, impossible to predict.

I don't know how to explain this to Isobel. It's hard to explain to people who didn't *know* him, and even Noah only got him in such small doses.

"I don't think they were that close," is all I say.

"Well, still." Isobel's voice is gentle. Thoughtful. "If they bonded over scary movies, maybe he's sort of projecting those feelings onto you? And that's why doing this is so important to him. Maybe Noah just, like, misses him."

"Maybe." I can't think of any reason that wouldn't be true, after all. Only that *I* don't feel that way, and I was his *daughter*. It doesn't feel right, that Noah's grief would influence him more than my own does me. I turn back to Isobel. "Sorry, I didn't mean to, um, bring down the mood. I know it's a lot."

"What? Oh, no, you don't have to apologize." Isobel shifts. The side of her palm brushes against mine for a moment, then withdraws. "Seriously, I'm, like, totally fine. Besides, you should be able to talk about this stuff, right?"

"Yeah." In theory. In practice, dealing with other people's feelings about my father's death is usually more trouble than it's worth. Then again, it's too dark to read much of anything in Isobel's expression. That makes it easier. "Thanks for listening. I'll talk to Noah in the morning about this. We'll figure something out." Already, our argument in the kitchen feels strange. I can't quite pinpoint what upset him. I can hardly remember what I said.

I must just be tired. My hand drifts, almost without my permission, into the space where Isobel's brushed mine. But she's already drawn away.

I fight a yawn. "I'll promise you one thing," I say. "This is the last night I'll ask you to sleep in a haunted house. I'll make sure of that."

Isobel giggles. "Thanks," she says. "Honestly, I'll probably feel better once the storm lightens up? I don't think this would be so bad if I didn't feel so trapped, you know?"

I nod. "That makes sense."

"I guess we should, like, try to get some sleep," she says. Her voice is warm, if still a little nervous. "Goodnight, Cleo."

Our hands aren't touching. But I think Isobel's must be close to mine, because I can feel the body heat radiating from her skin. Physically, it would be easy enough to close the distance between them and offer her the comfort that she so jokingly offered me. But emotionally, that space might as well be filled with spikes and serpents and traps that would put Jigsaw to shame.

"Goodnight, Isobel," I whisper. My hand, face-up on my pillow, remains still.

– 13 –

SCARE CHORD

MY BODY CAN only handle one night of anxiety-fueled insomnia before it overpowers my brain. In spite of everything, I sleep, and I sleep deeply. When I do wake, my eyes are thick and heavy with it.

I grab my phone from the nightstand, squinting against the harsh blue light of the screen. It's nearly 10 a.m., long past time to be getting up. Isobel's side of the bed is already empty and cold.

What's strange: the house is utterly silent, save for the howl of the wind outside.

What's stranger: the bedroom is dark as midnight. Past the glow of my screen, I can barely make out the silhouettes of the furniture.

Something is wrong. Trying to make sense of things, I pull myself up and out of bed. The floor is cold beneath my bare feet as I grope blindly to the window in the dark.

Outside is a blizzard. It must be. But it doesn't look like any blizzard I've seen in my eighteen winters living in Michigan. The sky is pitch black, speckled with white flakes that don't fall so much as flicker, rapidly blinking in and out of existence. It looks more like a television filled with static than a snowstorm.

Beyond that, I can't see anything. Not the glow of streetlights or the curve of the roads. No silhouettes of houses or skeletal branches or ground coated in its thick blanket of white. I can't even see the tree that fell on the roof last night.

A chill runs up my spine. The sudden cold is an expected byproduct of standing so close to the glass, of course. But the fact remains that I feel very uncomfortable in the dark.

I fumble my way to the light switch. It illuminates the room, but that light feels wrong. The shadows cast by the furniture and the door seem thicker than they ought to be, as though possessing actual weight. I blink, half expecting an optical illusion that will fade with enough exposure. But the impression remains.

Beyond the doorframe, the hallway is dark and quiet. Where *is* everyone? I should be able to hear muffled conversations, quiet footsteps. But there's nothing. It's as if I'm entirely alone here.

My argument with Noah resurfaces, along with

memory of his promise: *"If you tell the others to leave, I'll follow them right out the door."* It's ridiculous to think that he might have tried beating me to the punch by sending everyone home himself. It would go against everything he claimed to want. But the horrific quiet puts the thought in my mind, anyway.

I check my phone. Nothing from Noah, but there is a missed call from Mom. I sit on the edge of my bed, biting my cuticle. I should have called her last night to give her an update. She worries, I know. And in this particular instance, I can't say that I blame her. I'm worried, too: a pervasive prickling at the back of my neck. I'm never really sure if that worry is inherited from her or justified in its own right.

I select her contact and hold the phone to my ear. The line rings tinnily once, twice. Then it clicks, and Mom's voice replaces it.

"Hello?"

"Hey, Mom. It's, uh, Cleo. Obviously." I fidget with the blankets. At times like these, I hate talking on the phone. Conversations are difficult enough to navigate *with* the benefit of facial expressions. "I was just calling to check in. We're still stuck. It looks like the storm hasn't let up here."

"Were you expecting it to?"

I frown. Her tone is calm. Calmer than I expected, even. So why do I feel like she sounds accusatory? "The forecast said it would end by morning," I try.

"And you believed it?"

"I know, I know." I thread my fingers through my

hair, pushing pale blue strands away from my forehead. "Michigan weather, you can't predict it. Still, I don't think anyone could have predicted *this* storm."

I'm not sure who I'm trying to convince: her or me. But I find myself craving the validation anyway. I want her to tell me that there was nothing I could have done. That I don't hold any blame for this.

Mom has never been great at giving me that kind of comfort. So maybe it shouldn't surprise me as much as it does when she says, "It wasn't like you didn't have any warning. It was snowing when you left."

"I know." I begin to pace. "I tried to tell Noah, but . . ."

"But you didn't try hard enough." Mom sighs. The sound of it through the phone is skeletal, impossible to distinguish from the wind outside. "Now you're stuck."

Guilt curdles my stomach. The bedroom is too small to contain my pacing by this point, so I step out into the hallway. Someone closed the bathroom door in the night. The light that pours from beneath the crack at the bottom does little to combat the dark out here. I hunt for the chandelier's light switch.

"I'd offer to come get you," my mom says through the phone, "but I'd go off the road for sure. That would be *two* movies derailed by car crashes. And you, an orphan. Although you're eighteen now: a legal adult. 'Orphan' probably isn't the right word."

I stop dead in my tracks, light switch forgotten. "*Mom!*" I can't believe her. Not her words, and not the casual tone with which she speaks them. "Don't—Don't talk like that. It's . . ." I can't bring myself to finish the sentence. Mom's called me 'morbid' a thousand times. I never thought I'd be in a situation where it could describe her.

"No one's coming to help you." She almost sounds sad about it. But there's something beneath that sadness, an odd lilt that's near playful. "It's all hopeless. You were right, Clementine. You're not the Sydney Prescott, you're the Casey Becker."

This isn't right. It *isn't*. First, my mom hates scary movies. I suppose she might have watched *Scream* at some point in her life, but I doubt she'd remember the name of its final girl—much less the name of Ghostface's unfortunate first victim. And what does she mean, 'you were right?' It almost sounds like she's referencing my earlier joke with Noah, but she wasn't present for that.

There's one final thing, too. The most damning.

"You don't call me Clementine," I whisper. "It's always Cleo. Never Clementine."

"Do you like scary movies?" Another impossible *Scream* reference. A laugh issues from my phone's speaker. "I already know the answer. And you know what comes next. What's the line? Oh, that's right."

The voice no longer sounds like my mother. It's a drone, more like stone scraping against stone than vocal cords vibrating. It's an impossible voice.

A dead voice.

"Clementine, I'll *gut you like a fish*," it rasps.

A hand closes around my arm and pulls.

The phone drops from my grasp, landing with a muffled thud on the carpet. I should be screaming, I think distantly. The scream is what makes the jump scare so effective. There are horror actresses who have built their entire *careers* on screaming: Scream Queens, they call them. But no one expects the girl behind the camera to start screaming. I find myself woefully unprepared for it, my breath locked silent in my throat.

It occurs to me that, as far as final thoughts go, the one I'm having is patently ridiculous.

"Cleo? Cleo!"

Isobel. It's not a ghost—or a *Ghostface*—that's grabbed me, but Isobel. She's dragged me into the bathroom, and now she slams the door shut behind us before staring at me with wide, frightened eyes.

"Oh my god. What is going on?"

"I . . ." I can't process this. I keep thinking about the dead voice on the phone. *I'll gut you like a fish.* A line I've heard delivered countless times, but never with quite so much genuine malice. I can't stop shaking, any more than I can stop thinking about the line that comes next in that infamous scene.

I want to see what your insides look like.

Some part of me is still living in the horror movie version of this scene: the one where the hand grabbing me belonged to something far more nefarious. Something that croons horror movie lines at me while it devours me. But that isn't what happened. For

Isobel's sake, I try to get a hold of my careening thoughts.

"What are you doing in here?" I ask.

Isobel blinks rapidly, shaking her head. She's as lost for words as I am, evidently, which would probably make me feel better in different circumstances. "I don't *know*," she finally says. There's a note of hysteria to her voice, a jagged-edged pitch. "I woke up, you weren't in bed and I, like, thought I heard someone crying. Out in the hallway. I came out to look, but there was no one there, and I got, like, lost?"

"Lost?" I echo, as baffled as she sounds.

"It doesn't make sense," Isobel says. "It's like, none of the doors led where they were supposed to go? I just kept ending up back in the hallway. I started thinking that maybe I was having, like, a weird dream or something. So I tried the bathroom door, and *that* worked for some reason, and I tried to look in the mirror because reflections always look wrong when you're dreaming, you know?"

I can't say I do, but the question feels rhetorical, so I remain silent on the matter.

"My face looked normal," Isobel continues. "And that's when I heard you and pulled you in here." She stares, wide-eyed. "This *isn't* a dream, right? I mean, it feels weird, but it doesn't feel like a dream. Unless, like, *you're* the one who's dreaming, but I don't know what that would make me . . ."

She sounds as though she might genuinely be on

the edge of an existential crisis. I can't say I'm far behind her. No amount of horror movie consumption could have prepared me for this.

"I don't think I'm dreaming," I say. "I don't think any of this is a dream. I think something's wrong."

It's a massive understatement. I *knew* something bad would happen. I felt it, from the moment we drove through that storm to get to this house. But this goes so far beyond what I ever could have predicted. I'm not even sure I know what this *is*.

"You said I wasn't in bed when you woke up?" I ask.

Isobel nods. Her green eyes are glossy in the light.

"You weren't in bed when I woke up, either," I reply. "And it's past 10 a.m., but there's not even a little bit of sunlight. There's a blizzard outside, but it doesn't look like any blizzard I've seen before. And when I called my mom, she was . . ."

I don't know how to finish that sentence. Even with the strangeness of Isobel's story, I still have a hard time believing what happened on the phone. It's stranger than anything I'd ever write into one of my scripts. Could I have imagined it?

The door rattles.

When I heard scratching at the door that first night, I convinced myself I imagined it. There's no possibility of that now. The door shakes, kept from flying open only by the grace of the latch. Has Isobel locked the door? I can't find my voice to ask.

Isobel lets out a startled squeak, stepping

backward. Her shoulder bumps into mine, startlingly warm, startlingly real. I wasn't aware of just how far I'd managed to drift from my body until she shocked me back into it. All at once, I can feel my heart racing, my blood pumping through my veins. My chest is tight. My throat aches, and my mouth is dry. I've been breathing too shallowly.

The door rattles again. As if someone is throwing the full force of their weight against it.

Isobel presses her shoulder to mine, clutching at my arm. I reach up to cover her hands with my free one, but there's no feeling associated with the gesture, even though in other circumstances I'd be consumed with nerves.

I imagine a camera on us in this moment. Low moody lighting. An ominous soundtrack, full of strings. CLOSE-UP ON: our eyes glued to the door.

Slam! Slam! Slam!

Isobel's hands tremble beneath mine. Her fingers are cold and clammy against my skin. "Who's there?" she calls out.

I can't decide if it's a foolish decision or a brave one. Those sorts of questions, they're usually the precursor to a jump scare. Then again, the alternative is being trapped in this endless moment, surrounded by porcelain and fear.

The door stills. It stills, and I wait for the stinger, the moment where the doorframe shatters into splinters of wood and the door flies inward to reveal the horror beyond in all its glory. In movies, that moment is often less frightening than the buildup. I don't think that will be the case here.

On the other side of the door, there's a long, low rasp. The sound of someone trying to draw in a breath and only barely managing to do it. A death rattle. It's followed by a *thump* and then, impossibly, a dragging sound that gets slowly more distant.

As though whatever was throwing itself at us is crawling away.

I don't know how long Isobel and I stand there in silence, trembling, clinging to each other. Long enough for me to once again become aware of her warmth beside me as a tangible thing. I drop my hand, worried that it's unwelcome now that the horror has paused. Isobel flexes her fingers when I release them; I must have been clinging tighter than I realized. But she doesn't pull away.

"Do you think it's gone?" she whispers.

I shake my head in spite of what I heard. This feels like a trap. The classic horror movie fake-out. If we open that door, a shrieking specter will launch itself at us. Noose dangling around her neck, blood dripping from her mouth.

I know this. And yet, when Isobel steps forward, I can't bring myself to stop her. Can't bring myself to do *anything* to stop the inevitable. I've never been final girl material. What's the point in pretending? Isobel opens the door, and I resign myself to my fate. Cannon fodder after all.

Only when the door swings open, the hallway is empty and dark.

179

$$- \ 14 \ -$$

<u>**VANISHING POINT**</u>

For the first time, the ghost steps into frame. She can no longer be dismissed as a trick of the light.

She is real. She is here.

(Excerpt from THE WIDOW GHOST, written by Cleo Moss.)

I SOBEL LEADS ME into the hallway.

She holds my hand. I don't ask her to let go. Her palm against mine is an anchor, the only thing tethering me to the here and now. Even that is tenuous. I'm not entirely sure where *here* is, and I'm even less certain about *now*.

The house is, ostensibly, as it has always been. The balcony still overlooks the first floor, two tall windows flanking the front door. But the shadows that douse the hallway are thick and unnatural like the ones in the bedroom. The windows, full of that strange static snow, do not let in any light. And Michelle's painting is as unsettling as ever. I stop in my tracks, chilled by the way the woman's eyes seem to glitter in the darkness.

Isobel tugs gently on my hand. "Come on."

We walk downstairs. Voices echo down the hallway from the direction of the living room. Our friends. The relief on Isobel's face is palpable as she pulls me along toward them, her grip on my hand turning loose in her haste. "Guys?"

The others stand in a tight knot by the couch. When we arrive, Declan lets out a sharp laugh, his unusually bare face twisted with nerves. "Well, good morning. I don't suppose you two experienced anything out of the ordinary?"

"Oh my god, you guys, too?" Isobel asks. "What happened?"

Andrea huffs. "Zander and I woke up to the bed shaking. Like something out of, I don't fucking know—the movie where the girl sicks up pea soup?"

"*The Exorcist*," I reply dully. Like she's called for a line, and I'm providing it from behind camera.

My camera is here. Safe and plugged into the wall. I'm not sure why that seems so important in this moment, but it does.

"Right, right," Andrea continues. "Anyway, we got the fuck out of dodge."

"The lights were flickering," Zander adds.

"I didn't wake up to anything quite that visceral," Declan explains. "But when I left my room, someone—or something—was climbing the balcony.

I could see hands clinging to the banister. But when I looked down, nothing was there."

Rhiannon scoffs. "Come on."

Declan turns on her. "Are you still playing Agent Scully, darling? I think we're well past that."

"Are we?" Rhiannon crosses her arms. "It sounds like you all just had a bunch of weird dreams to me."

"I don't know . . ." Isobel recounts what happened to her, and then to us, her voice high and nervous. Against my will, I tell my own story, glossing over some of the stranger bits of the phone conversation. I worry that the others will be skeptical, but the only one who shows any disbelief is Rhiannon.

"Well, I didn't see anything," she says testily.

"Rhiannon, darling," Declan says. "I'm fairly certain that Virginia Barlow herself could come and scream in your face, and you'd blame it on a trick of the light."

I look around. Someone is missing here, and that seems more important than bickering. "Is Noah still asleep?"

Declan frowns. Without his makeup, he looks younger than usual. "I . . . I don't know," he says. "He wasn't in the bedroom when I woke up. Come to think of it, I can't recall him actually coming upstairs? He must have, though . . ."

A chill touches the back of my neck. "He was in the kitchen the last time I saw him," I say. "Wait, no. He went down into the basement for something."

All at once, it's not a haunting I'm afraid of. What

if Noah hurt himself? A twisted ankle, a tumble downward. The floor of the basement is cold stone, easy enough to break a neck on. He was frustrated. Distracted.

And whose fault was that?

I grab my camcorder from the charger. As if I can keep away the real horrors by clinging to the fictitious ones, the movie I'd been so quick to abandon. It does little good. Nothing I would ever write could be as tense as this room.

"Well," Andrea says. "Let's go look for him."

The kitchen is empty. Everything is as it was last night, but I still have a nagging sense that something is wrong. I stare at Noah's binder, still open on the kitchen table, before I realize what it is.

"His keys are gone." The others turn to look at me. None of them seem to understand what I'm saying. "Noah's car keys," I explain. "They were on the kitchen table, I'm sure of it, but . . . but they're gone now."

Zander's brow furrows. "You think he tried to leave?"

"I can't see his truck." Rhiannon peers out the window. "But I can't see anyone else's car, either. The storm is too thick."

"Cleo mentioned that he was, like, frustrated last night," Isobel says. At least she doesn't go so far as to assign blame to me. "He was annoyed that we wanted to leave."

Andrea lets out a frustrated groan. "Did that

fucker seriously storm out on us?" she asks. "That's just like him. He always gets pissy when things don't go his way, eh?"

Zander nods. "Remember when we did that thriller last year? I thought he and Thomas were going to get into a fist fight."

Isobel nods. "He gets, like, really frustrated when things go off-track? It's just because he cares so much, but it *is* intense."

It sounds like they're talking about a stranger. Surely they don't mean Noah. My cousin Noah, who can't seem to take anything seriously without turning it into a joke halfway through? That can't be right.

Only I think of our argument yesterday. Not to mention how effortlessly he kept things moving on this shoot, and his well-organized binder full of schedules and scenes.

I find that I have no choice but to defer to everyone else's opinions on this. The realization makes me feel strange. Noah is my family. Can my view of him really be so wrong? I guess I'm basing it on how he acted during *Slaughter!*, but that's not fair. He's done so many movies and shows since then.

I'm the one who hasn't.

I drift to the basement door, still clutching my camcorder. Do I expect to find him at the foot of the stairs in a death sprawl? I'm not sure anymore. All I can do is open the door and check.

There's nothing there. I peer into the darkness below, but the stone floor is utterly bare. The only sound that issues up is the tuneless hum of the boiler.

"Did you hide his keys?" Rhiannon asks.

I jump. "What?"

"I said, are you checking for him down there?"

That's not what she said. But what I heard didn't make any sense. I had no reason to think that Noah would try to drive home in the middle of a storm. I even checked the fridge to make sure he didn't drink anything that would impair his judgement. Why would I have bothered to hide his keys?

"Cleo?" Rhiannon tries again.

"Oh! Um, yeah. I'm checking for him."

"It's a good idea. Better to be thorough." Rhiannon steps around me and walks down the stairs.

I know that she's not afraid of ghosts, but the idea of letting her roam the basement of this house alone chills me. Splitting the party rarely leads to a good outcome in movies. But the others are too caught up in their conversation to notice.

Against my better judgement, I follow her.

It's so much colder in the basement. My breath plumes from my lips in a clear gray mist, and I have to wrap my arms around myself to keep from shivering. Rhiannon, even in her thick yellow hoodie, doesn't look any happier to be down here than I am. She looks around, frowning.

"I don't see him," she says. She moves toward the door to Michelle's studio.

"That's locked," I tell her.

She pauses, hand on the doorknob. "What?"

"That door is locked," I say again. "Michelle must have locked it before she left. I think it's her art studio. I tried to store these paintings I found in the upstairs closet, but . . ." I gesture at the paintings I left stacked next to the door.

Rhiannon jiggles the doorknob, as if she can't quite believe me. "That's odd. Why would she do that?"

I cross my arms against the chill. "Maybe she was afraid of Noah stealing another one of her paintings?" My eye catches on the stack. They're in a pile, face-up on the ground. Didn't I leave them leaned against the wall?

"She mentioned that the art studio was a storm shelter," Rhiannon says. "I don't think I like the idea of her locking something we might need."

Considering the tree on the roof, I can understand her worries. But for some reason, I'm far more concerned with the paintings. There's something wrong with them. I move closer, but even when I'm right on top of them, it takes me a moment to understand what my eyes are telling me.

The painting at the top of the stack—the one of Carrie's screaming face—is ruined. Her horror-widened eyes, her acne-studded cheeks, her blood-streaked crown, all of it is obscured by thick globs of black paint that shine wetly in the dim light. It's tacky to the touch when I reach out, but my fingertips don't come away stained. This has been done recently, but not so recent.

"Rhiannon, look at this." I flip through the paintings as Rhiannon peers over my shoulder. They're all similarly destroyed. "These weren't like this when I brought them down here. Someone ruined them."

I make it to the end of the stack. The final painting, the one of Rodrick embracing Madeline as the House of Usher collapses, has not been eradicated. But it has been altered. Before, the background walls had been riddled with thin, spiderweb cracks. Someone has gone through them with a thick brush, outlining each in thick black strokes.

I can't tell whether the perpetrator meant to widen the cracks or obscure them. But the effect makes the painting even more unsettling than it had been previously. The more I stare at it, the more those black lines seem almost to move.

"I don't understand why someone would *do* this," I murmur, more to myself than Rhiannon. "Noah was down here, but it couldn't be him, right? Even if he was annoyed with us, he wouldn't destroy someone else's artwork out of frustration."

I say this, but doubt makes a hollow of my chest. Can I say for certain what Noah would do? Apparently, I don't know him at all. Maybe he *is* the type of person who would ruin something just to do it. Maybe what I always perceived as *carelessness* was really a *lack of care*.

"I don't think he'd do that, either," Rhiannon says. She sounds more sure of it than I do.

Carefully, I replace the paintings. "If he didn't do it, what did?"

"I don't know," Rhiannon says. Her tone is clipped, curt. Too late, I realize my verbal slip up: *what*, not *who*.

I look at her, measuring my tone. "Listen, Rhiannon . . ."

Rhiannon sighs. "Please don't blame ghosts."

"I'm not blaming anything." This is less than truthful, and Rhiannon's face says she knows it. I try again. "I'm just saying. A lot of stuff is happening here that we can't explain."

"Everything can be explained," Rhiannon snaps. "Even if you weren't dreaming. There are other options."

"Like what?" I ask.

Rhiannon frowns. Behind her round glasses, her eyes are sharp and staring at nothing in particular. "Carbon monoxide poisoning can cause hallucinations," she says. "You'd be surprised by how many haunted house stories end with faulty detectors. Especially in weather like this. Furnaces running, windows frozen shut."

She says it so bluntly. I try to repress a shiver. "Isn't carbon monoxide poisoning, um, fatal?"

Rhiannon's expression falters. Through the cracks, I can see her angry frustration for what it is: fear, as raw and tender as an exposed nerve. In this moment, the shine in her eyes makes her look even younger than her sixteen years.

She takes a breath, and the moment is gone. "All the more reason for us to actually do something. Instead of chasing ghosts."

She stomps up the stairs.

I linger for a moment, in the cold and dark. I find that my body is just a bit too anxious to do much else. We need to do something, Rhiannon had said. But what does she suggest? If she wants to leave, she won't get far in that storm. And just waiting outside in the cold has its own risks.

Whether what's happening here is a ghost or a gas leak, does it matter if we can't escape either way?

"Cleo," Rhiannon says. She's halfway up the stairs by now, her voice impatient. "Are you coming?"

She seems rather reluctant to leave me alone. Carbon monoxide doesn't seem like it would benefit from a strength in numbers approach, but I'm not about to point that out to her. "Yeah, coming."

I follow her up the stairs.

The others have left the kitchen by the time we arrive back. I can hear their voices from the living room, their words swallowed by the howl of the wind. The overhead fluorescents flicker. It's so slight Rhiannon doesn't even comment on it, but the subtle shifting lights put me on edge. I cross my arms over my chest.

"Did you guys find anything?" Andrea calls.

Rhiannon stays silent, clearly expecting me to be the one to speak. I clear my throat. "He's not down there."

Andrea curses. She stomps into the hallway, the others trailing behind. "He must've actually left," she says.

I suppose I have to agree with her. Unless we want to entertain the notion of ghostly abduction, which I doubt Rhiannon is willing to do. What was he thinking, going out into a storm like that? Was he really that upset by the idea of not filming *The Widow Ghost?*

Was he really that upset with *me?*

I check the fridge. If he did leave, I want to make sure he wasn't drunk when he did it. Although drinking would explain how irrational he would have been to make that decision in the first place. When I check the twelve pack, though, it's still as full as it was last night.

"What are you doing?" Rhiannon asks.

"Oh." I shut the fridge hurriedly. "Just, um, checking. If we're going to be stuck here for a while, we should probably have a decent amount of food?"

Rhiannon can tell I'm not telling the truth. I can see it in her face. But she doesn't call me out on it, just pushes her glasses up her nose and her braids away from her face. "Okay," she says. "Let's—"

The flickering light gets more pronounced. The howl of the wind rises into a loud, womanish scream. All the hair on the back of my neck stands on edge, my skin slick with the same strange energy that comes before a lightning strike.

And long, ragged fingertips wrap themselves

around the entryway to the kitchen.

Somewhere in the distance, Isobel screams, and Andrea curses again. The grip on the entryway tightens. The fingertips leave streaks of old blood on the cased opening, a fetid brown smear.

Virginia Barlow pulls herself into view.

In many ways, the specter is exactly what I expected. Her feet are bare. Her fingertips are a ragged, bloody ruin. A frayed noose hangs from her neck, which is bent at a choking, impossible angle. Greasy blonde hair flops listlessly over one shoulder. Those are details that any veteran of horror media could guess.

But imagination—even mine, with its endless catalog of movie ghouls—falters in the face of reality. I catch on the strangest details: the bleach stain on her oversized shirt. The cuffs of her pajama pants rolled to reveal pale, swollen ankles. The chipped polish on her toes.

More than that, I'm shocked by the *presence* of her. The space she takes up in the doorway. This is no ethereal, intangible waif hovering transparently. There's a jerky, stop-motion flickering to her, but in spite of that, she is solid. She is real.

She sways. Her eyes hold the flat, colorless affect one would find on a deer carcass left on the side of the road. Her bloated lips are frozen in a joyless, rictus grin. She does not charge at us. She only stands, blocking the kitchen entryway.

Blocking our exit.

"Holy shit," someone—Declan, I think—breathes from the hallway.

I turn to Rhiannon, to see how she's handling this development. She stares at the ghost of Virginia Barlow carefully, dark eyes scanning every detail. She looks at her the way I sometimes look at complicated camera shots in movies. Like she's trying to find the trick to how it was made: the zipper on the back of the costume, the flaw that betrays the illusion.

Seconds tick by as she stares. And then, all at once, that stare hardens.

"Enough," she murmurs. And then, louder. "Enough!"

Rhiannon charges.

Above us, the fluorescent pops and goes dark. Rhiannon is a blur of yellow sweater, the metal beads threaded through her braids flashing in the dim light from the hallway. She collides with Virginia like she expects to pass through. For the ghost to vanish like the illusion Rhiannon so clearly believes her to be.

She doesn't.

Virginia's spectral form gives way with an oddly liquid sound, warping like the picture on an old television. But she doesn't disappear. Instead, the billowing folds of her clothing and the stringy masses of her hair envelop Rhiannon, their two bodies melding into one awful shadow dancing against the wall. They chart a stumbling dance back into the hallway. Rhiannon's cheek is phased into Virginia's collarbone. Her shoulder vanishes into Virginia's ribcage.

Rhiannon's face, half visible now, contorts in disbelief. Then disgust. Then raw, animal panic. Her hands scrabble for purchase against Virginia's shoulders, trying to push away, but she can't. She *can't.* Virginia's form clings to her like a glue trap. As Rhiannon struggles against her, the edges of her form seem to blur, stretching elastically but not giving.

"No." Rhiannon's voice is hoarse. "No, no, no."

Her palms stick to Virginia's shoulders in an odd mockery of an embrace. Threads of Virginia's . . . of Virginia *herself* spill across the backs of her hands with an odd, viscous texture. The consistency is not unlike the prop blood used in films. Corn syrup and water.

Virginia's fuzzy hand passes over Rhiannon's eyes.

Rhiannon screams.

I jolt, hands rising. Maybe to cover my own eyes, or maybe just to clap them to my face in my best Carrie impression. Either way, it's at that moment I realize that I'm still clutching my camera.

And for some reason, it's recording.

Virginia's head whips to face me, a movement so violent and sudden that several of Rhiannon's braids come dislodged from her and start swinging. The ghost's feral eyes widen, her head sagging even further into its unnatural, fatal tilt.

She takes one step toward me. Then another. Rhiannon does not come with her. The two of them part with a harrowing *squelch.* Rhiannon collapses to the floor, trembling, covering her face in her hands.

Virginia stares, wavering.

Then, in the viewfinder of my camcorder, she melts. She dissolves liquidly into the darkness, the shadows claiming her piece by piece until she's barely there. And then, she's gone.

All that remains is Rhiannon's harsh breathing and the relentless howl of the wind.

- 15 -

<u>OVEREXPOSED</u>

```
INT. HALLWAY - ????

A woman stands, staring pensively out the
front window. She's dressed in faded pajamas,
but she shows no signs of going to sleep.
She's waiting for something.

Or someone.
```

"**H**OLY SHIT."

WARM bodies crowd around me. In my peripheral, I see Andrea scoop Rhiannon up by the arms and sit her on the bottom of the stairs. I don't turn my head to look. I've long since lowered the camcorder, but it still feels like I'm viewing everything from its viewfinder. Removed, at a distance.

"What the fuck was that?" Andrea asks.

"A ghost," I say, toneless. That doesn't feel right, but I don't know what kind of tone I'd use if given the chance to try again. It reminds me, senselessly, of how

I felt during Dad's wake: watching people cry and mourn, knowing I ought to have been doing the same but finding myself unable to.

"Well then." Declan laughs, jagged, hysterical. "I don't know about the rest of you, but I've had my fill of all of this. I may be an aficionado of the supernatural, but even I know when things have progressed to a point of ridiculousness."

He moves towards the door, grabbing his coat off of one of the hooks.

"Where will you go?" Isobel asks. Her hands cup her elbows as her shoulders hunch, an oddly defensive posture on her lithe dancer's body.

"Not here," Declan says.

"But the storm . . ." Zander's eyes flicker to the windows, then back to Declan.

"Can be waited out from the safety of my car."

Declan zips up his boots, then straightens. One hand grasps the doorknob, his body tilted defiantly toward us.

"It's been an honor and a privilege," he says. "But now, I'm afraid, I must bid you good—"

He turns the knob. He pushes.

The door stays shut.

Declan frowns. "What on . . ." He shoves his weight against the door, harder this time. It barely budges. Snow spills from the narrow crack resulting from his efforts, glittering wetly against the hardwood. "What fresh hell is this?"

"It's the storm," Zander says quietly. "Snow must

have built up against the door."

"We're *trapped* in here?" Isobel's voice raises several degrees in pitch.

"No, no, fuck that." Andrea shoulders Declan aside. "Let me try."

But no matter how hard anyone pushes, the door doesn't budge. The windows, too, refuse to open. Zander suggests that they're frozen shut, which devolves into a spirited debate on the ethics of breaking one. That debate ends, quite spectacularly, when Andrea runs full tilt at one with a chair clutched in her hands.

She doesn't even make a crack.

That can't be explained away by the weather. But it doesn't surprise me. Of course, we won't be able to escape that easily. That isn't how these stories go, is it?

It's strange, because I've spent so much of this shoot in fear of something awful happening. But now that something awful is here, I no longer feel afraid. Only resigned.

Declan makes a strangled noise that only barely resembles a laugh. "Well, that's that. Cleo, darling, you couldn't have written a better plot if you tried. But let's look on the bright side. Death by ghost will look marvelous in an obituary. We'll be the talk of the town." He regards Rhiannon, still sitting quietly on the stairs, with a sideways glance. "Rhiannon. Darling. I said ghost. I don't suppose you have an opinion on that?"

At the sound of her name, Rhiannon turns to face

him. But she doesn't respond to his goading. She only stares at him, dark eyes wide behind her glasses.

"Quit it," Andrea says without any real venom. "There's got to be something we can do, eh? After all, Noah left."

"Did he?" I probably should keep the thought to myself. But what use is there in protecting the others from my pessimism at this point? "I mean, I thought he did. But after what happened to Rhiannon, I don't know. What if something in this house got him?"

A nervous silence settles over the group. Andrea is the one to break it. "I'm going to call him." She pulls out her cell phone. "He's probably at home sulking. If we tell him what's going on, he'll get us help, eh?"

Doubtful, considering what happened when I called Mom earlier. But Andrea already knows about that, so what good is bringing it up now? I stay silent as she dials Noah's number, putting it on speakerphone.

The phone rings once. Twice. Then it falls silent.

Andrea frowns. "Missed call." She tries again, but it doesn't even get past a full ring this time. Or the next. "That motherfucker. Is he blocking my call?"

For some reason, this chills me. I was prepared for fear, for a warped version of Noah hissing out horror movie threats. But the mundanity of being ignored is even worse. More real.

Andrea groans. "Oh, fuck this." She dials another number. It rings.

"Who are you calling?" Zander asks.

A pleasant female voice on the other end of the line answers this question before Andrea can. "911, what's your emergency?"

"Hello," Andrea says. "We're trapped in a house, and you need to send someone out to help us right away, the address is—"

"911, what's your emergency?" The voice asks again. "911, what's your emergency? 911, what's your emergency?"

With each repetition, the voice grows more distorted. Polite concern morphs into screeching, inhuman glee. Isobel lets out a quiet, horrified sound. I should take her hand. I don't.

"Shit." Andrea hangs up the phone, looking pale and disturbed.

"None of this makes any sense," Isobel says. "That call went through to, like, something. But Noah's didn't?"

"More proof that he's actually out there. Ignoring us." Andrea runs a hand through her sleek black bob. "It is weird, though. Noah left after the seance, and that's where things went bad, eh? But if he was able to get out . . ." She turns to Declan. "Aren't you the paranormal expert here? What do you think?"

"Darling, nothing about what just happened was in any research I've done." In spite of this, Declan's gaze is thoughtful. "Things did change during the seance, I suppose. But I did all the appropriate cleansing rituals after, so there's really no explanation for the sudden shift . . ."

He continues talking. Everyone talks, other than Rhiannon. Their voices are quiet and determined and not hysterical. But their words don't make sense to me. It's as though I'm buried beneath the snowbank piled up on the other side of the door, listening to them through layers of cold and ice.

And does what they're saying matter? Maybe Andrea is right, and something caused this. But I can't make the same cognitive leap that she has: that finding a *cause* means finding a *solution*. Just because you know why something has happened doesn't mean you know how to stop it.

Just because I know why Noah stormed out doesn't mean I could have kept him from leaving.

I couldn't have stopped him from grabbing those keys. Not even if I wanted to.

The others move to the living room. I linger in the hallway. My ears ring, the edges of my vision tunneling. It occurs to me that I may be on the edge of a panic attack. Only I'm breathing normally, and when I touch my fingertips to my pulse, it's steady and even.

Still, I can't think. Can't process anything past my bone-deep assurance that things are only going to get worse from here.

Only that isn't entirely true. Beyond the dizzy dissociation and the ringing, I can hear it. A noise in the kitchen. A clinking that is at once dissonant and musical.

CLOSE-UP ON: A pile of broken glass, being

swept up with a practiced hand.

I'm still holding my camera. I could close-up on anything I wanted with this. Stay safe behind the lens, where I'm not expected to be anything more than an observer. Where no one even looks at me.

Where nothing I do matters.

The kitchen is strange. In the flickering light of the dying fluorescent, it looks different. More lived in. There are dishes drying in the rack that we never used. A coat hung up along the back of a chair doesn't belong to any of us.

A set of keys sit on the kitchen table.

They aren't Noah's. Aren't any set of keys I recognize. But there's something in the casual sprawl of them, their plainness, that puts me truly on edge in a way that I probably should have been feeling for quite a while before this. I don't want to look at these. I want to hide them. Tuck them under a couch cushion, into a pocket, at the back of a drawer. Keep them from falling into the wrong hands.

Keep anyone else from going out in that awful storm.

Did Noah screen our calls? Or is he already gone, truck bed filling with snow as he sits crumpled in some ditch somewhere?

I blink. The keys vanish.

"Stop," I whisper. To the house, or maybe only to my own racing thoughts. "Please, stop."

The light brightens. The unfamiliar coat and the dishes are gone too. Had never been, just like the keys.

My head swims, caught between delusion and reality.

What is happening in this house?

Something clatters to the floor. I jump, whimper caught in my throat, and look around for the source. A moment later, I find it: movement at the other end of the table, a half-hidden figure crouched on the ground. Has Virginia come for me, then? No, I realize. There's someone else here.

I lean forward.

A girl kneels on the floor. Long blonde hair covers her face, too straight to be Isobel's and too clean to be Virginia's. She's entirely unfamiliar, clad in a low-rise jeans and a white t-shirt.

With a wet rag, she tries and fails to wipe up a mess of shattered glass and red matter. It looks a little as though someone dropped a jar of raspberry jam.

I know that isn't what it is, though. Not in a house like this.

"It's not his fault," she says. Her voice is soft, barely there. "It's just the way he is. I'll clean it up. It's okay. I don't mind."

Red drips on the back of her hand. *Plip. Plip. Plip.*

"I don't mind."

Plip. It drips from behind the curtain of her hair.

"I don't mind."

Plip. It drips from her face: the face I can't see.

"I don't mind. Can you hide his keys for me?"

She lifts her head.

She's a little older than I expected, closer to Declan's age than mine. Although it's hard to tell with all of the blood coating her face. Deep lacerations slice open her cheek, her hairline. The one on her forehead is so deep that it cuts through muscle and bone, revealing the gray meat of her brain. Half of her mouth twists into an unending sneer, but the other seems to be trying to smile. It's a sheepish smile, one that doesn't reach her pale, bloodshot eyes.

"He really shouldn't be driving," she says. "He could get into an accident like this, you know?"

The light is flickering again. Around us, the kitchen feels strangely malleable, caught outside of time. The window shows only that strange, static snow. We could be anywhere. We could be nowhere.

"Sorry to have to ask for your help," she says. "I'm just a little occupied, you know?"

She reaches up with one lacerated hand. Her skin is blurry, tacky around the edges. She could grab me like Virginia, pull me into her and show me whatever horrors left Rhiannon so silent. Or maybe, with no Andrea to haul me to my feet and no Isobel to grab me and drag me away, it will be even worse. Maybe if she grabs me, it will be to swallow me whole.

Only she doesn't grab me. She only holds out that hand, looking at me expectantly with her pale, haunted eyes.

A doomed girl, reaching out to another doomed girl.

And there's a part of me—instinctive, irrational, and impossible to understand—that wants to reach back. If my hands were free, I think they might reach for her without question.

But my hands aren't free.

I'm still holding the camcorder.

I lift it. I'm not surprised to see the screen glowing, even though I can't remember having turned it on. This is what I'm here for, after all. I can't save anyone: not this girl, not my friends, and certainly not myself. But I can do this.

In the viewfinder, the girl kneeling on the floor is not ruined. But she isn't cured, either. Her face is a misshapen blur, no eyes or nose or mouth. She's a perfect match for one of the figures in the painting we borrowed. The one Michelle hadn't finished, but hadn't obscured in black paint, either.

She tilts her not-face to the camera. Slowly, one blurry hand rises to touch her own unfinished cheek. Her fingertips trace the places where her features ought to be. Her shoulders slump forward—whether in resignation, or exhaustion, I can't tell. And then, she fades away.

I continue staring into the viewfinder. I'm too afraid to look up from it. I don't want to be ripped from my seat as an observer, forced to interact with the world again. I want to stay here, where the horrors stay safely on their side of the screen.

"Cleo?"

I turn. Isobel hovers in the entrance of the kitchen. Her face is clear, solid, real. And it is worried.

"What are you doing in here?"

I'm not sure how to answer her. What was I doing,

exactly? It had made sense in the moment. I hadn't even really been afraid, not completely. But I'm afraid now. In the viewfinder, Isobel's figure begins to tremble as my hands shake, my breath coming out in short, pained bursts. I keep staring at the camera, even as she gets too close for the tiny screen to hold her.

"Hey." Isobel's hands fold over mine, stilling them. It's only with that touch tethering me that I'm able to look up. In real life, her face is larger, more careworn. More fragile.

But there's a light, a life in her green eyes that no camera can really capture.

"Are you, like, okay?" she asks.

I laugh, rough and desperate. How am I supposed to answer that?

Fortunately, Isobel doesn't seem to need me to. She smiles, squeezing my hands. "Yeah, I get it. I'm totally freaked out here." She looks it. Still, her voice is steady as her gaze finds mine. "It's going to be okay, though."

She doesn't say it the way Noah would say it. It's not a dismissal of my worries, but an acknowledgment. So soft that all I can do is nod.

Even if I don't believe her.

Isobel continues clinging to my hand as we enter the living room. The others look up as I enter—even Rhiannon, wide eyes tracking me watchfully from behind her thick glasses. Beside her, Andrea peers at me from beneath Zander's encircling arm. "You look fucking rough," she says. "What's going on?"

"Well." I clear my throat. My voice wavers. "I sort of, um, saw something. I think?"

Isobel's hand tightens in mine—shock or sympathy. Andrea clambers to her feet, and Declan sits up, alert.

"What happened?"

"Um. I'm not sure if I can explain it?" That's an understatement. I hold up the camcorder, relieved that I won't have to try to put into words what just happened to me. "I got it on video."

Everyone other than Rhiannon gathers around me to review the footage. Part of me hopes that watching it back will help me make sense of it, but I feel more confused than ever. It doesn't feel like I'm watching something that just happened to me. Maybe it's because of how different the girl looks on camera compared to how she looked in reality?

"She looks like the painting," Andrea says. "Who do you think she is, eh? She almost looks like . . ."

"It's Virginia's daughter," Rhiannon says, and I startle. I hadn't even heard her come up behind me. "Not Michelle. The one who died in the car crash. Laura, right?"

"That's right," Declan says, eyes darting from the camera to Rhiannon and back again. "You . . . I'm surprised you remembered that. I didn't think you were paying much attention to my ghost stories."

Rhiannon shrugs, but her haunted gaze doesn't move from the camera. She speaks in a slow, detached tone. "She does look like the painting. She is the painting. She's not here. Not really. Not a spirit, not a soul. Just a memory. An echo. That's all. That's *all*."

She says it more like she's trying to convince herself. Her thin shoulders tremble, and finally, she looks away from the camera, eyes narrowing.

"I'm still *right*," she mutters. In that moment she sounds like herself: all stubborn will and diehard skepticism. I'm not surprised when Declan bursts into laughter, covering his face with one hand.

"Ordinarily I'd argue with you, darling, but all things considered I think I'm going to let you have this one." He slings an arm over Rhiannon's shoulders. She makes a show of grimacing at him, but she doesn't pull away. She even leans into the touch slightly, like a child seeking comfort from an older sibling.

"Soul or not, they must be here for a reason," Andrea insists. "And I don't think I buy that it's just the seance that did it. Maybe we summoned them, but what's keeping them here, eh? Especially after Declan did the cleaning or whatever."

"The cleansing," Declan and Rhiannon say in unison. When Declan looks at Rhiannon in surprise, she scowls. "I do listen," she grumbles.

"I don't know anything about ghosts," Isobel offers. "But if what we're seeing is like the painting? That's art. And art is about, like, saying something, right? Saying something, and being heard."

"You think they're trying to tell us something?" Andrea glances at Rhiannon. "Did Virginia tell you anything?"

Rhiannon's expression goes blank. But not with apathy. Her hands curl into fists, shoulders trembling. "Nothing," she says. "Nothing to do with what's happening here. Just. More memories. But they were only my own. Not relevant."

Her voice is sharp and tense and utterly impossible to argue with. Andrea clears her throat.

"Well, okay. She went away when Cleo filmed her. So did Laura. There's gotta be something to that, eh?"

Eyes turn to me.

Usually, the weight of my camcorder in my hands is a comfort. But that's because it encourages people to look away from me, not the opposite. "I don't know," I say.

"Well, it's still worth a shot." Andrea bounces on the balls of her feet. "Let's get these things on camera more. See if that fixes things."

She's looking at me like I'm holding the answers in my hands, like I have the keys to our salvation. She doesn't know that I can't be trusted with keys. I want to tell her, to explain to her that nothing I can do will make a difference. That if we're doomed, there's nothing I can do to stop it.

But telling her that won't do any good. It would just be cruel.

Instead, I tighten my grip on the camera. "Okay."

- 16 -

REFLEXIVITY

NARRATOR

... But when the storm was over, the remaining cast and crew had vanished. This footage is all that remains.

HAVING A PURPOSE, however flimsy, is enough to energize the group.

Andrea leads us on a thorough search of the house, her steps sure and decisive. Zander stays glued to her side, occasionally offering a murmured suggestion. Declan's jokes start to actually sound like jokes, and Rhiannon's voice loses some of its haggard edge. Isobel chimes in with theories in her sweet voice.

I stay silent, clutching my camcorder. I still don't believe it will save us. That's not the way these stories go. Not the way my life goes, either. No, I think that by the time the storm ends and police can finally make their way to this house, we'll be long gone. The footage I capture here will be all they find.

So instead of trying to film ghosts, I film my

friends. I take my time, capturing each of them in turn. Andrea with her determination; Zander with his gentleness. Declan with his wit and Rhiannon with her strength. Isobel with her gentle, irrepressible hope. I have years of experience filming candid moments, and it feels like it's all been leading to this: to preserving the truth of these people, if nothing else.

It's not enough. It's not what any of them—talented and wonderful and incredible—deserve. But it's all I can offer them. I'm as trapped as they are.

"Did you hear that?" Andrea asks. She looks around, dark eyes glinting in the low light.

"Hear what?" Isobel asks. Once relegated to the very edges of my frame, she now stands in the center of it.

"That." Andrea cranes her neck, peering up at the balcony. "It sounds like—oh, fuck it, eh?"

With no further fanfare, she bolts up the stairs.

"Andrea!" Zander cries out, upset. I can't blame him. Since what happened to Rhiannon, no one seems willing to dislodge from the group. The only exception is when I drifted into the kitchen to find Laura, but already, that feels like a dream. I still can't quite explain why I did it, only that it didn't feel wrong to do. It still doesn't, really.

Zander chases Andrea up the stairs, catching her by the wrist before she vanishes around the bend. She looks back, a crease between her eyebrows. "Whoa, hey, I was just checking the bedroom . . ."

"Well . . . don't rush off like that, okay?" Zander

laces his fingers with hers. There's a desperate, worried edge to his voice. "Things are scary right now. Please be more careful."

Andrea brings his hand up, pressing her lips to the backs of his knuckles. "Sorry, babe."

She waits for the rest of us to get upstairs before she enters the bedroom.

The jacket Zander wore as Patrick sits on the edge of the bed. In a kinder universe, we'd be filming the night version of the scene we filmed yesterday. It's a strange thing to feel heartache over, when I'd resented almost every moment of filming *The Widow Ghost*. But still, a part of me misses it.

"There's nothing here." Rhiannon sits heavily on the bed. "What now?"

"Can't say. There's not really a plan here." Andrea opens up the closet. "It just feels like they're trying to lead us to something. If they want to be filmed, it's because they want to get the word out about something, eh? Maybe about how Virginia died, or her daughter, what was it . . ."

"Laura," Zander reminds her gently. "Her daughter's name was Laura."

"Right, right," Andrea says. "Maybe that car crash was more, you know . . ."

"Are you suggesting foul play?" Declan asks, raising an eyebrow.

"I don't know!" Andrea waves a hand. "I'm just looking for something to point us in the right direction."

Isobel smiles faintly. I capture it in the viewfinder, taking care to get the lighting right. If nothing else, I want to commit that smile to memory. "Too bad there's not, like, a scrapbook for us to find. Like Halley does in *The Widow Ghost*." She turns to me. When she sees me filming, her smile turns confused. "Hey, what are you doing?"

I flush. Years of Mom snapping at me for filming family parties has conditioned a shame response, I suppose. "I'm just recording. And looking around. The way the ghosts show up in real life aren't the way they show up on camera, so I could catch something."

"What do you mean?"

It's difficult to put into words, but I do my best. "Well, in the camera, Laura looked like the painting," I explain. "But she didn't look like that when I saw her with my eyes. She was more, um, like Virginia, I guess. Closer to how she looked when she died. Her face was all . . ." I make a vague gesture with my hand. "Sliced up."

Isobel shivers. "That's *so* weird. Wait, did Virginia look different, too?"

"Oh." I'd never even looked at the footage I got of her. "I'm not sure, actually."

I rewind as Isobel comes to lean over my shoulder. Her honey blonde curls tickle my neck, and I can feel the heat radiating from her skin. It's a real, vital, living warmth. So at odds with the ghosts we're surrounded by.

In the camera, Virginia is alone—no Rhiannon in

her grasp or collapsed at her feet. And she isn't staring at the camera the way she'd stared at me. Instead, she's looking out the window with a worried, pensive expression.

"She's, like, waiting for something." Isobel's voice sounds sad. "Is it that night, do you think? Is she waiting for her daughter to come home?"

"Maybe," I say. "But Laura's already here."

"Her husband died in the crash, too," Declan points out, and I jump. I didn't notice him coming up behind us. "Michelle told us that, remember? And my research practically confirmed it. 'Predeceased by her husband, Gerald, and her daughter, Laura.'" He quotes the obituary in a matter-of-fact tone. "We've seen Laura, but I haven't seen any sign of Gerald's ghost wandering around yet. Maybe it's him we need to find."

"Did Laura seem like she was, like, looking for someone?" Isobel asks. "It's hard to tell in the footage. With her face all, like, you know."

"I don't think she was looking for anything." I hate to snuff out this thin hope for them, but I don't want to lie. "She was cleaning up this mess of, um, glass and blood. And she was saying how she didn't mind, and . . ."

Can you hide his keys for me? That's what she'd said. The memory strikes me low in the ribs, sending a chill up my spine that has nothing to do with ghosts.

"Do you think her dad was driving?" I ask quietly. "When they crashed."

Declan frowns. "The obituary didn't say. I can't imagine that information would be public knowledge."

"Why do you ask?" Isobel says.

"I don't know," I say, even though I do. "Back in the kitchen, Laura asked me to, um, hide his keys."

"His keys?" Andrea peers out of the closet, her black bob slightly disheveled from digging through clothes. "You mean Gerald's keys?"

"Yeah," I say. "That's why I think he must have been driving when they crashed. He was probably drunk."

I thought it was an obvious conclusion to draw, but it seems to take everyone else in the room off-guard. "What makes you think that?" Rhiannon asks.

I clutch my camera tighter, wishing I could go back to hiding behind it. "Why else would you hide someone's keys? That's what you do when someone's drunk, right?" The words come out more plaintive than I'd like.

Declan leans back, thoughtful. "I never would have come to that conclusion," he muses. "But it makes sense. Andrea, does that particular piece of insight fit into your theory?"

"Maybe?" Andrea wrinkles her nose, shrugging. "Keep looking around, I guess." She dives back into the closet, Zander close behind. The conversation moves on. I stay silent, even though I make no move to film again.

I hadn't meant to say anything out of the ordinary.

I thought everyone knew the trick to hiding keys. I used to do it all the time for Dad. I'd stash them in the backs of drawers, under furniture, in pantries and fridges. Even in the back of the freezer once. I tried to pick places where Dad could have reasonably left them himself, so that he wouldn't blame me.

He must have known. I had to switch up the hiding places often, anyway, because he'd get wise if I used the same one too many times. But he only ever got angry at me about it when he was *really* drunk. He rarely yelled at me about any of the things I did to manage him: the way I'd pour his beers down the sink, or listen for his footsteps in the kitchen after he was supposed to be asleep.

Because when he confronted me, we had to talk about it. And talking about it was something we didn't—couldn't—do.

"Don't go talking like that, Cleo," my mother had said, the one time I dared to use the phrase *alcoholic* in public. *"Your father's . . . problem . . . is nobody's business."*

Now, here in this bedroom, I feel that familiar shame curdling my stomach. Do the others suspect anything? I doubt it, but I still wish I would have kept my thoughts to myself. If nothing else, it's unfair to the Barlow family. Surely they deserve their secrets as much as mine does.

Only they do seem to be trying to tell us something, don't they? Why else would Laura have appeared in the kitchen? And why would I have been compelled to find her there?

Why didn't anyone else feel it?

I look around. The others aren't searching because they *have* to. No one else seems to feel the way I do about this house, like there's something leading them through its hallways. I shiver, clutching my camcorder closer.

In the viewfinder, Virginia still stares out the window, caught in a moment of quiet worry. How many times had she looked out that window, waiting for her husband to come home? I can imagine it. It's an expression I saw on Mom's face often enough, when I didn't come home early enough to hide the keys or Dad managed to find where I'd stashed them. She never said so, but I always thought she blamed me.

Who does Virginia blame?

I'm projecting. I *know* I'm projecting. But the similarities are too stark to ignore. There is one key difference, though: I was off filming the evening my father crashed, not sitting in the passenger seat. Laura didn't survive him.

Michelle did. I wonder what it must have been like for her, especially after her mother died. Bogged down with several times the grief, in a place with walls that echo with it. I'm beginning to understand why she seemed so ragged. Living in a house like this would weigh anyone down.

Above us, the lights flicker, and the wind raises to a howl outside. I look out the window, expecting to see the blizzard picking up in force. But it doesn't. The flakes don't seem to react to the wind at all; they just continue to flicker in that endless static pattern.

"Does the storm look . . . strange to you guys?" I ask. My confusion echoes Patrick's line from my script, in that final cut. *Does the sky look . . . too light to you?* It doesn't seem worth it to point it out. Noah might care, but Noah isn't here.

Would we be doing this at all, if he were still around? Part of me wonders if he'd still be pushing us to film. To make a movie in a house that seems to be defying all natural laws. I'm not sure how I feel about that.

With shaky hands, I hold up my camcorder.

Outside the window in the viewfinder is a still, white wall. Cracks run through its surface like fault lines, spidering out with surreal, shadowed weight. They remind me, oddly, of the *Fall of the House of Usher* painting downstairs. The cracks in the wall that someone went over with that thick black paint.

"Oh my god," Isobel breathes. She leans over my shoulder for a closer look at the viewfinder, lips parted in shock. Her warm weight at my back is less of a comfort than it ought to be. "Is that, like, snow?"

I shiver. The image that Isobel's question conjures is far more unnerving than my memory of the painting. We're on the second story, and surely the snow can't be *that* deep. Even a freak storm wouldn't move so fast.

Right?

Logically, it shouldn't be possible. But logic has little to do with what's happening in this house. Which is the illusion: the storm that we see with our eyes, or the wall in my viewfinder? Are we trapped in an endless storm, or are we buried under an impossible amount of snow and ice?

Are we waiting to die?

Or are we already dead?

A loud *thud* shocks me into nearly dropping my camera. Isobel utters a small cry. At first I think that maybe Andrea actually found something, but when she and Zander hurry out of the closet they look just as confused as the rest of us.

Thud!

It's not coming from the closet at all. It's coming from the other side of the room.

Against the back wall is a heavy wardrobe: an antique that looks to be more for decoration than practicality, considering the walk-in closet in the same room. Once, Isobel had tucked herself away between it and the wall, her black skirts playing at a ghostliness that feels silly now. She's talented, but no human can come close to the real thing.

With another violent *thud*, the doors of the wardrobe bulge.

"There's something in there," Andrea breathes. She's already creeping forward, quiet on socked feet. As if she expects to sneak up on whatever horror awaits her there.

"Maybe you shouldn't . . ." Isobel says, but Andrea just holds up a hand, quieting her. In my viewfinder, she's every bit the leading lady she so often plays. I shouldn't be surprised. Andrea's never been one to sit by and let life happen to her. Whatever comes her way, she meets it head on, taking hold of it before it can take hold of her.

No, she'd never wait for a door to burst open.

She'll fling it open herself with both hands.

I've always admired that about her, but right now, I don't know if it's a good idea or a terrible one. Then again, with my camera in hand, I don't have to pass judgement. All I have to do is record and let future viewers decide for themselves.

It's a comforting thought. Religious people probably feel similar, when they throw up their hands and declare some tragedy or another as God's will.

Andrea grasps the door handle on the wardrobe. But just before she can open it, Virginia flies through the wood, shrieking.

It should terrify me. Here it is, the archetypical jump scare playing out in real life. Only I'm still seeing it through the viewfinder of the camcorder. Watching my friends shriek as Virginia lunges at them. Not a part of it at all. For a moment, I can forget that any of this is real.

Then Isobel is dragging me out, and I'm forced to abandon that notion.

The Virginia in the bedroom is very different from the Virginia in my viewfinder. I knew she would be, but it's still a shock to see her as she appears to everyone else: her body broken and decaying, her teeth bared in a snarl. No wonder they screamed.

"Cleo, come on!" Isobel tugs me along, and I'm forced to keep moving, even as delayed fear roots me to the spot.

Virginia watches us go with baleful, glaring eyes. For just a moment, before I join the flight downstairs, I swear I see something peeking out from the wardrobe. Something with dark, unknowable eyes.

And I swear, that in that moment, it stares not at any of the others, but at me.

– 17 –

<u>MATCH CUT</u>

PATRICK
You don't get it, do you? We were always
meant to come here. We never had a choice.

(Excerpt from THE WIDOW GHOST, written by
Cleo Moss.)

"*I HATE* THIS."

Andrea clenches her hands into fists, throwing herself onto the couch. Zander sits down beside her, rubbing her back even as exhaustion clings to his features.

I'm not sure why we fled to the living room after being chased from the bedroom. Perhaps because it's the most well-lit room in the house, or maybe just because we haven't seen a ghost here yet. But, somehow, it feels safest. Ironic, considering the tree that sits on the roof just above our heads.

But I suppose that is the least of our worries, now.

It's worry that seems to have finally gotten to

Andrea. "Just what the fuck are we supposed to be doing here, eh?" She runs a hand through her hair in frustration. "I thought we were onto something, looking for the ghosts. But when Virginia came at me, I stopped thinking. All logic went right out the fucking window." She groans. It's strange to see her so defeated. "I just want to know what she fucking wants."

"I don't think she wants anything," Rhiannon murmurs. We all wait in silence, but she doesn't offer up anything more. She just stares at the darkened television, picking at the fraying sleeve of her hoodie as if the loose thread personally offends her.

"Are you, like, okay?" Isobel asks gently.

Rhiannon narrows her eyes, breathing out slow. "I can't believe," she says. "you've got me theorizing about *ghosts*."

Declan is the first to break, muffling a snort with his hand. Soon the entire room is laughing. The sound of it is a sweet shock, and I wish I had my camcorder in my grasp, instead of charging against the wall, so I could capture their expressions. Even Rhiannon hides a sheepish smile behind her hand, unable to truly keep her composure.

"Try to tell us what you mean," Zander says, when at last we all get under control. "It could help."

"What I mean is, I don't think she . . . or any of these things . . . are conscious," Rhiannon says. "So they can't really want anything. It's like saying a fire chooses what to burn."

"A poet, yet," Declan teases. Rhiannon rolls her eyes and throws an elbow at his side, which he nimbly ignores.

"I'm just saying," Rhiannon continues, undeterred. "We've been looking at this situation as though there's a reason for it. But what if there isn't one?"

It's the closest anyone's come to voicing my thoughts. But Rhiannon doesn't say it like it's an admission of defeat. No, she poses the sentiment as if it's a genuine question, as if there's a step that comes after acceptance.

Andrea seems to realize this, on some level. She frowns. "If there isn't a why," she says slowly. "How do we stop it?"

No one has an answer for her. Except, maybe, the wind as it howls, or the house as it creaks.

"Cleo, what do you think?" Isobel asks.

I startle. I'm not filming, but I still hadn't expected anyone to notice me. People usually don't. They go on with their conversations, and I'm content enough to listen silently. I'm an observer at heart, with or without the camcorder. I've gotten very good, over the years, at fading into the background.

Only Isobel refuses to let me fade. Her green eyes fix on me, all gentle curiosity. As if she could find me in any room.

"Um. I don't know." I stare down at my hands in my lap. My black nail polish is starting to chip. "Things are happening. And I guess they'll keep happening until they stop."

Or we stop. That's the truth we're all dancing around, isn't it? I can't bring myself to say it, but I'm still certain it's the most likely scenario. I've seen enough of these movies. I know how these stories go. Intrepid heroes locked in with murderous ghosts. One by one, they vanish, leaving only insufficient clues behind. It's a tale too morbid to be cautionary, fit only to chill bones around a campfire.

Help never comes when you need it to. Reach out a hand into the darkness, and you'll be lucky if it's only ignored. I know far better than to expect anyone to come to our rescue.

"Until they stop," Andrea echoes. Her expression is thoughtful, if a bit resistant. "You think we should just wait it out, eh?"

"I don't know," I repeat. The words taste acrid in the back of my throat. "Maybe." I turn to Isobel. "Why ask me, anyway?"

"Because you, like, understand them." She gestures at my camera, still charging. "When you film them, they're different. That's got to mean something, you know?"

I feel sick. It's one thing to have Andrea put me at the center of her half-baked theory. It's another thing entirely to have a girl who once told me that art was honest stare at me like I'm the one in charge of her salvation. The hope in her eyes makes me want to run somewhere dark and quiet where she can't find me with her gaze.

I can't save her. I can't save anyone. Why doesn't anyone understand that?

"I don't know." That seems to be all I can say. "I don't mean to do anything to them. It just happens. And it doesn't seem to be stopping them, so, um. I really don't think your answer is there. I'm sorry."

I wait for the disappointment in her eyes. The defeat. It will hurt to put that look on her face, but it will hurt more in the long run to let her believe a lie.

Isobel doesn't look disappointed. She just nods. "Well, there's still something to it, I think." She turns to Declan. "Don't you think? You're, like, the actual ghost expert here, right?"

Declan answers her, but I don't hear it. Rather, my brain refuses to process it. He might as well be speaking in the same Spanish he employs when he's frustrated or talking to his family. I can't understand him.

I can't understand any of this.

I get up from my spot on the couch, mumbling about needing to use the bathroom. It's the only excuse I can think of that won't lead to one of the others following me. I need to be alone, if only for a moment.

In the hallway, the shadows are dark. Michelle's painting takes on a strange, surreal life in my peripheral vision as I pass beneath it. I swear that Virginia cranes her neck to look at me, her eyes tracking my escape. Only when I look at her directly, she doesn't move.

Once inside the bathroom, all I actually do is sit on the closed toilet lid and try to catch my breath. The white porcelain sink and bathtub seem over-bright, stinging my eyes to look at. My ears ring, and my chest is tight with panic.

I squeeze my eyes shut, forcing myself to breathe in, then out. This is utterly ridiculous. When I saw Laura in the kitchen, I held my camera steady. When Virginia appeared in the bedroom, I'd been supernaturally calm. Why is it that I'm going to pieces now, over nothing?

Fight, flight, or freeze. My responses are always the wrong ones.

I breathe in, then out. In, and then out. I imagine myself as a character in some nameless film. INT. BATHROOM — EVENING. Shot from above, with a distorted lens to make the figure sitting in the frame even smaller. She'd have her arms curled around herself protectively, shoulders trembling. Warding off a threat that doesn't exist.

In a movie, this would be a turning point. For a more traditional heroine, this would be the moment that she digs deep and finds the strength she didn't know she possessed. In the sort of narrative I enjoy, it would be a more tragic story beat, where the escalating threats finally descend on the sacrificial lamb.

The thought should frighten me. It doesn't. In spite of everything, I don't think I'm in danger when I'm alone here.

Because Isobel is right. I understand something

about this place.

It doesn't change anything. I don't have any illusions about my role in this story. I will never be the one who saves the day. I'm just the girl with the camera. And no matter what the others think, the girl with the camera isn't supposed to fix anything or figure anything out. My job is not to interpret. Not even to experience. Leave that to the actors and actresses of the world, or the critics who analyze, or even the casual audiences. None of that has anything to do with what I am here for.

I am here, as always, to bear witness.

My heart rate slows. My breathing settles into an even push and pull. I lower my hands, blinking away the stars that linger from the pressure of my touch against my eyelids. The brightness of the bathroom is no longer overwhelming: I'm able to frame it, clinically, the way I would frame any shot in my camera.

It seems so obvious. That's what I'm here to do. I'm here to record the truth of this house, capture it on film so that the tragedy of it can no longer be ignored. To make sure that myself—and my friends—aren't forgotten.

To wish for anything else is a folly. Our end is already written. *My* end is already written. Some people are just doomed. At least I can leave behind proof that I existed, something that will last even after I'm gone.

Isn't that what artists are supposed to do? Isobel

can talk about honesty, Andrea can soak up the attention like a sponge, Noah can stick to his binders. But in the end, art is this: leaving a mark on the world. That's all any of us can hope for.

Dad didn't leave much. He always had a way of eluding even my frame. He preferred to be on the other side of the camera, making suggestions for shot composition, praising my work.

I'd asked him, once, if he ever wanted to make movies. The question made him irrationally angry, as questions often did. Even the most innocent of inquiries could send him off on a shouting fit. I don't want to make him sound worse than he was, because his anger wasn't frightening. He never harmed me and rarely insulted me. But the bursts of tantrum were still off-putting. Like watching a grown man revert into a toddler without reason.

But maybe there was a reason. Maybe he did want to make movies at some point, but he had to put those dreams aside. Now he's dead, with nothing to show for it.

I can be different. And my friends, they can be different, too. That much, however little, I can do.

A chill runs down my spine, and the lighting in the bathroom seems to shift. There's something on the other side of the door. I can see its shadow in the crack between wood and floor, blotting out what little light comes in from the hallway. There's no sound. Just that still shadow, and the wind.

Is it one of the others, come to fetch me? Or is it

something else?

The shadow shifts and grows darker. Bloody fingertips poke underneath the door.

I stand, then kneel on the ground. I can't quite bring myself to get within reach of them, but I get as close as I can, quieting my voice to a whisper. I don't want the others to hear me speaking to a ghost. They'll think I've gone mad.

Maybe I have. Maybe only a mad person feels more calm when the scare happens than waiting in anticipation for it.

"I don't have my camera with me," I whisper. "You'll have to wait."

The bloodied hands still. On the ring finger, the nail has broken off entirely, and the nail bed oozes blackish blood. Hemp rope fibers burrow in the ragged fingertips like splinters. I wonder how hard Virginia must have struggled against the noose in those final moments, to have remnants of it still clinging to her incorporeal form. How much it must have hurt.

Would it have been better for her not to struggle at all? To go limp and let the rope claim her? Is a person capable of doing that, or does the reflexive will to live always kick in, for better or for worse?

"Just wait," I say again. It sounds almost like a plea.

The fingers tremble, just once. Then they withdraw. Faintly, I hear the sound of faltering footsteps, walking down the hallway until they're swallowed up by the wind.

I stay there, kneeling, until a more solid set of footsteps come my way.

"Cleo? Are you, like, okay?"

I shiver at the sound of Isobel's voice. I'm aware, all at once, of the stiffness in my joints, the pain in my neck. How long have I been kneeling here? It's not as though I don't remember doing it, or my thought process for doing so. But trying to make sense of it now is like trying to make sense of a dream. I certainly couldn't explain it to Isobel.

"I'm fine." My voice comes out surprisingly steady. I open the door. Virginia's ghost is nowhere to be seen. There's only Isobel, looking at me with open concern. "Sorry," I say. "I didn't mean to worry you."

"That's okay." Isobel smiles, but it doesn't reach her eyes. Even her optimism is worn thin at this point. "I think we've all decided to just chill in the living room for now. Or not *chill*, obviously, it's like . . ." She puts her face in her hands, and my heart twists in sympathy. She doesn't deserve to feel like this. "This is all so totally crazy, I don't . . . How are you even supposed to react to this, you know? I feel like I'm . . . I don't even know . . ."

"About five seconds away from a nervous fucking breakdown?" I offer. "I mean, I certainly don't feel that way. But if you do, that's understandable." It's a weak attempt at levity, but Isobel deserves that much, at least.

It has the desired effect. Isobel, giggling wetly,

lowers her hands from her face. "Oh, totally. I'm completely normal about this, too." She sniffs, her green eyes damp. "Cleo, can I have a hug?"

Oh.

I like to think of myself as having a fairly large vocabulary, really. But words fail me in this moment. I barely manage a squeaky 'yes' before Isobel steps forward, wrapping her arms around me. Her head rests on my shoulder, face tilted into the crook of my neck. Slowly, I let myself press my palms to the backs of her shoulders. My forehead fetches up on the top of her scalp.

Isobel breathes out slowly, the tension unfurling from her body in increments. I should have done this sooner. For as often as she's reached out a hand to me, I should have realized that she was seeking comfort as much as she was offering it. Of course she was.

I let her take that comfort now. Let her hold me for as long as she likes, if that's what it takes. With the warmth of her body against mine, the camcorder has never seemed less important.

"Come on," she says as she pulls away. "Let's head back to the living room with the others, okay?"

I think about Virginia's fingers, poking under the doorway just now. With Andrea, she had burst right through the wardrobe. Trying to scare her away. She's different with me. This whole house seems different with me, somehow. Different when I'm alone.

But Isobel looks at me expectantly. I can't turn her away.

"Okay," I say quietly. I let her lead me back to the living room.

- 18 -

<u>VERTIGO EFFECT</u>

WHEN ISOBEL AND I enter the living room, the others have already settled in. Declan curls like a cat in the armchair with his eyes closed. Rhiannon is at one end of the couch, her back to the room and her face buried in the cushions. Zander lays on the floor with his head pillowed in Andrea's lap. She runs her fingers through his curls, the only one left awake.

"We can't really tell if it's night or not," she murmurs by way of explanation. "But we all figured we're tired enough for it to be. And it's not like there's anything else we can do." Her jaw tenses for a moment, then releases. "We'll figure something out. But for now, it feels safe to rest here." She shakes her head, a wry smile on her lips. "It's fucking weird. That tree could come crashing down at any second, but still. I guess there are worse things, eh?"

Worse is a matter of opinion. But I understand what Andrea means. A small, irrational part of me hopes that the roof will collapse. Collapse and let in the wind, the snow, the world. We're too isolated in this house. Bugs trapped in a killing jar. And like a bug, I can't truly comprehend the arbiter of my end. Only feel the truth of my death by inches under my carapace.

Isobel takes the other end of the couch, opposite Rhiannon. She looks up at me, patting the space beside her. "There's room for you, too."

There isn't, really. The two of us would barely be able to fit side-by-side like that. Still, Isobel's green eyes are full of hope. I can understand that. It's natural to want another body near you in the frightening dark. Isn't that why she hugged me earlier?

I wish I could be the one to provide that comfort for her here and now. But I would make a poor bedmate in these conditions. "Maybe later," I say. "I'm, um, too restless to sleep. I'd probably just end up kicking you."

If Isobel is disappointed by my failure to help, she takes it in stride. "That's totally fair. Feel free to come up later if you change your mind."

She curls in on herself and drifts off. So does Andrea, still sitting upright with Zander's head in her lap, her hand slowed to stillness in his hair. I settle into the alcove by the bay window. The chill of winter against my back helps, oddly, with the skin-crawling jitters of insomnia. I know without even trying that I won't be able to sleep.

Instead, I review the footage on my camcorder. I'm not sure what I'm looking for. Trying to imagine what others will think if they find it, I suppose.

What will a stranger see, when they look at this footage? They'll see Andrea, effortlessly taking charge. Zander loyally at her side. Declan, snarking and throwing out theories and existing, so wholly as himself. Rhiannon with her quiet logic offering a new perspective. And, of course, Isobel: the least knowledgeable of the genre, but fitting in as seamless as the rest.

All my friends, captured in a moment of time. Forever preserved, no matter what happens. And me, on the other side of the camera. Will I be remembered at all?

I think there's at least a chance of it. There's Noah to consider, after all. Assuming he really did get out before all of this began. I honestly believe that's the most likely option: if the ghosts had gotten to him, surely we'd have found evidence of that by now. And if he'd gotten hurt on the drive home, he wouldn't have been able to screen our calls.

I don't wish ill on him, but if I'm being honest, his escape seems unfair. It wasn't good sense that led him away, just good luck. No wonder he was always so dismissive of my worries. Some people are charmed like that. They never have to anticipate the worst, because for them, the worst will never come.

And then, there are people like me. A Cassandra unable to change the course of her own fate.

Maybe it will be through Noah that I get remembered. Wouldn't that be an ironic twist of fate? He'll grow up, become a famous director like he always wanted. And this doomed production will be relegated to an interesting footnote on his Wikipedia page.

I'll be lucky if it mentions me by name.

The idea is a far cry from the giddy daydream I'd entertained before the seance. But deep down, I'd always known that kind of success wasn't for me. There was a reason I never really let myself consider *The Widow Ghost* as anything more than a passion project, or *Horrorfest* as anything other than a terrible idea.

It all seems so trivial as I watch the footage replay.

I've caught up to the most recent recording by now. In the viewfinder, the scene in the bedroom erupts into chaos as Virginia's ghost bursts through the wardrobe. I hadn't really had time, in the moment, to process what she was doing. In real life, she'd lurched at Andrea. But here, she presses a finger to her lips, her free hand flat against the door of the wardrobe. She looks, for all the world, like a frustrated mother trying to calm an unruly sleepover. It makes the horrified reactions of the living on camera almost comical in comparison.

How will people react to this? Will they see the

horror for what it is, or brush it off as some strange shared delusion?

The camera jerks as I'm dragged away, the picture blurring into disarray. But right before it vanishes from frame, the door of the wardrobe moves. It creaks open for just a flash before Virginia's restraining hand slams it shut again.

In my tiny corner of the living room, shadows flicker like the snowfall outside as I rewind the footage. I let it roll again, finger hovering over the pause button until I'm able to stop it at exactly the right moment.

The door *does* open. I swore it had, when I was fleeing. From within, a pair of eyes shine wetly among the shadows. They stare at the camera. There aren't any other features to discern in the dark, but I can't help reading emotion into that gaze. Deep down, I think they look surprised.

Deeper down, I think they look pleading.

It doesn't feel like an accident, that I caught this on camera. It doesn't feel like an accident, that I noticed the ghosts long before the others. It doesn't feel like an accident, that I knew from the moment we set out that something would go wrong.

It doesn't feel like an accident that we're in this house, with a family history that mirrors my own in such a hideously intimate way.

Rhiannon's convinced that the ghosts aren't sentient and therefore can't want anything. But is that really true? Maybe fire doesn't choose what to burn, but the blaze does still reach ever higher when given the opportunity. Is that not a kind of wanting, even if it isn't conscious?

I wonder. And I also wonder if neither Isobel nor I had the right idea about art. Or maybe we both did, in our way.

Maybe, in the end, art is about being recognized. And maybe that's all these ghosts want, too, in their own way of wanting. To be recognized by someone who understands them.

It isn't as though I think I'll save us all with this effort. I can't believe that salvation is an option, even as I unplug the camera and sneak out into the hallway on quiet, socked feet. I'm not a hero.

I'm just an artist. And I will do what an artist does.

Outside, the wind howls, snow flickering in nonsense patterns beyond the tall windows. It's distant to me now, part of a world I'm no longer a part of. The bite of the cold, the damp burn of the snow, the chill seeping beneath layers of clothing: these are all sensations that my skin once knew, but they feel very unimportant now. It's like I'm a corpse buried deep in the earth, unreachable by the elements that rage above me.

But much like a grave, this home is colder.

I make my way up the stairs, palm skating across the banister. It's strange how familiar this place has become in such a short amount of time. When I take in the house—its pale blue-gray wallpaper, its high archways, its oak-lined balcony—I no longer feel as though I'm looking at it with the eyes of a stranger. My body knows these steps as sure as it knows the hallways of my own home.

The door to the main bedroom is closed. I'm almost certain we left it open as we fled downstairs. But I can't say I'm surprised to see it in this state. I press my palms flat against the wood, leaning forward.

"It's okay," I murmur. "It's just me."

The ghosts are different when I'm alone. They've never grabbed me like they did with Rhiannon or rushed at me like they did with Andrea. Laura's hand in the kitchen, Virginia's fingertips beneath the doorway, neither of those were violent. They were desperate. Reaching out for help.

Just like it feels as though something—someone— is reaching out to me for help now.

"It's okay," I whisper again. And I open the door.

The bedroom is dark. Ordinarily, one of the streetlights outside would provide at least a little illumination, but none of that reaches here now. The only light comes from the screen of my camcorder's viewfinder, a bluish glow that spills across my pale fingers.

I don't fumble for the light switch. It would feel wrong, like disrupting someone while they're sleeping. I walk carefully through the darkness instead, guided only by the version of the room I can see through my camera's lens.

With the ISO settings pushed to their extreme, the wardrobe door is thrown into sharp relief. The handle casts a harsh shadow against the wood. When I reach for it, the shadows of my fingers turn long and spindly before shrinking the closer I get. I grip the doorknob, then open it.

The screen version of the wardrobe is empty of everything, even clothing. I can see all the way to the back corners, twined with cobwebs. Dust motes swirl at the disruption.

Slowly, I lower the camera. I know even before I look that it isn't telling the truth.

There's something inside.

I can't make out more than the huddled shape of it. But it's there, and finally I start to feel something other than a dull sort of resignation. Fear trickles in like the wind that howls through the foundation of the house. What am I doing here? If I really don't think this is going to save us, what is it that I'm hoping to accomplish?

Why did I come up here alone?

Even as I ask myself these questions, my body continues to move. My hands tremble as I pull out my phone, but that doesn't stop me from turning on the flashlight, shining it into the wardrobe.

Inside is a man with no face. He wears a rumpled button down and stained jeans, and there are scuffs on his shoes. He's crouched down as if speaking to a child, balanced precariously on the balls of his feet. His long arms dangle between his knees, knuckles brushing the wooden floor of the wardrobe.

Above his neck, all is covered by an angry black scrawl.

Black like the splotches destroying the paintings in the basement.

Black like the scribbles over the man from the painting in the hallway.

This *is* the man from the painting in the hallway. Michelle's father, Gerald—or what remains of him. He doesn't react to the light, or my presence. He only sways uncertainly, as if unable to keep his balance. His hands come up to paw at his obscured face in clumsy, uncontrolled movements.

I can't run. Can't move at all. I shouldn't be seeing this. I can't do anything for this man. I can't even film him. He eludes my camera, further proof that all of this is wrong.

His shoulders heave. His spine contorts. A slushy, muffled groan issues from the black ruin of his face. He sounds like my dad used to during particularly violent hangovers. The comparison makes me feel even sicker.

I take a step back. And I collide with something. It's cold but yielding, with a strange static cling that sends all of the hair on the back of my neck on end. The acrid scent of fresh paint fills my nostrils.

I'm still trying to make sense of it when ten cold fingers wrap around my throat. They squeeze.

My camera drops from my hands, thudding to the carpet a world away. I reach up on instinct, clutching at the hands around my throat much as Virginia must have clutched at the noose, all those years ago. But, like Virginia, my struggles are ineffectual. The hands squeeze tighter. My lungs scream silently for air.

In front of me, the faceless man continues to lurch, oblivious to my presence. But his clumsy movements are no match for mine. I thrash, arms flailing, legs kicking out. My foot collides with something solid and painful and sends it flying into the wardrobe. It crunches on impact.

The grip around my throat loosens. Rather, it *fades*, as if the hands themselves are vanishing from existence. I don't spend time questioning it or looking around for answers. I don't even freeze, as I am wont to do in such situations. Here at the end of it all, a more powerful instinct takes over.

I flee.

I burst from the bedroom, turning for the stairs as soon as I clear the doorway. I nearly stumble on the first riser, but momentum pushes me forward, sending me careening down another step.

Another.

And another.

Alfred Hitchcock, of *Psycho* and *Rear Window* fame, was known for producing a certain kind of camera technique. It's even named after one of his movies: it's called The *Vertigo* Effect, sometimes referred to more simply as a dolly zoom. In this kind of shot, the camera would be moved toward an object while simultaneously zooming out, or vice versa, creating a surreal effect where the object doesn't appear to change sizes despite moving closer to the viewer.

I am running down the stairs. But the first floor isn't getting any closer. It remains the exact same distance away, as if caught in Hitchcock's camera instead of my own ineffectual eye.

"No!" Speeding up does nothing. I chance a glance over my shoulder, and my heart hits my throat, choking me with fear.

Virginia Barlow is pursuing me. No *Vertigo* Effect on her: she's gaining with a slow, dreamy terror, but she *is* gaining. Her face, even stretched in its perpetual grimace-grin, is a mask of hate. Her eyes gleam like those of a predator.

I had it wrong. What I saw—who I saw—in that wardrobe, I was never meant to see it. And I can't imagine that Virginia will let that go unpunished. Not when she's looking at me with such hate and fury in her gaze.

"Please!" My throat burns, lungs working overtime in the wake of Virginia's hands around my neck. "Please, someone, help!"

No one is coming. No one ever does. But reflex always kicks in at the end, and my hand, just as thoughtlessly as it struggled against Virginia's strangulation, reaches out into the darkness, groping for a salvation I don't believe in.

A hand wraps around my wrist. It pulls.

Behind me, Virginia lets out a cheated scream. I hardly register it through the dizzy disorientation as reality struggles to orient itself. I'm no longer on the stairs. I'm in someone's arms, a pair of familiar green eyes staring at me in abject alarm.

Virginia is gone. And Isobel, startled and concerned, holds me.

– 19 –

<u>IRIS</u>

"CLEO? OH MY god, are you okay?"

Isobel's hands are like bird wings, fluttering before settling on my shoulders. She peers at me with shock, with fear, with the sort of unfiltered concern that I never quite feel like I deserve. I want to look away. Only I can't find the wherewithal to do much of anything right now.

"Cleo?" Her green eyes widen in horror. "What happened to your neck?"

Andrea peers around the corner. "What's going on out here? Everyone alright?"

An excellent question. One I find myself thoroughly unable to answer. Isobel saves me the trouble. "I heard screaming, so I came out here! It was all dark and, like, weird, I don't even *know*. But then I heard Cleo call for help, and her hand sort of reached out of the dark? So I grabbed and pulled, and . . . poof, Cleo!" Her arm twines with mine as she turns to look at Andrea. "Something's wrong. She's hurt."

"Hurt?" The others are spilling out of the living room now: Declan adjusting his gray shirt, Zander with his blonde hair in disarray, Rhiannon unfolding her glasses as she walks. Everyone is here, and they're looking at me with concern. I don't know what to do with it. I don't know what to do with any of it. I don't understand how I'm not still on those stairs.

Since when do people actually come when I call for help?

Now that it's happened, I feel guilty. They're all as scared as I am. They shouldn't have to waste their energy on taking care of me.

"Shit," Andrea says, pulling me out of my thoughts. She puts herself between me and the stairs, narrowing her eyes. "That looks bad."

"What happened?" Zander asks.

I swallow. I'm not sure how to explain what just happened, what led me to the stairs or what I found up there. I hardly understand it, and I understand even less how I managed to escape. That isn't how these kinds of stories go. That isn't how *my* story is supposed to go.

"I left my camera upstairs," I finally say. My voice is hoarse.

The others exchange a confused glance. Finally, Rhiannon speaks up. "Give her a minute," she says.

"If the g—if something happened. You should give her a minute."

Not even Declan has the heart to call out her almost slip up. Isobel presses closer to me, her temple a warm weight on my shoulder. An anchor. Before I can second guess myself, I slip my hand into hers and squeeze.

She smiles at me.

Andrea steps on the bottom stair. Panic slices through my chest. "*Wait—*"

She waves me off. "Someone's gotta get the camera, eh?" But she must remember Zander's worry from the last time she charged up the stairs like this, because she pauses long enough to look back at him. "Babe?" He follows her, and the two of them ascend the stairs hand-in-hand.

I track their movements with an anxious eye. The stairs do not stretch or distort or give any sign that they're about to turn back into the nightmare that befell me. Andrea and Zander reach the top without incident and vanish around the corner.

Seconds tick by in silence. I'm not sure how long it takes for everyone else to get as nervous as I feel, but eventually Declan calls up. "Are you two alive up there?" He winces and shakes his head, visibly regretting his glib tone the moment it passes his lips.

Andrea responds immediately. "We're okay!" She doesn't sound like she's lying, exactly. She just doesn't sound like she's telling the whole story. "There's nothing up here, it's just . . . fuck." She and Zander reappear at the top of the stairs. Their expressions of sympathy are eerie in how similar they are.

"I got the camera," Andrea says, "but . . . shit, Cleo . . ."

The camera's viewfinder dangles at a sharp, obscene angle, reminiscent of Virginia's neck. As Andrea walks back down the stairs, more damage becomes apparent: the chipped casing, the shattered lens. And, still, when Andrea pushes the camera into my hands, I press and hold the power button.

Nothing happens.

My camera is destroyed.

"Oh, Cleo." Isobel's grip on my arm tightens. "I'm so sorry."

Sorry. A word I've grown far too used to hearing. I stare at the camera, turning it around slowly in my hands. It was already an older model when I got it, not impressive in the least. But it's been a constant companion for me over the years, accompanying me on every trip and outing that I could justify bringing it. I've seen so much of the world through its lens.

I never finished a movie with it.

Now I never would.

And what of my footage here? My final project, the one thing I could give in this awful situation? I try to eject the memory card, but it's caught in the shattered mess of plastic. When I finally do recover it, it's as bent and mangled as the camcorder itself. Ruined.

It's cruel. Crueler than even I could have suspected the universe of being.

"Cleo?" Declan's voice is wary. I suppose he's expecting sobs, if not outright hysteria.

"It's fine." The words come out on reflex. I blink rapidly. I don't want to break down in front of everyone. I have no *reason* to break down. I've lost far, far worse, and I didn't cry then.

Why should my eyes sting now?

"It's a camera." I breathe out carefully, locking my heartache somewhere deep where it won't show on my face or in my voice. "It's just a camera. I'm fine."

I'm not sure if the others believe me. It's hard to say 'I'm fine' in a way that's convincing, even when it's the truth. But before anyone can call me on it, Zander speaks. His quiet voice has never sounded more thoughtful.

"Does the house feel . . . different, to you guys?"

He's frowning up at the balcony. It reminds me, strangely, of the scene where Patrick stares out the window and asks Halley about the sky. Only this is all Zander. Zander and his quiet tendency to pick up on things that others wouldn't.

Andrea leans against the wall beside him, arms crossed over her chest. "What do you mean?"

"It's just . . . I'm not sure how to explain it." Zander looks at Andrea, as though she alone can pull the words from him.

She presses two fingertips to the back of his hand. Her voice, low and gentle, has the cadence of an old comfort. "It's okay, babe. Just try."

"I've always felt . . . watched, in this hallway,"

Zander says, his voice faltering. "And there's been a . . . a shadow, I guess? I thought it was my mind playing tricks on me, or something with how the house was made. It didn't really seem worth commenting on, anyway, with everything else going on. But it's gone now."

Now that he's pointed it out, I sense it. There's something about the air in this hallway that's different from before. It held an oppressiveness that is noticeable only in its absence. While the shadows are still long and dark, they hold less weight than before.

"That's interesting . . ." Declan presses the side of his finger to his lips. A holdover from when he used to bite his nails as a nervous habit. His brown eyes find mine. "Cleo, do you think you can tell us exactly what happened to you up there?"

He speaks, still, with that careful sort of tone that people use when they think you're liable to burst into tears. Out of a desire for him to stop looking at me that way more than anything else, I speak. "I was filming when Virginia grabbed me by the throat. From behind. I dropped the camera, I was struggling, and I . . . must have kicked it into the wardrobe."

The words taste like ash on my tongue. I didn't do it on purpose. But the fact remains: the camcorder is broken because of *me*. It was shattered not by ghosts, but my own careless limbs.

"And then?" Declan asks. His eyes hold a strange light. "What happened then?"

"Virginia's grip loosened enough for me to get

away," I explain. "I tried to run, but the stairs just kept going. And Virginia kept chasing me until Isobel pulled me out."

Isobel squeezes my arm. There's comfort in that small gesture, as intangible as the shift in the air. I lean into it.

"She *chased* you," Declan says. "but she didn't *catch* you?"

There's an odd emphasis on his words. Like he's come to a conclusion that I can't follow him to. "Well, no. Like I said, Isobel pulled me out before that could happen." I glance at Isobel, who smiles up at me wanly. I try on a smile back, and I find that it comes easier than I thought it would. It means something that she helped me.

"I don't think that's what's happening here," Declan says. His voice is quiet, contemplative, somewhat removed from its usual transatlantic affect. "At least, not entirely."

Rhiannon crosses her arms over her chest, dark eyes narrowing behind the thick lenses of her glasses. For once, it's not skepticism that colors her tone. "What are you thinking?"

"The ghosts—or the entities, if you'd prefer that terminology—are only getting stronger. Not only are they apparently warping the house to their own ends, they've managed to cause physical harm." He gestures at my bruised throat with one slim hand. "But, when Cleo destroyed the camera, that did something."

"Hey, you're right." Andrea speaks slowly,

working it out as she goes. "I just guessed that the ghosts wanted to be filmed. But I've been wrong before. What if it's the opposite, eh? Maybe the filming just made it worse."

She doesn't say it as a condemnation of me, personally. But the idea still makes my stomach ache. All this time I spent reminding myself that I wasn't a savior, and it never occurred to me that I might in fact have been holding the tool of our damnation.

"It makes some degree of sense," Declan says. He sounds excited now. "It's emotional resonance. The more we focused on them, the more we created them, the realer they became."

"Like art, in a way," Zander muses in his quiet voice. Isobel nods, her blonde curls bouncing with the force of the movement.

I don't like this. Not even Rhiannon is disagreeing, only staring solemnly as the others unravel this theory as far as it can go. But I'm afraid of what will happen once they reach the end of the thread. I'm afraid of what will happen when they decide where to place the blame.

Who else would it lie with, other than the one who held the camera?

"That doesn't make sense," I say. The others turn to face me. I grip the camcorder tightly, even though it can't offer me any protection now. And, if the others are to be believed, it never did. "The camera's broken, but the ghosts are still here, and we're still trapped." I gesture at the window and its unchanged static snow.

"Besides, there were always ghosts here. They only really got bad after . . ."

"After the seance," Zander finishes.

"So we're back where we started," Rhiannon sighs. She looks tired. "Why are we trying to put logic to this, anyway? It's all nonsense." It's not a dismissal this time as much as a resignation.

"Not necessarily," Declan says. "Breaking the camera still had an effect. If there's something else like that we can do, something we're missing . . ."

There's a long silence. Then, beside me, Isobel jerks as if struck. "Oh my god. It's the painting!"

She points. Above us, Michelle's half-finished painting looms. And now that she mentions it, some of that aura—what Zander referred to as a shadow— does seem to cling to it. Virginia's painted eyes glare with active malevolence, and Laura's half-finished face radiates misery.

"Zander's right," Isobel says. "It *is* about art. And that art was made by Virginia's daughter. Of course it's going to be charged with, like, emotions or memories or whatever is making this happen!"

"When Cleo filmed Laura in the kitchen," Rhiannon says quietly, "her face was blurred out like it is in the painting. It's all connected."

Declan grins at her, a shock-burst of light. "Oh, honey, we'll make a conspiracy theorist out of you yet."

Rhiannon rolls her eyes.

Andrea interjects before the conversation can go

too far off-track. "Okay, painting, we're all on the same page. The question is, what do we do about it, eh?"

"Could we rip it up?" Zander asks.

The idea makes me uncomfortable. I don't want to destroy another artist's work, even in a situation as terrible as this.

Thankfully, Declan shakes his head. "I don't think that's enough. The painting would still exist, just in pieces. It's not like the camera. Burning it would be safer."

"Ah, yes," Rhiannon says flatly. "Lighting something on fire in an enclosed space. Where we can't leave. Safer."

Declan rolls his eyes. "Much as I'm loath to admit it, you may have a point. Although, I wonder . . ." His brow furrows for a moment, deep in thought. "When I performed the cleansing after the seance, it was generalized. More of a precaution than anything. If I did something similar, more targeted against the painting itself . . ."

Andrea raises an eyebrow. "You want to *exorcise* the thing?"

"Exorcisms are for demons, not ghosts." Declan stares up at the painting. There's a distance to his expression, as if he's too lost in thought to really give the conversation his full attention. "Besides, only priests can perform exorcisms."

Rhiannon actually chuckles at this. "And you're a stickler for religious rules?"

This gets his attention. "Listen. Our goal in this particular endeavor is to create less ghostly activity, not more. And while my *abuela* took me coming out remarkably well, even she has her limits. If I performed outright blasphemy, she'd rise up to haunt me herself." He blinks, then adds, almost as an afterthought, "Besides, I don't know how to do an exorcism. They don't exactly cover that in catechism."

My knowledge of such a ritual is similarly lacking. I could offer the fact that they used porridge colored to look like pea soup for the scene where Regan projectile vomits in *The Exorcist*, but I don't think such horror movie trivia would be particularly useful in our current situation.

It's just as well that I'm still too emotionally stunned to voice *that* thought out loud.

"Well, let's focus on what you do know how to do, then." Andrea presses her palms together, determination in her gaze. "Let's do the cleansing ritual."

- 20 -

<u>ACTION</u>

CLOSE-UP ON:

The patch of wall where Michelle's painting once hung. The wallpaper is more faded than it should be.

DECLAN SETS UP the cleansing.

It involves more candles than the seance had, in various shapes and sizes scavenged from around the house. He sets them around the painting, now removed from the wall and laid flat on the floor. But one thing remains the same: he asks all of us to sit in a circle around it. "It will help if you lend your energy," he explains.

Rhiannon, long past clinging to her skepticism, sits beside him, her round glasses reflecting the flickering lights of the candles. I, without my camera, have no choice but to join as well.

I sit in the circle with Declan on my left and Isobel on my right. I wonder if cleansing rituals, like seances, require the participants to hold hands. Or maybe it's more that I hope that's the case with Isobel by my side. What I feel now is not the giddy crush that I'd harbored my freshman year, back when all I really knew of Isobel was the slope of her shoulders, the curl of her hair, and the way she twirled across the stage like she was made for it.

And, yet, those feelings are a part of it, too. A part made ever deeper by the fact that now I know the cadence of her speech and the shape of her thoughts. I know that she can wax philosophical about art and drop the occasional morbid joke. I know that she can, sometimes, be afraid of the dark.

I know that she reached a hand into that darkness for me.

And now, all I want to do is reach back.

I want to hold her hand because it would comfort me, yes, but I want it to comfort her, as well. I wish I would have stayed with her on the couch when she asked me to. But even with that abandonment, she still looks at me out of the corner of her eye. As if by some absolute fucking miracle, she wants to hold my hand, too.

"Alright." Declan sighs. He's usually so unflappable, with his immaculate make-up and his quick wit. It's unnerving to see him so careworn. "Alright, just . . . give me a moment." He folds his hands, presses his knuckles to his lips and mumbles something in Spanish. I don't recognize the words, but they hold the cadence of an old comfort. When he lifts his head, he seems steadier. More like himself, with that solid confidence that I'd always assumed came naturally to him. "It's time to begin. Everyone join hands."

Isobel reaches out at the same time that I do. Her hands are solid and warm, her fingers slotting into the spaces between mine with a lack of hesitance that's a little dizzying.

The mood now couldn't be more different than during the seance. Before, there had been a light air of curiosity, easily broken with jokes and laughter. But there's no sign of laughter now. Only the howl of the wind outside and the slow, ominous creaking of the house as it settles.

Although *settles* feels too calm a word for what's really happening in this place. *Suffocates* might be better. The walls seem heavier somehow, bowed with weight. As though the tree on the roof is weighing down the space spiritually instead of physically.

In spite of this ambient noise, the intake of Declan's breath seems very loud. "Spirits," he says. "You are no longer welcome in this place. It is time to move on."

The lights flicker. The wind picks up, howling louder and more insistently through the cracks in the house's foundation. Outside, the snow continues its endless static strangeness at odds with the sound. My head spins just to look at it. It's the same detached dizziness that led me to walk into the kitchen on my own. The same feeling that compelled me up the stairs.

I hear whispers. They call to me. But Isobel's hand in mine, the heat of my friends' bodies around me, those things keep me grounded in the here and now. Not chasing after ghosts for reasons I can't articulate to anyone, let alone myself.

"Spirits," Declan says, louder, his voice gaining confidence. "Be gone from this place. It—" He falters here for a moment. "It isn't natural for you to linger on like this. Your time is over. You need to go."

The candle flames splutter but don't go out. By their light, I can still see the painting on the ground. Virginia's glare. Laura's blurry, indistinct face. Gerald's body, and the black paint obscuring him from the neck up.

The paint drips down his shoulders, covering the top parts of his arms. Had it been like that before?

No. No, the scribbles hadn't gone past his neck before. But as Declan chants, as I continue to stare at the painting, I realize that the black paint is spreading.

It happens slowly, so slowly that at first I think it's an optical illusion brought on by the flickering candlelight. But it's not. The black paint, scrawled across Gerald's face in a moment of frustration, creeps. It spreads downward, obscuring his plaid shirt, his half-finished hands, his tan pants. It keeps spreading until it swallows him, right down to the brown tips of his shoes.

"Be at peace," Declan says, voice unsteady. Does he feel as uneasy as I do watching this scene play out? Maybe it's the artist in me, still stinging at my own work's destruction, but it's hard for me to find anything peaceful about this.

Laura might turn to look at her father. It's hard to tell, with her unfinished face. There's just the barest tilt of that featureless oval before the black paint jumps from Gerald to her. It wraps her in spidery tendrils that spread like cracks. Soon, those inky gashes across her skin widen into chasms. She bows her head, shoulders slumping before being consumed by the paint entirely.

"Be at peace," Declan says again. If he hadn't sounded uneasy before, he does now.

The wind shrieks ever louder. It no longer sounds like it's coming from outside at all. During the seance, I had almost been able to make out words in that toneless screeching. But there's none of that now. Only an endless drone that sounds near feral.

"Virginia," Declan calls out, authority tinged with desperation. "It's time to move on."

The black paint spreads, winding around Virginia's neck. I feel a phantom vice around my own bruised throat, sympathy pangs that turn more concerning as I struggle to breathe. I gasp, trying to keep it quiet so that I don't interrupt the cleansing.

Isobel notices. She squeezes my hand, but it does little to comfort me. "Cleo," she whispers, "Are you okay?"

I don't answer. Because I'm not okay. I can breathe again, but that doesn't stop the burning ache in my chest, the panicky flutter in my heart. It doesn't stop the truth: a simple, stark truth that I knew from the moment Noah and I skidded across the ice.

Something is wrong.

We're going to die.

The blackness doesn't consume Virginia the way it did her family. The canvas ripples and bulges once. Twice.

Bloody fingertips burst from the paint.

Isobel shrieks. The pitch of her voice is horror-movie perfect, the sort of scream that would be at home in any slasher trailer. A moot point, since my camera is destroyed. There is nothing shielding me from the horror of what's happening here, now, in real life. In front of *me*.

Fingertips are followed by hands, then arms. Palms slam themselves against the canvas, elbows bending at harsh, unnatural angles. I can *see* the tendons in the wrists strain with effort as they shove. The round tips of shoulders appear, then sink back into a sea of black paint. For a moment, that paint leeches up the skin. Then it recedes, overwhelmed.

And Virginia bursts from the painting.

Even trapped in the canvas from the waist down, she's horrific. Her stringy blonde hair hangs in her face, her eyes bulging from her skull. Her skin is swelled taut, her pallor ghastly. She looks exactly like she must have hanging from that noose all those years ago.

Except her dead face now moves. And it's twisted in rage. Her jaw unhinges, and she howls a wordless keen of anger.

"Virginia!" Declan needs to shout to be heard. He really does sound, despite his insistence against the term, like the priest from *The Exorcist*. Specifically the scene right before he dies of a heart attack. "You don't belong here anymore. You need to move on."

Black paint leeches up Virginia's arms in drips. It wraps around her throat and squeezes. She thrashes against it in pure animal rage. One of her flailing arms knocks over a candle.

In a movie, that candle would fall over onto the painting and be the thing to destroy her. There would be a nice narrative weight to that, to having her consumed by her own anger. Even if the rest of the house went up with it, even if we all died in the blaze, the viewer could still walk away feeling satisfied, knowing that the story ended in a way that made sense.

But there's no sense in this. The candle tips in the other direction instead. The flame finds Isobel's shirt and brightens as it catches.

Isobel screams again. Her hand rips from mine.

Andrea curses and shoves her backward, tearing off her jacket and smothering the flames. It all happens so quickly, it isn't until the fire is out and Isobel is sobbing that I realize *I* should have done something. I was right there. But instead of helping, I froze while the girl who reached out her hand to me burned.

I want to apologize. I want to offer comfort. But I can't move. I can only stare while Andrea mutters reassurances that are nearly lost to the sound of

Virginia's raging. The remaining candles flicker ever more violently, as though making up for the one that's snuffed out.

But their light is not the only light in this house.

There, over Isobel's shoulder, sit the remains of my broken camera. And although it should be impossible, the viewfinder is glowing. Pale blue light spills out over the stairs where I'd left it, casting wide shadows across the banister.

I stand. Not because of some strange force compelling me. This is not the madness that consumed me when I walked up the stairs by myself. This is something else. Something I don't have a name for.

As the cleansing ritual spins out of control, I rush to the stairs. The camera is still broken. But when I look at the cracked screen of the viewfinder, I see the footage I shot while I was alone in the bedroom. The footage of Gerald's ghost crouching in the wardrobe flickers in and out of existence.

So, too, do the scribbles covering his face.

They don't vanish entirely, but I see flashes of him: a bit of pudge around a jawline, dark circles under his eyes. Receding hair that's the same auburn as Michelle's. It's too quick for me to get much of a sense of his expression, but when Virginia screams again, I decide that I have better places to put my energy.

"Here!" I shout, thrusting the camera into her flailing hands. "Here, take it!"

Even the candles seem to cease their flickering as Virginia stills, chaos dissolving into quiet. Her pale, dead eyes fix on the footage. A string of saliva caught between her teeth thins and breaks, shining wetly against her chin.

Then she screams, and it's a scream that makes every howl that came before sound like a whisper in comparison. She slams the camera down again, and again.

The black paint creeps up again, and this time, she doesn't struggle against it. She's too busy trying to destroy what remains of my camera. Too angry to pay attention until the blackness covers her face, swallowing her whole.

The candles, all at once, burn out.

"Fuck." Andrea's voice is the first to break the silence. "Shit, fuck, hang on . . ."

She switches on her cell phone's flashlight, flooding us in its artificial glow. The others follow suit. I see Declan, wide-eyed; Zander and Andrea clinging to each other; Rhiannon solemn, already getting to her feet. Isobel, her face tear-streaked but unharmed, the fire put out.

Virginia is gone. So is my camera, and so is the painting. All that remain are shattered scraps of plastic, glass, and paper.

"Is it over?" Isobel's voice is heartbreaking in its hope.

"I think it might be," Rhiannon says. She's moved to the window by the front door. "Look."

We join her. Outside, the storm is still raging, but it's no longer the strange static against black that it was before. The cars are too far away to see clearly, but I can see the driveway choked with snow. Tree branches laden down with ice.

In the distance, streetlights flicker like stars.

Rhiannon turns on the overhead chandelier as Andrea tries the front door. "Still stuck," she says. "We could try breaking a window again, I guess, but . . ."

She doesn't finish her sentence. She doesn't have to. Breaking a window would get us out of this house, but where would we run to? And more importantly, is there really anything to run from anymore? How would we explain the property damage in less drastic circumstances?

It's as though the real world, with its logic and rules, has reasserted itself. Andrea must agree, because she dials and puts her phone on speakerphone with no further explanation. A voice answers almost immediately.

"911, what's your emergency?"

This is not the droning script that we'd been given earlier. The operator on the other end of the line sounds tired. More human than the last one ever did.

"Yeah, hi," Andrea says, talking fast. "My friends and I, we're stuck in this house we were staying at. Snow's built up against the door and we can't get out. Can you send someone?" She rattles off the address, pulled up on Zander's phone in anticipation of her.

There's a moment of silence on the other end. I can hear the tinny sound of other phones ringing, operators talking in muffled voices. "Are any of you in active danger?"

Andrea glances around. She must see the same uncertainty I feel mirrored on every face, because her voice is cautious when she responds. "I guess not. But we're stuck here."

"Yes, and I will be sending a dispatch out to you as soon as possible," the operator says calmly. "But our emergency services are stretched thin because of the storm. We need to prioritize more time-sensitive calls. Cheboygan County is under a shelter in place, so you wouldn't be able to go anywhere right away anyway."

Andrea bounces on the balls of her feet. "How quickly can you get out here?"

"It might not be until tomorrow."

Which means another night spent in this house. And yet, the prospect is not as harrowing as it once was. I still don't particularly enjoy the idea, and I can tell that the others are similarly unenthused. But none of us can come up with a reason that we can't stay. At least not one that this operator, living outside in the real world, will believe.

In the end, it's Andrea who makes the call, as she is so often wont to do. "Okay," she says, resolute. "Okay. We understand."

Outside, the snowflakes begin to slow.

- 21 -

<u>**AVAILABLE LIGHT**</u>

INT. BEDROOM - NIGHT

Maybe I don't want there to be a script for
this.

W E OPT TO spend our final night in the house upstairs instead of in the living room again.

There's something almost superstitious in the way we all go back to our tenuous routines as they were before the house went strange. Rhiannon takes Noah's bed in lieu of the couch, but the rest of us return to our usual rooms. As if, by behaving normally, we can convince ourselves that the ghosts of the Barlow family really are at rest.

I'm still anxious. But the nerves are more akin to what I felt in the early days of filming, back when the ghosts were only whispers and shadows. Destroying the painting—and my camcorder—has managed to rob this house of its crushing, malignant aura. I may not feel settled, but I also don't feel like there's danger here. At least, not in the way there was before.

I don't know what to think about it. Unfortunately, I'm left alone as Isobel showers, and thinking about it is all I can do. Obviously, I'm glad that the house isn't the way it was before. The ghosts here—Virginia especially—were a true threat to our safety. I only have to touch my throat and feel the ache from her bruises to understand what could have happened, had they been allowed to linger. A bit of destroyed art seems a small price to pay.

And yet . . .

It isn't the destruction itself that sits uneasily under my skin, prickling like television static. It's the fact that the destruction worked. I can't help but compare it to *Slaughter!*, and how that production ended. Obviously, it's ridiculous to believe that my filmmaking caused my father's death. But isn't it equally ridiculous to believe that it caused the ghosts to become malevolent?

I imagine talking to Noah after all this. Assuming he really did screen our calls, he has no idea what we've gone through. What will he say when I tell him? Will he brush off my concerns with the same eyeroll he always gives? I think he will. But I think it will be a long time before he invites me to another set. We can use my broken camera as an excuse, but we'll both know the truth.

Some people are just doomed. Better not to let them too close.

In the distance, the shower turns off. Moments

later, Isobel appears in the doorway, dressed in pajamas with her blonde curls damp.

"Oh my god, I think that was the quickest shower of my life." She rolls her eyes dramatically, her expressions dialed up to stage-performance level. "Like, I really think we're all good now, but I still kept thinking it was going to be like that scene in, oh, what was that movie with the lady in the shower? You know . . ." Isobel pantomimes gripping a knife in one hand, holding her fist aloft in a fairly accurate impression for a movie she can't remember the title of.

"*Psycho*," I tell her, smiling in spite of myself. "That wasn't a ghost, though. Just a run of the mill serial killer."

Isobel laughs. The idea of Isobel Vernier of all people laughing at my morbid humor is still a bit startling. "Well, still. I don't think I'm cut out for this horror life, Cleo." She flops down onto the bed. "No offense."

"None taken." I scoot over as she climbs up beside me. "It's, um, much more fun watching on the screen than it is experiencing it in real life."

Isobel hums. "Sure, that makes sense. Maybe I should take this as a cue to watch more horror movies, like, build up my tolerance." She leans back, weight balanced on her palms. Her blonde curls tumble down her back as she cranes her neck to tip me a wink. "I'll watch any movie *you* make. You might have to, like, hold my hand through the scary parts, though."

A laugh darts from my lips, and I'm too flustered

to respond with anything but the truth. "I don't think you have to worry about that anytime soon." Isobel frowns at me. I hurry on, "Me making another movie, I mean. I can hold your hand through other scary movies if you want, though."

My clumsy, belated attempt at returning her flirtation goes ignored. Isobel's brows furrow, genuine confusion coloring her tone. "Why wouldn't you make another movie? It totally sucks that your camera broke, but you can get another one eventually, right?"

"It's not the camera," I say, even though the reminder does send a pang through my chest. "It's just . . . I don't know. With the way this shoot has gone, it sort of feels like the universe is trying to tell me something."

Isobel's eyes soften. Her fingertips brush the back of my hand. "Cleo, none of what happened here is your fault."

The attempt at comfort, as sweet as it is, rings hollow. "Isn't it, though? It might not have been my idea. But I'm still the one who held the camera, Isobel. Me filming made everything worse."

Isobel wasn't there for *Slaughter!* But she knows how it ended. She's perceptive enough to put the pieces together. And yet, she's not looking at me with dawning horror or even with pity. Instead, she's looking at me like the things I'm saying never even crossed her mind.

"The ghosts were always here, though," she says.

"Maybe. But I'm the one who made her mad." My

fingertips find the bruises Virginia left against my throat and press down. Like I need to remind myself of the pain my actions caused.

Isobel reaches out and takes my hand, pulling it away. "Virginia was mad, I think. But, like, it looks like she was more angry at her husband than anything. That's the footage you showed her from the bedroom, right? I saw it before she smashed the camera."

"That's right." Considering all that happened with the candle, I'm surprised she even noticed. "He was, um. Well, I couldn't actually see him. Do you think it's fair for Virginia to be mad at him? I mean, I know he was probably d . . . driving. But it was still an accident, right?" I amend my statement at the last minute, remembering how everyone reacted the last time I'd voiced my assertion that her husband had been drunk.

And if he'd been anything like my dad, he couldn't help himself, could he? I'm not sure if you're *allowed* to be mad at someone like that.

Isobel doesn't know the extent of it, though. And she doesn't seem particularly interested in debating the morality of Virginia's emotions. She just shrugs. "I don't know. My point is, it wasn't ever about the filming. The real problem here was the painting all along, right?"

"What makes you say that?" I ask.

Isobel blinks at me, wide-eyed. "Because it wasn't finished."

She says it like it's the most obvious thing in the world. I, for one, can't follow the logic. "What do you mean?"

Isobel's brow furrows. "Well, it's like I said earlier. Art, it's about, like, being honest about stuff? And part of being honest is admitting when you've said all you can say, or done all you can do. I don't think all art needs to be sold or shared or anything like that. But at some point, you've got to let it go. Like, if I just danced the same thing every day, obsessed with getting it perfect, I really would go all *Black Swan*. That's not healthy."

"How does that work, do you think?" I ask. "There has to be art that's unfinished that's still fulfilling, and art that is finished that's haunted." I'm not trying to poke holes in her theory. I'm just trying to understand.

Isobel seems to take my question in the spirit I meant it. "You've got a good point. I think it comes down to, like, intention? What do you think?"

I don't answer right away. Before all this, I compared making art to burying my hands in the soil and letting worms crawl over my skin. But I never once thought to ask why I was digging. Am I planting something meant to bloom one day? Or am I exhuming something better left to sleep under the dirt?

Am I a gardener or a grave robber?

Does the distinction matter when the ground is too frozen to dig?

"Hey." Isobel's hand squeezes mine, gently pulling me out of my thoughts. "You still with me?"

I laugh, rubbing my eyes with the hand not pinned under Isobel's palm. "Yeah. I'm just thinking. Or . . .

not *just*, I guess. I don't know."

The size and scope of my thoughts feel too big to hold. These conversations Isobel and I have, they're challenging. The way her mind works is fascinating. I wish I had time to ask her a thousand questions: not just about her view on art, but on life, too. I want to know so much about her.

"Can I ask you a question?" I ask. "A kind of personal one?"

In the dim light, Isobel's eyes twinkle. "Ooh, I *love* kind of personal questions. Hit me."

"Is there anything that would make you want to stop dancing?"

With anyone else, I'd be worried about them dismissing my question at best, or getting offended at worst. But by now, I trust Isobel enough to give me the benefit of the doubt.

Her expression turns thoughtful. "I don't know. I mean, like, stuff happens, right? I could get sick, or injured, or something. But that's not really what you're asking, is it?"

"No," I whisper. I expected her to understand me, but not quite so much. "It isn't."

"I think even if something like that would happen, I'd still find a way to make dancing part of my life." She props herself up on her elbows, blonde curls tumbling over her shoulder. "Or at least performing in some way. It's not even that I love it, it's like . . . it's who I am, you know? I try to imagine a version of me that doesn't do that, and it's like imagining a stranger.

It's like . . ."

"It's like even if you tried to run from it, it would still find you," I finish. My chest aches.

"Exactly," Isobel says. "It's a part of me." She tilts her head to the side. "Is that how you feel about filmmaking?"

The question hits harder than I'd like to admit. I haven't tried making a movie in three years. But not a week went by where I didn't at least think about it. I'd tinker with half-finished scripts, take my camera on walks or to parties, shoot meaningless footage around my room. I couldn't stop, even if I wanted to.

"I do." My voice trembles. As self-righteous as he was, I wonder if Noah didn't have a point, dragging me along on this venture. I still wish he'd have gone about things differently, but I think I'm beginning to understand what he saw in me.

Isobel smiles, and I push all thoughts of Noah from my mind. "Well, that's settled, then. You can't give up on it. Why would you want to?"

"I don't know." It's an honest answer. But also, it isn't. "I'm scared, I guess."

Isobel nods. "I get that. It *is* scary. Even if you're not in a literal actual haunted house. I mean, like, I get stage fright all the time, right? God, the first time I had a solo, I fully barfed in the wings before going onstage." Her candor startles a laugh out of me. Luckily, she doesn't take offense, only smiling wider. "No, seriously! It was, like, a total disaster. But that just proves my point. Fear's not a good reason to not do something. If even *that* can't stop me, I don't think anything can."

"Yeah." I can't help the fond smile that curls up my lips. "You're pretty unstoppable, Isobel."

Isobel laughs. "Cleo! You flirt."

It's just as casual and carefree as any joke she's made this whole time. But it's not exactly lost on me that she's still holding my hand, and that she's been closing the distance between our bodies by inches this whole time. Her green eyes are soft and curious, her head tilted toward mine.

In a script, I'd find a smooth line to transition on. In a script, we wouldn't have been talking about stage-fright-induced vomiting mere seconds ago. But this is not a script, so what I blurt is, "Can I kiss you?"

Isobel's eyes widen, her eyebrows shooting up into her bangs. She's smiling, but I can't tell if it's a smile of relief or one of pure, shocked amusement. Fuck. Words, imperfect and unscripted, continue to tumble out of my mouth.

"I mean, you were looking at me like you wanted me to kiss you. I thought you were, anyway. But if you weren't and I was reading it wrong, that's okay, and I just wanted to make sure because I don't want to do anything you don't want to do, obviously, but I—"

Isobel kisses me.

Isobel *kisses* me, and I don't think about ghosts, or art, or fear. I don't picture this moment from outside of myself, framing it in close-up with a gaussian blur. I don't even think about the softness of Isobel's lips or the warmth of her body, at least not in a way I feel compelled to describe.

My mind is, for once, blank. And I am happily inside of it.

Isobel pulls away. Her forehead tilts to press against mine. "I've kind of been flirting with you since day one," she says. "Thanks for noticing."

Warmth rushes to my cheeks. "I mean, consider my social circle. I spend a lot of time around theatre nerds. A lot of you are just like that, so I didn't want to assume."

Isobel giggles. The sound is sweet in the darkness. "You're cute," she says, and presses me back against the mattress.

She kisses me again, soft and gentle to match the slowing snowflakes outside. It's lovely, but when Isobel's hand creeps beneath my shirt, I pause. "Wait." Isobel stills instantly and starts to pull away. I grab her by the waist. "I mean, don't *stop*, just, um . . . I haven't ever, actually . . . I mean, I'm still a . . ."

"Oh." Isobel relaxes into my arms. Her fingertips twine through my pale hair. "Okay, that's fine. Are you saying that because you want to slow down, or . . .?"

"I don't *know*." I bury my face in my hands. This was much easier when my brain wasn't involved. "Sorry, I'm being ridiculous."

"Hey, hey, none of that." Isobel tugs my hands away, giggling. "I'm fine with whatever you want, honestly! But, like, you do have to tell me."

I groan. Isobel's hands wrapped around my wrists are the only things keeping me from covering my face again. "This goes so much smoother in movies." I close my eyes, screwing up my courage. "I want to keep going. I want you. I'm just nervous, but, um . . . 'Fear isn't a good reason to not do something?'" Isobel giggles softly when I quote her. I open one eye. "As long as you want to, obviously."

Isobel gives me a look that manages to be both fond and utterly exasperated. "So, like, I'm *literally* straddling you right now."

"Okay, okay." I laugh, my chest fizzing with emotion too complex to name. "I just want to hear you say it. Is that alright?"

"Well, fair is fair, after all." Isobel leans forward. Her lips brush my ear as she whispers. "I want you, too."

Her hands resume their exploration under my shirt. This time, I let them.

The fear doesn't go away. Like every time I've gotten this far with someone, there's the instinctive reflex to flee, to stop. To draw away before I let myself become too vulnerable. "You know, I think I have to confess something," I babble.

"Hm?" Isobel hums against my throat, sending shivers down my spine.

"It's just . . . God, when I was a freshman? I had the biggest crush on you. You were actually the first girl I ever, um, liked."

"Wait." Isobel leans back to grin at me. "For real?

I was your *closet key*?"

She sounds delighted. I resist the urge to hide behind my hands again. "Stop, it's embarrassing."

"What? Oh my god, don't be embarrassed, I'm flattered." Isobel giggles, and I'm gratified to see that she's a little pink in the cheeks. "I had no idea, honestly."

"Well, I was too scared to really do anything about it. I could barely talk to you."

Isobel grins. In the low light, her eyes shine with a warm cheer that somehow doesn't manage to feel cruel. "Are you scared now?" she asks sweetly.

Yes. I could say that. Could stop things here, and let that fear rule me, as I've let it rule so many other aspects of my life.

Instead, I lurch forward and kiss her.

Isobel's hands go to the waistband of my pants, and this time, I don't stop her. I pull her shirt over her head instead. When I look to where the candle burned her clothes, I see that the skin beneath is undamaged and whole.

I quickly find more to look at. And, with some coaxing, to touch.

This is not like the love scene I wrote between Halley and Patrick. It's clumsy, and awkward, and it takes a lot of whispered check-ins and gentle encouragement. But Isobel knows what she likes and isn't afraid of telling me. When I stumble, she just laughs and pulls me in for another kiss.

It's good. Good in a way I didn't think I'd be able

to feel anywhere, much less in a house like this one. But in this room, there's no horror. There's only the soft sound of Isobel's sighs, the gentle sweetness of her body against mine, and the hypnotic shadows of snowflakes rippling across her bare skin.

And for just a moment, I let go of fear.

- 22 -

<u>**SMASH CUT**</u>

```
          HALLEY
        (dismayed)
     We're still here.
```

(Excerpt from THE WIDOW GHOST, written by Cleo Moss.)

I WAKE UP with a start, breath catching in my throat as my heart rate spikes.

The bedroom is almost poetic in its calm. The blankets are warm, and Isobel's head is pillowed on my shoulder. Was it a nightmare that woke me? I could have sworn I heard something, but Isobel is still asleep, her breathing deep and even. Maybe it was all in my head.

But then it comes again: a low, ominous *crack*. The walls tremble with the force of it. Downstairs, something falls and shatters with a discordant *crash*.

This, at last, is loud enough to wake Isobel. She stirs, her hair tickling my chest. "Mn," she mutters sleepily. "Cleo?"

"Something's wrong." My voice is even. Calmer than it has any right to be. "Get dressed."

I gently disentangle my limbs from hers, feeling next to nothing as I do so. Subconsciously, I think I've been waiting for something like this to happen. Our victory had felt too easy, too cheap. I'd let myself forget in Isobel's arms, but deep down I knew that the horrors couldn't be over.

Outside the window, there is no moonlight, no stars. Not even snow. Just an endless wall of black. Isobel rolls over and turns on the bedside lamp, but its glow is faint and does little to dispel the shadows that haunt every corner of the room. I can barely make out the worry on her face. "Did the storm stop?" she asks.

"I can't tell," I reply. I don't tell her that I fear there might be something worse out there.

The others are already in the hallway by the time we finish dressing. I can hear their murmured voices, and light spills from behind the crack in the door. Fear prickles the back of my neck. I can't make out what they're saying, but I can make out the tone: quiet, tense. The same tone my mom would use on the phone when she was worried about Dad getting home safe.

She was right to worry, wasn't she?

I almost want to stay hidden in the bedroom on instinct, the way I did then. Let the responsibility fall to someone else, someone more equipped to deal with it. But Isobel takes me by the hand and pulls me along.

We walk together into the hallway.

The others are already gathered downstairs. Isobel leans over the railing, blonde curls dangling. "What's going on?"

Below us, Andrea gestures vaguely to the wall behind me. "See for yourself."

I look over my shoulder, bracing for ghosts or ghouls or any manner of strange, supernatural horror. But that's not what I find when I turn.

It's the wall. It's covered in cracks.

They start from the place where Michelle's painting once hung, spidering out from floor to ceiling. One particularly wide crack runs horizontal across the entire length of the wall, gaping like an open maw. The wallpaper above and below it sits out of sync. It's as if the top of the house itself is about to slide right off.

It's also familiar.

I stare. Why do these cracks stir such a strong sensation of *déjà vu* in me? After a moment, I realize: it's Michelle's painting. Not the portrait of her family, but the *House of Usher* piece, with Rodrick embracing Madeline as the house collapsed around them. The walls in the background had looked exactly like this. The resemblance is so uncanny, I actually press a fingertip to one of the finer cracks, half expecting them to be tacky and wet to the touch.

They aren't. I can feel the ragged edges of the wallpaper, and beyond that, a chill. A gust of wind.

"Oh, my god." Isobel peers over my shoulder. "Oh my god, this is bad. Did the tree do this?"

"I don't know." I shake my head, pulling away. "I don't think so."

"There's something distinctly stranger going on here than a fallen tree, I think," Declan says. "Take a look from down here, you'll see what I mean."

Isobel glances over her shoulder at me. When she looks at me like that, I have no choice but to move. We walk down the stairs together, arm-in-arm.

I see what Declan means at once. The thinner cracks could, conceivably, be caused by the weight of the tree pressing down on the roof. But the thick one along the length of the wall is another matter. It's less of a crack and more of a gap, as if that part of the house simply crumpled away, leaving nothing behind. Through it, I can see outside: snow-laden trees and distant rooftops. Snowflakes drift past, even though every window remains pitch black.

"Whoa, okay. Weird." Isobel stands on her toes, but the gap remains well above her reaching hands. "How's it staying up like that?"

"It doesn't make any sense." Rhiannon crosses her arms over her chest in a tight, defensive curl. "It shouldn't be able to do that."

"It is, though." Andrea pulls her phone from her pocket, staring at the gap. "And maybe we couldn't explain ghosts to the cops, but we sure as hell can explain this, eh? I'm calling 911."

She dials, putting the phone on speakerphone. It doesn't taunt us with a distorted voice or even a ring. Only the hollow sound of the wind, made tinny and indistinct through the phone speaker.

"Holy wah, am I *done* with this house." Andrea hangs up the phone and shoves it back into her pocket with an air of genuine disgust. Then, she looks up at the crack with steely-eyed determination. "Okay. Fuck it. I'm going in."

What is she talking about? Surely she doesn't sincerely intend to climb through that crack in the wall. For one thing, I don't know how she'd even reach it. It's too far above the first floor, and too far below the balcony. Also, it's barely wide enough to fit into. She'll be lucky if she doesn't get stuck halfway through. Or, worse, get her innards scooped out on some unseen edge.

The others seem similarly concerned. Rhiannon says, "No," at the same time that Declan says, "Absolutely not." The two of them exchange a glance, visibly surprised to be on the same side for once.

"Why not?" Andrea is already backing away, swinging her arms back and forth in half-hearted stretches. "Before, there was no way out. Now there is. Seems pretty straightforward to me."

She jogs up the stairs, all easy confidence. I suppose her logic shouldn't surprise me. Not because I agree, but because I know her. Andrea's the type of person who always feels like there's something that can be done. When it was just searching through a haunted house for ghosts to film, that seemed harmless enough. But this is something else entirely.

"What are you doing?" Isobel asks worriedly. She

presses against my side.

"Well, I can't exactly get to it from down there." Andrea grips the banister, and I realize with a dawning sort of horror that she actually intends to jump over.

"Andrea!" Zander bolts after her. But once he reaches her, he stalls. He stands with his arms at his sides, eyes pleading. "Please, be careful."

Andrea turns to him. Her entire face softens, and her fingertips find a tender, familiar place along his jawline. "It'll be okay. Trust me."

I eye the gap. It looks wrong, the depth of it all out of proportion to the rest of the house. It won't just be a matter of wiggling through and finding herself on the other side. Andrea will have to *crawl*. There are horror movies, based on true stories, about cavers that have found themselves in similar conditions. Very few of them ended happily.

I want to tell her this. I want to ask her to think it through. But if she won't listen to any of the others, why would she listen to me?

"Don't worry about this, guys," she says. "I've got it."

She sounds so sure of herself. I suppose she's used to watching different genres, where things like this turn out better. Is that what puts such a confident gleam in her eye? It would make sense. So much of what I know of Andrea, from how she tackles a role to how she takes care of her friends, is defined by that same confidence.

How can any of us stand a chance against that? Zander only gives her wrist a squeeze before releasing her.

Andrea lets out an audible breath. We all watch as she peers over the balcony, gauging the distance before climbing over the railing. Isobel slips a hand into mine. Her palm is cold from where she'd touched the wall, but I don't think the slight tremble has anything to do with the outside elements. I squeeze it gently, more out of reflex than anything. I am as focused on Andrea as I would be if I still held my camcorder.

"Okay. Sit tight, eh?" She grabs the banister and slides down. For a moment, she dangles from the balcony, her feet swaying in midair like Virginia's must have. She swings back and forth, gaining momentum. Her hand slips. Beside me, Isobel gasps.

"Careful!" Zander lunges, arms reaching over the balcony even though part of him must know that if Andrea *does* fall, he'll be too late to reach her.

But she doesn't fall. "I'm fine." She re-adjusts her grip and tries again. Zander clutches at the railing with a white-knuckle grip as she swings, then releases, letting herself drop.

She catches herself on the lip of the gap. Her sneakers thud against the wall as she braces herself. Several more hairline fractures spread where she kicks, splitting across the wallpaper. She scrambles for purchase. Sawdust rains down to the floor.

The house groans.

"Andrea . . ." Rhiannon says, but Andrea only makes a dismissive noise.

"Wait, just wait." Finally, the toe of one sneaker catches on the gap. She levers herself up, sliding in feet first. Her legs vanish into the darkness, then her waist, then her torso. Her head, sticking out of the wall like some strange mount, shakes in disbelief. "Damn. This wall is thicker than I thought."

The house groans again. The wall shifts, the top and bottom of the gap moving further out of alignment. Isobel's hand tightens in my own. "Maybe you, like, shouldn't . . ." Her voice wavers. I don't think I've ever heard her quite this afraid.

"Fuck that, eh? The only way out is through." Andrea slides deeper, ducking her head to fit in the gap. She wiggles her way further in, her now muffled voice excited. "I'm making it out, though! I can *feel* the wind, okay, I just have to . . ."

The wall, finally, crashes down.

Most of Andrea's body is crushed instantly. Pulverized, I assume, to a pulpy mass of blood and skin and shattered bone. Her fingers, still gripping the ledge, are severed at the knuckle. They patter to the floor with a sound similar to rain hitting a rooftop. Her scalp starts to slide down to join them, but it's caught by the strands of black hair still stuck in the gap. It dangles instead, twirling slowly to reveal the mess of tissue and blood on the other side.

Zander screams, wordless: a wail of grief that rivals Virginia's supernatural moans. I can't look away from the wall, even as blood oozes from the crack where Andrea's body once was.

I didn't say anything to stop her. But everyone else tried to talk her out of it, and she didn't listen to them. What could I have possibly said to convince her of anything different? What could I have done?

What could I have done to stop any of this?

The others rush for the stairs. Isobel's hand is still clutching mine, so I find myself dragged along. I'm not sure if it's on purpose or not, but I let myself be led away from the carnage either way.

Zander leans over the banister, his face pale. He stares at Andrea's remains like a man grieving. Which is to say, his face doesn't hold much expression at all. Some horrors are too big to wear. His mouth opens and closes, but no sound comes out.

"Zander . . ." Isobel tries, but falls silent. I don't blame her. There are no words for this.

He turns to us slowly. It would make an interesting shot composition, I think: all of us gathered on the staircase, and him on the other end of the hallway. I'd capture it as an aerial shot, if I could. If my camcorder was still functional, and I was still allowed to remain separate from this.

"You were wrong, you know," Zander says. His voice is dazed, listless.

Behind him, the light shifts. It almost looks like someone is stepping out of the bedroom behind him. No one is there. But a shadow, its shape reminiscent of Virginia, slides along the fractured wall.

"Virginia wasn't angry at her husband," Zander says slowly. A chill runs up my spine. Zander hadn't been *there* when Isobel said that. "She wouldn't let herself be. She tucked her frustration into the back of the pantry, folded her annoyance in with the blankets, pressed her rage into every shadowed corner. It's how that rage continued to live here, long after she stopped."

The shadow on the wall tilts its head to the side. It's like the ghost I saw our first night in this house: impossible to perceive in a way that's tangible.

Zander's head drifts sideways until he's a match for the shadow behind him. "Rage isn't what drives someone to tie a noose to a balcony. Rage wasn't what filled her heart, in those final moments it beat."

One tear trickles from the corner of his eye, curving in the valley of his temple. The shadow presses a not-hand against the banister. Zander, as if in a dream, follows suit.

"It was grief."

The shadow hurls itself over the balcony. Zander follows it, headfirst.

It takes longer than it should for him to land, as though the house is stretching to accommodate his drop. When he finally does hit the floor, it's with a crack so sickening that my stomach lurches. He lands in an ugly, unnatural sprawl of limbs, his neck cocked at an impossible angle not unlike Virginia's.

Blood seeps from the open crack in his skull to join Andrea's, still dripping down the wall.

- 23 -

<u>INTO FRAME</u>

CLOSE-UP ON:

A locked door.

THE WALLS RUMBLE. Isobel presses herself into my side as cracks spread across the wall and spider up to the ceiling. Dust drifts down. A banister cracks and falls away, landing next to Zander—Zander's body, his *corpse*—with a wooden *thunk*.

Declan curses in Spanish. "The whole house is coming down," he says.

His statement can't elicit more horror than I already feel. My ears echo with the *squelch* of Andrea being crushed, the *crack* of Zander hitting the hardwood. Some shock-deadened part of my brain keeps trying to think of how I would frame their deaths on a camera. What kind of shot would really sell the horror to an audience? It's impossible to imagine with the blood still drying. I'm too close to this to fictionalize it.

"Come on." Rhiannon's voice is hoarse with horror, but determined. "We're going to the basement."

Declan stares at her, nonplussed. "So that even more of the house can fall on us?"

"So that we can break into the art studio." Rhiannon is already moving toward the kitchen. "Let's go. Michelle mentioned that it doubles as a storm shelter. We'll be safer there."

This is enough to startle the sarcasm right off of Declan's face. "That makes sense."

Rhiannon pauses. "Well, with the storm, it's been in the back of my mind." She must know that the door will still be locked, but she doesn't let that deter her from continuing into the kitchen. "Come on."

We follow her. The lights flicker, cups and plates rattling in their cabinets. Isobel shrieks as the window shatters, raining glass into the sink.

In the basement, it's almost possible to forget the chaos upstairs. The walls here have not yet begun to fracture, and with the door closed, the sounds of furniture falling and breaking are muted. But there are still signs that not all is well: the single light bulb won't turn on, and a subterranean *thrumming* sets my teeth on edge.

At some point in our flight, Isobel stopped holding my hand. I wish, now, that I still had the warmth of her palm. It would be nice to have the reminder of her bare skin on mine last night, and how for a fleeting moment, everything felt like it might be okay.

Rhiannon turns on her phone's flashlight. It skids across Michelle's ruined paintings, then lands on what she's looking for: the putty knife sitting on the ground beside them. "There."

I didn't even notice that when I examined Michelle's paintings. But Rhiannon did. Had she, even in that moment, been preparing for something like this? Not a supernatural collapse but a worsening storm? I'm a little in awe of her. I would have taken that fear and frozen with it, not run through contingency plans.

Black paint coats the edge of the putty knife. Whoever ruined the paintings must have used it. I suppose I have better things to worry about than who did so and why, but there's still something distinctly unnerving about seeing the evidence just sitting there.

Declan picks it up, gripping it in one hand. "Who here has the most strength, do we think?"

Andrea is the obvious choice, but Andrea is gone. Her death, and Zander's death, are both so sudden and awful that I can't even begin to process them. The loss echoes against the stone walls as we stand in silence, the house rumbling above us. The defunct lightbulb sways with the force of whatever it is that's happening up there.

Finally, Isobel speaks up. "I'll, like, try? Ballet is more about leg muscle, but . . ." She shrugs, and I can't deny her. Of those of us left, she's unambiguously the most athletic.

Declan hands the knife over without complaint. Isobel approaches the door with some trepidation, but she doesn't let that trepidation stop her from jamming the knife between the door and the doorframe. It sticks against the lock, but the door jamb splinters. Cracks run along the wall, as though the collapsing house is doing half the work for us.

As though something—or someone—wants us to get in.

Just like something wanted me to go upstairs alone. My throat burns with the memory of Virginia's hands around my neck. I'm suddenly, horrifically sure of one thing: there is no salvation here.

But it's too late. With a final shove, the lock breaks. The door swings open.

And I don't think any of us—not Rhiannon with her plans, not Declan with his wits, not Isobel with her hopes or me with my fears—are prepared for what's inside.

The room's primary function as an art studio is evident. There are easels with half-finished paintings scattered about, canvases stacked against the wall, paints left out on a bench. There's also evidence of it being a storm shelter: a shelf lined with non-perishable foods and water, sturdy metal benches and tables.

On one of those tables lays a corpse.

It isn't fresh. Its skin is dry and damaged, and it wears no clothing. And yet, it retains a grotesquely human shape. Its shriveled hands are laced over its sunken chest, its legs neatly together.

It does not have a head. It ends at the ragged, pulverized stump of its neck.

This is not like the specter of Virginia's body, or the macabre vision of Laura, or the strange ghost of Gerald. This is different. This is real. I can smell the rot. I clap a hand over my mouth and nose, but it isn't enough to block out the horror.

"Oh my god," Isobel breathes. She's the only one who makes any sound.

I blink. For a moment, the corpse is replaced by a blurry watercolor image of a man lying on his back. It's too quick to make out his face, but I can see thin wisps of ginger hair and a still, sleeping face. Then it vanishes. Only the corpse remains.

Behind us, there's an ominous groan. When I glance over my shoulder, the ceiling of the basement has begun to buckle, cracks spreading across the stone walls.

Rhiannon sees this. "Fuck it," she mutters, and shoves us inside. Even after everything we've seen, practicality still outweighs horror for her. The walls out here are collapsing, and the ones in the art studio are not. Evidently, that's enough for her.

I half expect the corpse to sit up at the intrusion. That's what would happen in a horror movie. But it doesn't so much as stir. It really is just a corpse, not another apparition sent to haunt us.

But that doesn't mean we're alone in here.

There's an obscene black smear on the far wall. It's

paint, layered so thick that it's still sticky and damp. The edges of it are ragged and splattered, as though thrown from a bucket at full force.

Caught in the center of that paint, like a fly in a glue trap, is a woman.

She hangs from the wall with her arms outstretched, her head dangling. Her reddish-brown hair is pulled back in a ponytail. Her eyes are closed, but her expression is twisted and haggard. Thick ropes of black paint wind around her wrists, her arms, her legs, her torso.

It's Michelle.

When did she get back? The question is fleeting, because the answer is obvious: she never left. When we scattered in the wake of her grief, she came down here. And instead of coming back up and going on her trip, she stayed. She locked herself in her art studio. And now . . .

Did the paint trap her here? Or did she submit willingly to this?

And what does this have to do with the corpse in the center of the room?

I step toward her slowly. I'm not sure why I do it. Surely, it's not that I think I can help her. But she's so much like me. A horror fan. An artist. Someone who once found herself listed as *survived by* in an obituary that came too soon. Someone with a loss shaped just a little like my own.

Doesn't that mean anything?

Even when I get close enough to touch, she doesn't

stir. She's breathing, but it's fitful. Her brows furrow, the lines around her eyes growing more pronounced. Her lips move but do not form words.

There's something clutched in her right hand. A cell phone with a chipped screen and a red phone case. It's familiar, but it isn't until I tap the screen and see the *Friday the 13th* screenshot on the lock screen that I know for sure.

This is Noah's phone.

Why does Michelle have Noah's phone?

Isobel screams.

She could be screaming for any number of reasons. The corpse could be sitting up. Another ghost could have come to torment us. The roof could be caving in, trapping us all beneath rubble. But it's not any of that, and deep down I know it isn't. Noah's phone is in Michelle's hand.

And there's another corpse in this basement.

"No." It passes from my lips in a breathless, almost soundless whisper. In spite of everything, for just a moment, even I can't believe that the universe could be this cruel. But of course, it is.

It's Noah. He's crumpled behind a table, not visible from where we walked in. But he's there, and he's dead. His glassy eyes stare up at the ceiling, the roof of his head caved in around a wound that has long since dried. A muddy shovel lays beside him. Blood and flecks of bone matter cling to the spade.

"Oh, my god." Isobel stumbles forward, then back. Caught between wanting to help and realizing that he's beyond it. Tears fill her eyes and spill over her cheeks. "Oh my god, Noah . . ."

He'd been down here all along. Michelle must have been the one screening his calls, must have taken the phone after she hit him with the shovel. But why? Why do any of this? And why didn't we realize it sooner? Why didn't *I* realize it sooner? I should have known that he wouldn't just leave like that, I should have . . .

What?

Would it have done any good for me to know that he was here in the dark? His skin going cold, his blood and brain drying? I couldn't have saved him. He was already dead.

He was already dead, and our last conversation was a fight.

Noah. *God*, Noah . . .

I stumble back. It's too much. Too much to put into words, or thoughts, or feelings. My mind is blank of scripts, and my mouth is blank of screams. There's nothing but the stark, ugly reality of what's in front of me.

My back hits the wall. Paint leeches at my skin with a sticky, burning sensation. It wraps around my waist.

"What—" I pull away, pure reflex. But it's as useless as fingertips against a noose. I'm caught, sinking into the wall with no power to stop it. My chest constricts with a crushing sensation that is too big to simply be called fear.

I turn my head. Michelle's eyes are open. She's

staring at me.

"I'm sorry," she whispers. Her voice is hoarse, her lips dry and cracked. "I didn't . . . I didn't want to do it. But I couldn't let anyone see. No one was supposed to know."

In the spaces where her body isn't covered with paint, I can see blood flecking her shirt. Even though I knew she must have been the one to wield the shovel, the realization still hits like a gut punch.

"You killed him," I whisper. It's not a question. "Why would you do that?"

"He wasn't supposed to see," Michelle says. "I'd just left to see if you were still there . . . but then I saw the paintings. I couldn't stand them. I tried to get rid of them but . . . he walked down. And I hadn't shut the door. He saw."

Saw the corpse on the table. Saw that she was hiding more than paintings behind the locked door.

I open my mouth, even though I don't have the faintest idea what to say. I don't get a chance to say anything, because paint fills my mouth and covers my eyes. I can feel it wrapping around my limbs, pulling me back. I'm dragged deeper. Away from the art studio. Away from the house. All of it vanishes in the black.

In my last moments, I think I hear someone call my name. But then even that is gone.

– 24 –


```
INT. KITCHEN - EVENING

Please.

No.

I don't want to be here.
```

IT IS DARK, and it is silent.

I cannot even hear the sounds of my own body. I must be breathing, because my lungs don't burn, but the sound doesn't reach me. Nor does the sound of my heart beating, or my blood rushing through my veins. Even the faint ringing in my ears is gone.

Slowly, shapes swim out from the blackness. I'm standing in a room. I can make out a table, a fridge, a stovetop. They're familiar. This is my house's kitchen. Only there's a strange overlay over it. A film grain, or maybe a paint stroke. Either way, it looks odd and unreal.

I wrap my arms around myself, looking around. I need to find my way out of here. I need to get back to where I was, before . . . before . . .

My mind swims. For a moment, I think of Isobel's curls spilling across her pillow. But the image is flickering and warped. No match for Andrea's blood on the wall, Zander's bones twisting and snapping. Noah with his skull caved in, his eyes staring out into nothing forever.

An object appears on the table. It's more real than anything else in the room, which is ironic, because it's also the most impossible: my camcorder, unbroken. It's a trick, it must be, but knowing that doesn't stop me from picking it up.

Through the viewfinder, the kitchen looks normal, if slightly desaturated as the light over the table flickers. Out the window, the sky is dark but not *pitch* dark. Night has only just begun to set in. And there's a set of keys on the kitchen table.

Behind me, a voice that sounds a little bit like Noah's speaks. "Take one. Action!" A clapboard falls.

A girl walks into frame. It's me. Only not as I am now. I'm younger here, my hair bright red instead of pale blue. I'd freshly dyed it, I remember, in honor of *Slaughter!* I have a bag of filming equipment swung over my shoulder, my camcorder resting at my hip. I peer out the window as headlights spill across the kitchen.

"Mom? Declan and Noah are here. I'm heading out." The me in the viewfinder pauses, waiting for a response. "Mom?" Another pause. The me in the viewfinder doesn't say anything more. She just wrinkles her nose and leaves.

Moments later, a tall figure walks into the room. I can only see the back of his head, his sand-colored hair hanging limp and greasy. He stumbles into the table, mutters a curse, and picks up his keys.

"No," I whisper, staring through the viewfinder as my father leaves the house with keys in hand. "No, no, no. Cut!"

The screen flickers. The keys reappear back on the kitchen table as though they'd never left. The voice that only sort of sounds like Noah speaks again. "Take two. Action!" The clapboard falls.

Younger me walks into frame as headlights fill the kitchen with their glow once again. This time she notices the keys on the table. She frowns, eyes flicking back and forth. "Mom? Declan and Noah are here. Do you have a second?" A pause. "Mom?" A beat as she realizes the truth—that Mom isn't home. "Shit." She peers into the living room from the kitchen. I don't follow her with the camcorder, but I know what she sees: Dad, passed out on the couch. "Dad? Are you asleep?" No answer. The me in the viewfinder sighs. "Fuck it." She leaves.

A moment later, there's the ominous creak of couch springs.

"No." My voice turns desperate as my father walks into the kitchen, scraping raw against the lining of my throat. "Do something. You have to do something.

Cut!"

The scene resets again. My entire body feels like an open wound, pulsing to the beat of my heart. Behind me, the voice that actually doesn't sound much like Noah at all speaks. "Take three. Action!"

Again. This time the me in the viewfinder actually picks up the keys, looking around. Nerves rise in her face as she looks around for a suitable hiding spot. Declan honks his horn, and she flinches. In one jerky movement, she stuffs the keys in the back of the fridge, behind the ever-present case of beer on the bottom shelf. It's a sloppy hiding place, one she's used before, but she doesn't have time.

"You coming, Cleopoke?" *That's* Noah's voice, so familiar that it sends a fresh pulse of grief through me.

"Coming, coming, shhh! Dad's sleeping." The girl in the viewfinder hurries out the door.

Dad appears in frame after a few beats of silence. He curses, opening drawers and muttering to himself. He opens the fridge. He moves the twelve-pack.

"No," I moan, but it's too late. He's fishing the keys out, grumbling obscenities. "There has to be a way to fix this, please. *Cut.*"

My father vanishes. The keys reappear on the kitchen table. The voice that is not Noah's voice, the voice that grates like the voice on the phone that told me it would *gut me like a fish,* speaks again. "Take four. Action!"

This time, younger Cleo puts the keys in her own pocket before sprinting out the door. There's a whir like tape fast-forwarding, and the footage speeds up. Dad paces the floor like a caged animal. When the younger version of me returns home, he explodes in anger. The obscenities he screams are too fast for me to understand them. But younger Cleo hears. She sobs as he snatches the keys out of her hand.

I can't cry. Or I won't. I'm not sure that I know the difference anymore. "Cut," I say.

"Take five. Action!"

Younger Cleo tries calling Mom. There's no response.

"Take six. Action!"

Younger Cleo refuses to leave with Declan and Noah, saying that she doesn't want to make *Slaughter!* anymore. It makes Dad so angry that he storms out of the house with his keys anyway. He shouts at her that she's being a goddamned idiot, wasting her talent like that.

"Take seven. Action!"

Red and blue lights fill the kitchen as the police arrive.

"Take eight. Action!"

Mom, who returned home hours after Dad left, holds a hand to her horrified mouth.

"Take nine. Action!"

Younger Cleo stands in the center of the kitchen. She tilts her expressionless face up toward the ceiling. Her jaw unhinges. She screams, and screams, and screams.

"Cut." My voice is hoarse, my hands trembling.

I'm gripping the camera tight enough to hurt. "Cut, cut, cut."

The keys sit on the table. They're so small in the viewfinder. So inconsequential. They don't look like the sort of thing that could ruin everything. The sort of thing that could inspire icy cold dread at the pit of my stomach, even now.

"Take ten. Action!"

Younger Cleo walks into frame again. I watch as she steps past the kitchen table, out the door to Declan's waiting car. She's beaming. She's so excited about filming that she doesn't even look at the keys. Is this the way it happened? I can't remember anymore. Just like I can barely remember that single night of filming. All I remember is what came after.

My father stumbles into frame. My throat aches, and this time it has nothing to do with the injuries Virginia gave me. "There really was nothing I could have done," I whisper. "I couldn't have changed anything." I'd known this. I'd *always* known this. So why does it hurt?

In the viewfinder, my father stills. "Isn't that what you wanted, Clementine?" His voice is flat, utterly without affect. It's a world of difference from how he spoke in life. But it's still his voice. And it's his words. He was the only one to ever call me *Clementine*.

"Dad . . ." My voice cracks. Not with tears, but with their absence. Or maybe with what all their absence implies. I didn't want this. Of course I never wanted him dead.

But that isn't what he's saying. I know it, and he must know that I do, because he keeps talking.

"Remember when you asked me why I never went to rehab?" He laughs. It doesn't sound like his laugh, just a poor imitation of it. "Well, asked is a nice word for it. We were arguing, so you weren't really expecting an answer. But I gave you one anyway. Do you remember what I said?"

I blink rapidly against my tears. I do remember it. Although I don't want to. It's one of the only times we talked about his problem so bluntly. It hurts to think of now. I knew it wasn't right to get mad at him, but I'd heard stories. I knew other people got help for this. But he never even *tried*.

"You told me . . ." I swallow. "You told me it wouldn't do any good."

"That's right. Some people are just doomed, Clementine." His hand hovers over the keys on the table. They vanish like a cheap filming trick. Easy to do in post. "There's nothing anyone can do to stop it. So why bother trying? It's just not worth it."

I think of Isobel's smile. The hope in her voice when she talked about her future, even when she knew it wasn't guaranteed. Her fear, and the way she always came back from it. "I'm not sure that's true," I whisper.

Dad's head tilts to the side. His unwashed hair, falling over his shoulder, is eerily reminiscent of Virginia's. "So there was something you could've done? It's your fault?"

The suggestion is a knife to my chest. "Of course not. It's just, I—I can't . . . If we're going to have this conversation, can't you at least fucking *look* at me?"

Seconds tick by in silence. My hands tremble. Then, my father turns to face the camera.

For one awful moment, it's like I'm staring at a stranger. Is that really what he looked like when he was alive? Were his eyes that far apart, his nose that narrow? Had his jawline been that shape, or had it been rounder?

His features morph with every unvoiced question. At least, I think they do. He's so small in the viewfinder. It's hard to tell what's real and what's my mind playing tricks on me.

"Are you really him?" I ask. "Or just my memory of him?"

"Oh, Clementine." His voice is even. Calm. I don't think I ever heard him so calm in life. "Memory is all that's left of me. That's how this works."

It's this, of all things, that makes my eyes fill with tears, the pain in my chest finally overflowing. It's not fair. I couldn't stop him from drinking. I couldn't stop him from driving. And now, I can't even remember his face with any certainty. What kind of daughter am I?

"Why are you crying, Clementine?" Dad's voice is too flat to sound curious. But he still asks.

"I miss you." My voice wavers and breaks. "Oh, Dad. I think I spent so much time trying not to feel guilty about this, I forgot to miss you."

Dad laughs. It's closer to his real laugh this time:

rough, with an edge of self-deprecation. "I didn't make myself easy to miss."

"Stop." It comes out too harsh, dangerously close to an argument. "I would never say that about you. I would never think that about you. Don't say that."

"I'm not the one saying it," he says. "You already know that, Clementine."

Because this is my memory of him. Does that mean it's my words in his mouth? I shake my head against this, against all of this.

"I'm not . . . I'm not mad at you. I don't want to be. I don't want to end up like Virginia, so consumed with anger that it's all I have left. Or Laura, cleaning up your mess forever. Or . . ."

I focus on my hands, still clutching the camcorder. They're covered in black paint, so thick that I can't see my skin.

Because that's what's real, isn't it? Not the camcorder. Not the kitchen. Not even my father, trapped in my best reconstruction of his final moments. Just the paint.

"I'm not like them," I say quietly. "I'm alive. I'm like Michelle."

"Is that what you want?" There's no judgement in my father's voice. "To be like her?"

The question gives me pause. I don't want to be like Michelle: the sort of person who would dig up a grave and kill the first person to see the evidence. It's a horrifying thought. But that brings me right back to the start. If I'm not like any of the Barlows, then what am I?

What do I feel about the memory of the man in my viewfinder?

The question isn't as easy to answer as I'd like. Because in many ways, him dying left our home calmer, easier to live in. I stopped having to worry about checking the number of beers in the fridge or finding hiding places for his keys. I stopped having to look over my shoulder at school events, worried that he'd show up slurring his words and stumbling. I stopped having to listen to Mom's sighs and rants.

But our family holds one more similarity with the Barlows. His death also left our home colder.

I think about my father's laugh. The stupid jokes he'd tell just to make me smile. The way he'd compliment all of my scripts, even the ridiculous ones. The way he'd be so excited to share his favorite scary movies with me, telling me all about the technical behind-the-scenes trivia. The smile on his face when he gave me my camcorder, just weeks before he died, and told me he knew I'd do great things with it.

It's been too long since I thought about those things. That's not fair, either.

"I can't carry this anymore, Dad." My eyes sting brutally, even though I'm no longer crying. "Not like this. I need to let it go."

My father stares at me through the viewfinder. "If you let it go, then what will be left?"

I shake my head. "I don't know. But I can't keep living like this." I taste something sharp and acrid in the back of my throat as my hand hovers over the power button. It might be paint. "I'm sorry, Dad. But this doesn't help either of us."

I press the power button.

In a movie there would be a moment. Where my father's features would coalesce and he'd look at me with pride. I'd get closure, understanding. But that's not what happens here. Instead, the camera shatters in my hands, and my father vanishes. The room around me breaks apart as black paint consumes me.

Because my father is dead, and the figure in the viewfinder was never him. Whatever closure I find, clumsy and inelegant as it is, is closure I'll have to find for myself.

− 25 −

DENOUEMENT

<pre>
                    FATHER
      If you let it go, then what will be left?

                   DAUGHTER
      I hope it's love. I want it to be love.

FATHER's face continues to fade as the
kitchen around them warps nightmarishly.
DAUGHTER looks at where his eyes used to be,
even so.

                   DAUGHTER
         I love you, Dad. Still.

   (Excerpt from A COLDER HOME, written by
   Clementine Moss.)
</pre>

THE PAINT LEECHES away, leaving me gasping for air.

I stumble back from the wall, clutching my chest. I'm in the basement again, and it doesn't seem like any time has passed. Isobel is beside Noah's corpse, the horror on her face still fresh. Declan and

Rhiannon are nearer to the wall. Nothing has collapsed in on itself in my absence.

Except, maybe, my heart.

The black paint pulls back, sliding off of Michelle with a strange *shlooping* sound. She drops from her pinned pose against the wall, hitting the ground hard with a cry. She'd go sprawling without me to steady her.

There's a part of me that wants to let her fall. She killed Noah. I should hold no sympathy for this woman, no matter how unconscious she was of the horrors her grief would unleash. And yet, I grab her arm as reflexively as I might have grabbed my father's, when his tenuous balance failed him.

"I don't . . ." Her voice is hoarse. "Please, don't tell. Don't tell on me."

Declan mutters something low and venomous in Spanish, and a similar stab of revulsion twists in my gut. But I don't let go of her arm. "Why did you do it?" I ask.

Her eyes dart to her father's corpse. She thinks I'm talking about him, not Noah. Does the body on the floor even matter to her? "I know I wasn't supposed to," she whispers. "But I couldn't get his face right. In the painting, I mean. I needed to see him. I didn't realize, the accident, it . . . it was a closed casket. I didn't know."

Didn't know that her father's corpse was headless, she means. Why did she bring him back here after she discovered it? Had she hoped, maybe, that his body here would be enough to manifest his ghost? If so, it didn't work. The only specters we saw were born from Michelle's imperfect memory. And, if Zander was to be believed, the lingering energy of repressed emotion. Then again, that could have been from Michelle's memory, too. I have no problem believing that she picked up on her mother's anger, no matter how hidden it was. I certainly knew whenever *my* mom's patience with my father was wearing thin.

My chest aches. I find that I understand Michelle completely, and that I don't understand her at all.

"This isn't how it's supposed to be," I tell her.

"But I couldn't get it right," Michelle insists.

Her desperation is a fractured mirror. I've spent enough time agonizing over scripts: the bits of dialogue that don't land, the descriptions that don't translate from brain to page. It's why I've been frozen all of this time, unwilling to move forward with any project until forced.

Michelle's been frozen, too, beneath a mountain of grief. The weight of it is crushing her, and us with it.

"Maybe it doesn't need to be right," I say. "If you'd painted him how you remembered him, that would have been enough. It would have been okay, if it wasn't perfect. As long as you . . ."

As long as she what? I still don't have the words for it. I don't think Isobel had it quite right, when she said art was about telling the truth. I don't know if I had it right, either, when I thought it was about bearing witness. Maybe it will be years before I truly understand what it is that compels me to return to filmmaking, time after time.

But I'd rather spend those years creating than standing still, caught in a trap of my own making. I don't know what I want to be, but I don't want to be this.

"This isn't the answer," I tell Michelle. "It can't be."

The walls begin to shake. Cracks spider across the stone, starting where Michelle was pinned and then working their way out. After the paint, there's something almost mundane about the ordinary fault lines, the way they emit clouds of dust.

The cracks are small. For a moment, I think that maybe the shelter will hold.

Then the ceiling splits open.

There's nothing mundane about the house as it collapses. It shatters the way a mirror would shatter, with twice the chaos. I leap backward to avoid a couch as it separates Michelle and I. Isobel dives out of the way of a falling table.

And there are the ghosts. Like Virginia's shadow, they're more shade than substance, ephemeral memories given brief form. They laugh, sob, and scream as they tumble down. When they hit the floor, they splatter into a mess of black paint.

A hand reaches out to me. I grab it, catching a glimpse of blonde hair and thinking that it's Isobel. But it isn't. It's Laura, half-remembered and sobbing, blood dripping from her wounds.

"Please," she says. "Please."

Ghostly hands clutch at my face. For a moment I'm back in my family kitchen, stuck in that worst moment. I push Laura's specter away, and the image of the kitchen vanishes with her just in time for me to dodge a falling chair.

Rhiannon shrieks. I find her with blood splattering her face, no sign of Declan beside her. Only the shattered porcelain remains of a bathtub, and beneath it, a lurid red smear of matter that *can't* be the remains of another friend, it doesn't even look *human* anymore, it doesn't—

The house gives another impossible groan. A chunk of the ceiling misses me by inches.

I look around wildly. My gaze lands on Michelle.

She's standing by her father's body. Her shoulders tremble in time with the shaking walls. I reach out to her. "Michelle, please!"

Michelle looks at me for one single moment. Then, she looks up at the collapsing ceiling. In a moment of devotion, a moment of choice, or maybe just a moment of instinct, she throws herself over her father's corpse, shielding it with her own body. A wooden railing from the banister skewers her through the back. There's enough of a gap between her and her father that I can see when it comes through the other side. Her head jerks up, her eyes bulging out, blood running from her mouth. Then it drops. Her body goes limp and still.

On the other side of this awful display, Isobel stands. Her horror-stricken gaze locks with mine. "Cleo!"

There's a hard shove at my back. I tumble beneath one of the sturdy work benches just in time for the house to collapse in on us with one final, terrible shudder. Everything goes pitch black.

I'm not unconscious. Nor am I dead.

It takes my mind several long moments to accept the fact that I haven't been flattened. The bench I fell under held. I take in one breath. Another. The air in my lungs is cold. It has the harsh bite of ice that only outdoor air brings.

The rubble around me is silent.

Carefully, cautiously, I push my way through. The remains of the house give way with a clatter. I'm surrounded by debris, *buried* in it, but far above me is a small pinprick of light. Cold wind blows down on me, chilled but bracing and fresh.

I claw my way toward it like a drowning woman swimming to the surface. Rubble stabs my hands and scrapes my body as I flounder upward, but I don't stop, even as my body aches. The light grows brighter, a clear yellow so pale it's almost white.

Behind me, the ruins shift. Someone is climbing up in my wake. I look over my shoulder, hoping blindly for one of the others to appear from the wreckage. A friend to help me through this.

But it isn't them.

It's Gerald—Michelle's father.

The corpse that climbs through the rubble is not the flesh-and-blood version that Michelle dug up in her grief. But it is headless, the bloodless stump careening wildly as the body thrashes. One hand reaches out and narrowly misses my ankle.

I shriek, flailing upward. Gerald—or what's left of him—makes a low, wheezing noise, the exposed muscle of his throat contracting with the effort. His hands flail, groping sightlessly for me.

"No!" The word tears out of my throat. I clamber up through the wreckage, toward the light.

I don't dare look over my shoulder to track his pursuit. But I can hear it: the shifting rustle of debris, the whisper of rubble against fabric, the hideous whine of his breath. It's terrifying. My blood turns to ice in my veins, making my limbs even stiffer and harder to move.

It would be easy to stop. The light is so far away. Do I really think I can reach it before Gerald reaches me? Wouldn't it be easier to let the horror come to me on as close to my own terms as I can manage?

Some people are just doomed, Clementine. That's what my dad's memory told me. And I don't know, I'll *never* know if that was true of him. He's dead, and the dead are beyond change. They're preserved in amber, stagnant.

I'm still alive.

I keep climbing.

The light gets closer, closer. Close enough that my fingertips numb from the cold, wind biting my cheeks.

Close enough that I could reach out and stick my hand into the open air, if I weren't occupied with climbing for my life. I clutch at the topmost rubble and pull, trying to drag myself out of this nightmare.

The rubble slips. I slip with it, sliding downward. Gerald's hand wraps around my ankle and pulls.

I'd scream if I had the breath to. I lash out, kicking with all my might. My foot collides with something—I'm not sure what, I don't have time to look—and the grip loosens. And then I'm scrambling, not thinking, just desperately clawing my way to freedom.

My hands break the surface, then my arms, my shoulders. Cold air slaps against my face and snow falls down the front of my shirt but it doesn't matter, doesn't stop me. I drag myself forward and up until I'm rolling across the snow-covered ground, away from the hole I clawed myself out of.

I'm free.

For a moment, it's all I can register. I blink up at the sky. The storm has finally ended, and the night is clear. The moon shines brightly above me, and my breath plumes out in clear white clouds. The cold is uncomfortable, and already I'm starting to shiver, but it's better than being in the wreckage.

I sit up. The house is a ruin now, so much jagged rubble. The hole I climbed out of is still and silent. Gerald's ghost is gone, if he'd ever been. If he wasn't just one remaining memory there to keep me in the dark.

I get to my feet slowly. The wind pulls at my hair,

sending pale blue strands into my face. "Hello?" My footsteps crunch across the snow. I pause to pull a coat—it's Andrea's, I recognize with a pang of grief—out of the rubble and wrap it around my shoulders. "Is anyone there?"

"I'm here."

A hoarse voice sounds from around the other side of a ruined wall. I stumble through the snow, limbs aching, to find Rhiannon. She's crouched down with a duvet wrapped around her shoulders. Blood drips sluggishly from a superficial wound in her temple, but she looks otherwise unharmed.

She's also alone. No sign of Declan. No sign of Isobel.

I lean against the rubble, breathing heavy. My ascent has left me exhausted. "Are you okay?" I ask.

"Fine. I got lucky. Declan . . ." She blinks. Behind her miraculously unharmed glasses, her eyes are glassy. "I saw him get crushed. He didn't make it."

I think of the pulpy remains beneath the shattered bathtub, the mass of blood and bone that my brain refused to register as human. My legs give out beneath me, and I land heavily beside Rhiannon in the snow. I'd known it, on some level, but I'd still hoped.

I can't remember the last time I'd let myself do that.

"One of those . . . things . . . grabbed him." Rhiannon stares out into the snow, still shying away from the word 'ghost' after everything. Only now Declan isn't here to tease her about it. "I don't know if it was like when Virginia grabbed me, but . . . he didn't move. The bathtub fell on him, and he didn't even flinch."

I sit with the weight of that for a long moment. The snow is cold beneath me, but I can't find the strength to stand. Even my stinging eyes are too exhausted to shed tears.

"Rhiannon," I say quietly. "What happened to you? When Virginia grabbed you? Did you see something?"

Rhiannon bows in on herself. Her dark-skinned hands curl into fists against her knees. "I heard my sister's voice," she murmurs. "Like a bad recording. Sounding like she had in the hospital, in the weeks before she died. I kept trying to fix it, make it so that her voice was clear. But I couldn't . . . quite . . . make out her words."

My heart aches. I didn't know this about Rhiannon. It must have happened before we met. But I find it isn't difficult to fit the knowledge into what I know of her. "I saw my dad," I offer, vulnerability in exchange for vulnerability. "But it wasn't really them. Just memories. You were right all along."

Rhiannon's lips quirk in what can only charitably be called a smile. "I've never cared less about being right." Her voice cracks on the final syllable.

There isn't really anything to say to that. I look out at the horizon. In the distance, lights flash, emergency vehicles making their way carefully down the icy roads. Is someone finally coming to our aid? It's too late to do much good, I suppose. Still, maybe it means something. A hand reached out into the dark *has* to mean something, even if it misses its grip.

Rhiannon sees them too. "It'll probably take them a while to get here," she says. "The storm's done, but the roads are still iced over."

"Should we wait in the cars?" I ask. "It would be good to get out of the cold, at least."

"In a minute. I'm dizzy. Might have a concussion." She touches the cut on her temple and winces.

I doubt I'll be much help supporting her—after my ascent, I'm not in much better shape. Still, I can't get over how lucky I was during the collapse itself. It isn't as though I'd meant to hide under the bench. Something shoved me. Now that I think about it, it had almost felt like hands at my back, pushing me to safety when I didn't know how to get there myself.

Declan and Michelle had already been dead. Isobel had been in front of me.

"Rhiannon, did you push me?" I ask. "When the house was collapsing, did you push me under the bench?"

Rhiannon shakes her head. She's looking at me more than a little strangely, but it doesn't matter. There's a more pressing question, one that I've been avoiding. One that I haven't been able to bring myself to ask. But I think I have to.

"Did you see Isobel?"

Another head shake. "She was on the other side of the basement when the house came down. I'm not sure, but I think . . ." She sighs, shaking her head. "I don't think anyone else made it. It's a miracle *we* made it."

I turn back toward the wreckage of the house. Rhiannon is right, I know. It's foolish to think that anyone else could have survived that awful collapse. Foolish to think that Isobel might be stuck but alive, trapped beneath the rubble. Trapped, perhaps, in her own version of the black paint, unable to free herself. Waiting for someone to reach a hand out to her the same way she once reached a hand out to me.

I stand. I start toward the ruins.

"Don't," Rhiannon says, sharp. "While I was crawling out, I saw . . ." She doesn't finish. She doesn't have to. I'm not quick to forget Gerald's corpse chasing after me, trying to drag me back to the depths. He could be waiting for me in there. Him, or countless other terrors.

In a horror movie, that would be the final sting shot. One more victim dragged to her unfortunate end. Cut to black on her helpless screams.

I don't want to live my life like it's a horror movie. I don't want to live assuming I'm doomed.

So I dig through the rubble. I dig as the sirens draw closer, as Rhiannon huddles beneath her blanket, as the moon shines and the wind blows and the snow hardens to ice beneath my feet. I reach into the darkness as far as I can.

And when a hand clutches mine, I let myself hope.

MORE BY JILLIAN MARIA

The Songbird's Refrain

There's Magic Between Us

Curiouser And . . .

Jillian Maria is a sapphic author who loves stories with big feelings and a lot of heart—even if that heart is a little bloody and bruised. When not writing, you can usually find her doting on her cat, listening to music, or gently obsessing over whatever piece of media has currently grabbed her attention. More information on Jillian and her works can be found at www.byjillianmaria.com.

9 781733 863537